Off-Limits Roomates

A Reverse Harem College Sports Romance

Rebel Bloom

Copyright © 2024 by Rebel Bloom

All rights reserved.

No portion of this book may be reproduced in any form without written permission from the publisher or author, except as permitted by U.S. copyright law.

Contents

1. ***Ella*** — 1
2. ***Ella*** — 7
3. ***Vaughn*** — 11
4. ***Ella*** — 16
5. ***Ella*** — 20
6. ***Vaughn*** — 24
7. ***Ella*** — 28
8. ***Ella*** — 33
9. ***Ella*** — 37
10. ***Ella*** — 41
11. ***Ella*** — 46
12. ***Ella*** — 51
13. ***Fisher*** — 56
14. ***Fisher*** — 60
15. ***Ella*** — 65
16. ***Ella*** — 71
17. ***Ella*** — 75
18. ***Ella*** — 80

19.	***Fisher***	85
20.	***Ella***	91
21.	***Vaughn***	97
22.	***Ella***	102
23.	***Booth***	108
24.	***Ella***	113
25.	***Ella***	117
26.	***Ella***	122
27.	***Ella***	127
28.	***Ella***	133
29.	***Ella***	138
30.	***Ella***	143
31.	***Ella***	147
32.	***Fisher***	152
33.	***Booth***	156
34.	***Ella***	161
35.	***Ella***	165
36.	***Fisher***	170
37.	***Ella***	175
38.	***Ella***	181
39.	***Vaughn***	186
40.	***Vaughn***	192
41.	***Ella***	197
42.	***Ella***	202

"Ella! You can't say things like that to me! Are you trying to give me a heart attack?" She groaned. "Honey, just come back home. This is all too much. You can take off a semester and transfer back to Penn in the spring."

I ground my teeth together. "I'm not letting Billy cost me an entire semester of school."

"Then maybe I should come there. I could rent a place and we could live together again. You know how much I miss you when you're gone. I could even enroll and take a few classes. It could be just like that movie we watched together about the mom going back to college with her daughter. They had so much fun together, Ella! We could go dancing!"

"Mom! I already had to see my boyfriend eating out another woman today. I can't handle any other trauma." I grabbed my purse and keys and held my breath before opening the door and rushing out to my car. No one looked up from what they were doing. I might as well have been invisible.

"I heard a door. Are you in your car? Are you okay? Ella?"

"I'm fine, Mom. Apparently no one is all that interested in me, even the guys doing drug deals in the parking lot." I started my car and locked it, just in case anyone decided I was worth a look. I put Mom on speaker and loaded the GPS with the address I'd been given.

"Oh, Ella, people want you. I want you." She laughed. "Just in the clingy mother way, though."

"You're going to give me nightmares."

"Sorry. Anyway, tell me again about how Billy was going down on this other woman."

I pulled out of the lot, careful not to disturb the guys arguing about their dealings. "You're kidding me."

"No. I want to hear it all again so I can come up with an appropriate punishment for the asshole."

"Fine. I got here a day early to surprise him before classes started. I went to his house and one of his frat brothers let me in. I should've known

1

Ella

"He was face down in someone else's vagina, Mom! He had to pull himself out to look at me!" I paced in front of the window in my cheap motel room. Outside I could see a few guys loitering in the parking lot and I watched what definitely looked like a drug deal go down. Hurrying back to the other side of the room, I shook my head and tried not to think about how I wasn't sure the flimsy lock on my door would hold if anyone even pushed the door too hard.

"I just hate when men slip and fall into other women's vaginas. You know, that's never happened to me. Not even once. Not a single man has ever tripped and landed in my vagina. And it's not like I've been keeping my legs closed tight. Not during these dry and trying times."

I stopped pacing and grimaced. "Mom."

She laughed her belly deep laugh that usually made everyone around her laugh along. I just wasn't in a laughing mood. "Sorry!"

A text came through on my phone and I had her hold while I read it and replied. "I got a hit for a potential room. Talk to me while I go out to the car? I'm less likely to get murdered if I'm on the phone, I think. Or something like that."

43.	***Ella***	206
44.	***Ella***	211
45.	***Vaughn***	215
46.	***Ella***	218
47.	***Ella***	222
48.	***Ella***	226
49.	***Vaughn***	230
50.	***Booth***	234
51.	***Ella***	238
52.	***Fisher***	243
53.	***Ella***	248
54.	***Ella***	254
55.	***Ella***	258
56.	***Vaughn***	263
57.	***Ella***	267
58.	***Ella***	272
59.	***Ella***	278
60.	***Ella***	282
61.	***Ella***	287
62.	***Vaughn***	292
63.	***Ella***	296
64.	***Booth***	300
65.	Epilogue	306
66.	Free Preview of Grumpy Makes Three	313

something was up when the guy just giggled and ushered me in. Billy was in his room with the door wide open, eating some pretty blonde woman out. It took him a while to notice me, Mom. I was just standing there in shock. Then, he tried to chase me out to talk to me but he had vag breath and some of his frat brothers were standing around watching. So I throat punched him and got out of there."

"What?! You didn't tell me you throat punched him! Way to go, Ella! I-" She grunted. "You're just messing with me, aren't you?"

"Of course. I would never throat punch anyone, even if I wanted to." And I'd really, really wanted to throat punch Billy. "I'm so embarrassed, Mom. I came all the way here to be with him. I left my dream school for this. I took a chance on him and he's been cheating on me for who knows how long. I hate him. I hate him so much."

"You have nothing to be embarrassed about." She snorted. "Do you know how many times I've been cheated on? I don't want to give you any negative views on men, but men cheat and men kind of suck, baby."

I turned onto a service road next to the interstate and continued following the directions. "Mom, I don't want to be mean, but you had me with a man who disappeared as soon as the responsibility showed up and you've dated a long line of losers since. What negative views are you worried about giving me that you haven't already?"

"Hey! That's not nice. They weren't all losers." By her silence I could tell she was about to say something I wouldn't like. "Speaking of the one who wasn't a loser... You know Vaughn goes to school there. You could always call him for help. I'd feel a lot better about you going to Vaughn than I do about your little motel spot."

I laughed. "Vaughn? You want me to go to Vaughn? Are you crazy?"

"You don't have a lot of room to be choosy, Ella. Your step-brother might be your only option."

"He's not my step-brother, Mom. You and Paul got divorced so long ago." I shuddered. There was no way I was going to call Vaughn. Not a chance in hell. "I'd rather go crawling back to Billy."

"Shut your mouth. You better not!" Mom's raised voice was a clear indicator that I'd struck a nerve. "We don't do that in this family. No Daughton woman has ever taken back a cheating loser. If that starts with you, I'll disown you."

I turned away from campus and looked up at the houses as I slowly drove. The farther I got away from campus the worse the houses looked. "That should show you how much I want to call Vaughn. Also, don't threaten to disown me. I'm too old to become a parentless kid. I wouldn't handle it well."

I pulled to the curb so I could say goodbye to Mom before pulling into the driveway of the house I would hopefully be moving into. I flipped up my visor and glanced around, always conscious of my surroundings. Too bad that didn't translate into relationships.

"Mom?"

She didn't complain about me cutting her off, probably able to hear in my voice that I wasn't doing great. "What is it, Ella Rae?"

I heaved out a great sigh. "Why didn't I see the signs? I finished my first year at Penn with a 4.0 GPA. I'm a smart woman. Yet... I really thought Billy loved me. I moved here for him. How could I have been so stupid?"

She matched my sigh. "You weren't stupid, Ella. You trusted the person you were supposed to be able to trust. He was your first boyfriend. Your first everything. You followed your heart and I don't want you to lose that, baby. It's a beautiful thing to be able to trust. It's just also a very dangerous thing at times."

"Don't talk about my first anything. I can't handle that." I groaned and let out a frustrated scream. "I hate feeling like this. This isn't a productive emotion."

"Funnel it into finding a new place to live because I'm not going to be able to sleep if you don't get out of that motel room. It feels like I've already lost my only kid to the seedier side of life. I'm not cut out for mothering a high-risk child, Ella. We each have our limits and we need to respect that."

Dropping my head forward on my steering wheel, I couldn't help agreeing with her. "You're right. I'll figure it out. Just because campus housing is full doesn't mean there aren't a hundred other great options, just like the one I'm going to see now. I'm sure it'll be amazing."

"I hope so. I'm minutes from flying there to live with you."

She was just crazy enough to do it, too. With a shudder, I sat up straight and locked eyes with a guy jogging down the sidewalk next to my car. I momentarily lost track of what I was thinking as he came closer to my car and I noticed the way his bare chest muscles flexed. "Wow."

"Wow? Wow, what?"

Tall, muscular, and tan, the guy jogging towards me was stunning. He had bone structure that would've made Captain America jealous and a knowing smirk loaded and ready just for the moment he caught a woman gawking at him, I was assuming. As soon as he passed me, I let out a breath I hadn't even realized I was holding.

"Ella Rae Daughton? What is it?" Mom sounded like she was getting frantic on the other end of the call. "Answer me, child, or I'm seriously booking a flight right now!"

I shook my head at myself. "Sorry, Mom. I just... I got distracted."

"By what?"

"By nothing. I've got to go, Mom. I think this neighborhood might be okay, after all." If the guy who just jogged by lived there, it was a nicer neighborhood than I'd thought. He looked like he was captain of the rowing team. "I love you. Don't come here! Okay?"

"Rude." She blew a raspberry. "I love you, too. Call me later and update me."

I hung up and looked in the rearview mirror to see Mr. Rowing but he was already gone. Not that it mattered. He could've jumped on the hood of my car and flexed his impressive pectoral muscles in my face and I still wouldn't have been interested. Not after Billy and his public cunnilingus.

I took a deep breath and prepared myself for being on. I needed a place to live. Fast. The last thing I wanted, besides living with Billy, was Mom showing up on campus and screaming my name to find me. That was the only thing that could embarrass me more than Billy's cheating.

I got out of my car and life smacked me again as I stepped onto the sidewalk. I heard a deep shout a split second before I got hit by what felt like a train. I waited to hit the ground but found myself clinging to sweaty muscles mid-air instead.

"Whoa, there." Mr. Rowing grinned down at me, white teeth on full display with deep green eyes sparkling in the sunlight. "You okay?"

"Where did you come from?" I looked around, belatedly realizing that I was still clinging to him. Forcing myself to let him go, I took a step back and looked around. He really had appeared out of nowhere.

"Right now or in general?" He put his hands on his hips and his stomach muscles flexed.

Taking a step backwards, I cleared my throat and forced a smile. I had to get away from his muscles and his pretty eyes. My brain scrambled to find a witty reply, but the moment his smirk deepened, every clever thought I had evaporated. I was officially fluent in gibberish. "I'm, uh... really late. Bye!"

Turns out, I didn't need Mom's help to embarrass myself—I had that covered. As I bolted away like a raccoon on meth, I mentally added 'Learn how to run like a normal person' to my to-do list. Because clearly, life wasn't going to give me a break any time soon.

2

Ella

"And this is where you'd sleep." Jamie, the forty-two-year-old woman wearing hot pink Uggs and her hair in pigtails, grinned as she whipped back a fabric curtain to reveal a bed shoved into the closet of her room. "It's cute, right?!"

My mouth opened like I had something to say but I had nothing. I felt like I could've stood there a thousand years and still nothing would've come to me. The house was a shrine to 2000's pop and Jamie was looking for someone to have sleepovers with. She wanted a friend to pillow fight with and play Dream Date on a fake plastic telephone from the late 90s. Most of those things I learned directly from the things she was saying to me.

"My parents live in the back of the house but they know not to come out when I'm hanging with my friends." She blew a bubble with her bubble gum and it popped over the tip of her nose. She casually stuck her tongue out to work the gum back into her mouth. "It's totally cool. You won't even notice them. And we're only a little ways away from frat row. The parties are great there and if we get blitzed, my parents will come and pick us up. Can you say personal uber?"

I shut my mouth and opened it again. "I...can?"

She blew an even larger bubble and giggled when it popped over the edges of her glasses. "Did you see that? Wow."

I was kind of impressed but mostly I felt like I was in the home of a serial killer. "I did. Well, I should-"

"Oh, my god! I didn't even show you the best part of the house!" She grabbed my arm and tugged me back into the living room. Pushing me down on the powder blue couch, she rushed over to the entertainment center and grandly opened the cabinet doors at the bottom. "I have every season of *Friends, Buffy,* and *Angel*!"

I watched in horror as she pulled out the first season of *Buffy* and put a disc in the DVD player. She wasn't seriously about to start a season of a TV show, surely. There was no way.

"Stay right there. I have to get something." She ran out of the room, her jelly slides *clacking* against the wood floor. "Don't you dare move, bestie!"

I glanced at the door and screamed when I saw an older woman standing on the other side of the glass storm door. Jumping to my feet, I stumbled backwards into a glass table with a set of Destiny's Child dolls starring on top of it. Beyonce fell over and Kelly Rowland fell completely off the table.

"Bee! Kelly! You have to be careful, Bella!" Jamie rushed back into the room with an unpopped bag of popcorn just as the theme music to *Buffy* started. "Oh, my god, Mom! You scared Bella! Go back to your room!"

The woman with her face pressed to the glass pouted. "Jamie, I just need to use the bathroom!"

"Mom! God!" Jamie straightened the dolls and tossed the popcorn on the floor. She even stomped her foot. "Leave me alone in front of my friends! You promised!"

I wasn't sure why but I felt the need to correct Jamie. "Um. My name is Ella."

"What?" She stared back at me with pieces of the bubble gum balloon still stuck to her glasses and the dolls clutched in her fists.

"Nothing. Sorry."

"Jamie, I'm sorry to bother you but I need to pee. You know I get infections if I hold it." Her mom pulled open the door and wedged her way past Jamie. "And your father is going to need to poop soon. Did you tell your new friend we all share the bathroom? The last girl wasn't very good about sharing. Your father had to poop his pants that one time and I still can't get the smell out of the washing machine, Jamie."

"Mom! You're embarrassing me!"

I moved towards the door but Jamie all but transported to appear in front of me and pushed me down on the couch. She sat down next to me, still squeezing poor Beyonce and Kelly, and nodded to the TV. I looked at the TV and back at her, unsure of what she wanted. All I knew was that she wasn't all that sane and I wanted to escape before she turned me into a giant doll that she enjoyed squeezing.

"Push play, Bella. We can just turn it up so we won't hear my mom peeing. She pees louder than anyone I've ever known. I think she has a medical problem." She waited for a second and then slammed the dolls down on the couch to push play herself. "God. Do you ever have such a bad day that you just want to scream, Bella? I mean, I could just scream. I-"

She screamed and it scared me so bad that I screamed too. Grasping my chest, I leaned away from her on the couch just as the opening scene of *Buffy* started.

"*Welcome to Sunnydale, Buffy.*"

Oh, hell no. I jumped up, vaulted over Jamie's legs, and nearly ripped her storm door off its hinges as I busted out of her house. I climbed in my car, locked the door, and started it just as Jamie came running out of her house, shaking Beyonce at me. I gunned it out of her driveway, nearly took out a soccer mom and her van of merry kids, and then peeled away from that house of horrors like a bat out of hell.

I had to shout at google a few times before it understood my command to call my mom. As soon as the call connected, I screamed at her. "She was a crazy person, Mom! She had dolls and she tried to make me watch *Buffy*! She wanted me to sleep in her closet and share a bathroom with her loud peeing mother and her poopy father! I had to run out of there before she murdered me."

Mom was silent.

"Did you hear what I said? She wanted to skin me alive and stuff me with that cheap polyfill so she could play with my dead body, Mom!"

Mom's laughter oddly enough helped calm me down. She laughed so hard that I could tell she was crying. "You're so dramatic!"

"I wish. I really wish I was being dramatic, Mom." I took a deep breath and pulled over on the side of the road, being sure to keep an eye on the rearview mirror for signs of a Beyonce wielding Jamie. "I give up. Send me Vaughn's number. Please."

When she finally stopped laughing and sent me the number, I'd almost calmed down enough to rethink what I was about to do. Then a kid on a bike rode by my car and I jumped so hard that I pulled something in my back. Admitting defeat was never easy but admitting defeat when it was over a guy who'd spend three years bullying you? It was just one step up from living as a life size doll with Jamie.

3

Vaughn

I walked into the coffee shop I'd agreed to meet Ella at and nodded at the guy working the counter. I'd completed three practices in less than twenty-four hours and I was fucking exhausted. The only reason I'd agreed to meet my ex-step sister was to see what she wanted and to see if she was still a nerdy kid with a too-big head for her body.

"Can I get a coffee? Black. Nothing fancy." I leaned against the counter and looked around as I held my card out to the guy. The place was mostly empty. It was farther from campus than anyone I knew liked to go. There were only three tables occupied in the entire space.

"How's it going? You going to bring home a championship ring this year, you think?" He charged my card and handed it back before grabbing a basic mug. "I caught most of the games last year and y'all were robbed, man."

"Last year can suck my dick." I growled. I hated thinking about how close we'd been to a championship the year before. "We're going all the way this year."

The guy said something else but I missed it. I'd been clocking the tables and when I got to the one in the back, I couldn't believe what I was seeing. I did a literal double-take and then searched the rest of the shop to see if I'd missed the real Ella Rae somewhere.

"Here you go."

The last time I'd seen Ella Rae Daughton, she was just a weird kid with features that didn't work together, but the woman staring back at me with the pained smile was a far cry from that little girl. This woman was sinfully hot with a perfectly proportionate head size and features that not only worked together, they fucking sang.

"Bro?"

I jerked my gaze back to the guy behind the counter and cleared my throat. I saw that he was holding my coffee out to me and took it with a little too much gusto. A bit spilled on my hand but I just wiped it on my pants and thanked the guy before heading towards Ella.

She looked up at me with wide green eyes and the poutiest mouth I'd ever seen. It made me think things I had no damn business thinking about a girl who was once my step sister. She was wearing a sundress that clung to her tits and from where I stood, taller than her, I could just see down the front of it. Again, shit I shouldn't have been looking at.

Ella swept her long brown hair over her shoulder and stood up. "Vaughn... Thanks for meeting me."

I still stared down at her. Despite the growth spurt she'd had since I'd last seen her, she was still almost a foot shorter than me. She'd filled out, though. Gone was the skinny kid. In front of me was a woman with curves that made my mouth water. That sundress stopped mid-thigh and I could see a lot of tan leg that felt too interesting.

I shook my head and forced my brain to get real. Ella had been family. Looking at her like she hadn't been was fucked up. "Of course. It's not every day a ghost from the past calls you up."

She pulled a sweater off the back of her seat and pulled it on before sitting back down. It covered most of her curves like a bad magic trick. "I don't know about ghost..."

I pulled out the chair across from her and sat down. My knee bumped hers and my fucking stomach reacted like I was a pre-teen trying to kiss a girl for the first time. Grinding my teeth together, I spoke a little gruffer than I meant to. "What else do you call someone you haven't spoken to in...seven years?"

She wrapped the sweater around herself tighter and rested her elbows on the table. Looking at her closer, it looked like she'd been crying. There was also a degree of crazy to her hair, like she'd been running her hands through it a ton. "If I had any other options, I wouldn't have called you. I don't mean that in a rude way... I just... We're not friends. I know you don't owe me anything. I hope that you can help me despite that."

"We're not friends? We shared a bathroom during your most awkward years, Ella Rae. We go way back. Doesn't that automatically mean a friendship exists?"

Those forest green eyes flashed and I felt a lick of flame up my spine. She adjusted her face as soon as the annoyance showed, though. "I'm serious, Vaughn."

Forcing out a breath, I sat back in my chair and then realized with a jolt of annoyance that I'd forgotten all about my coffee as soon as I'd seen her. "What do you want, Ella Rae, and why do you want it?"

She looked away and then stood up suddenly. "I'm sorry. Give me just a minute, please."

I stared after her as she disappeared into the bathroom behind her. I knew she was crying and it felt like shit. I chocked it up to having been like a big brother to her for three years. Some of those familial feelings must've still existed. By the time she'd come back to the table, I'd already decided to help her with whatever she needed. I was an asshole, but I wasn't a monster.

She sat down and dabbed her nose before looking up at me again. Her eyes were red and it somehow made the green glow. Her bottom lip quivered before she sank her teeth into it and bit down hard. She took a deep breath and nodded to herself. "I moved here to be with my boyfriend and I found him cheating on me this morning. Campus housing is full and I just had to run out of a house where I'm pretty sure a woman wanted me to be her doll. She offered me a bed in her closet and pillow fights for a thousand dollars a month. I checked into a motel and I've already seen a few drug deals and it's the middle of the day, Vaughn. I need somewhere to stay. I wouldn't ask you if I wasn't desperate."

I traveled on that rollercoaster of a story with her, but where her voice dipped with an emotion that sounded like sadness, I felt rage. I pushed my coffee away from me and tapped my knuckles on the table. "Who's the guy?"

She shook her head. "It doesn't matter. It's over."

I felt like it mattered. "You don't have anywhere else to go?"

She shot me a look that I instantly understood. I was the guy who'd driven her crazy for three years. There was no way in hell she would've come to me if she had anyone else to ask.

I thought about the empty bedroom in the house I shared with my best friends and tilted my head as I studied her. That time it was more clinical than perverted. "You still got all your cleaning supplies, Cinderella?"

Her face shifted with another flash of her anger but she fought it back. "Just tell me what you want."

I felt bad for her but I was still the same asshole she'd known before. If I was going to rush in and save her, she was going to pay for the rescue. "You can stay with me but I don't just need another roommate messing up the place. We need someone to clean up. The house gets disgusting and the maid service Fisher brings in is full of women who bitch at us the entire time they're cleaning. You clean the house, and I mean all of the house, and you can stay for free."

Her eyes narrowed in fury and she sat back in her chair. I could see the anger radiating through her. She hated me. "You want me to clean your house."

"I don't call you Cinderella for no reason." I smirked as the tops of her cheeks turned red. Making her angry had always been fun and nothing had changed. "So, Cinderella. Are you going to be my maid?"

4

Ella

I wanted to take his coffee mug and slam it over his head. I wanted to stuff him in the trunk of my car and drive back to Jamie's to give him to her. I wanted... I wanted to move into his house and have a place to stay. I swore under my breath and nodded. "Fine."

He grinned and I felt even angrier when I saw just how handsome he'd become. I didn't even know if that was the right word, though. He was devilishly good looking. He looked like trouble and he made it look fun. "Cinderella, I think this is going to work out just fine."

"Don't call me that, Vaughn. Call me Ella or just don't call me anything." I realized I was coming to him as a beggar so I took a deep breath and forced a smile. "Please."

He ran his hand through his dark blonde hair, pushing it off his forehead and leaving just a strand hanging down in front of his pale blue eyes. With dark, thick eyelashes I wished I had, that little hair was like an arrow pointing out his perfect features. I wanted to cut it off.

It was a cruel twist of fate that the guy I remembered had grown into a version of himself that made my stomach flutter. He rubbed his sharp jawline with his giant hand and the smirk just grew wider. "You've learned some manners in the years since we lived together. That's good. You were just shy of a feral animal back then."

I felt my lips pulling back in a sneer and quickly covered my mouth with my hand. I watched him laugh and balled my other hand into a fist. Hitting him wasn't a good idea, but I really wanted to. Oddly enough, I kind of wanted to hit him more than I'd wanted to hit Billy. "I'm not a little kid anymore, Vaughn. You don't have to keep up the big brother bully act."

He leaned across the table towards me. "But you liked it so much."

I stood up and pushed my chair in before grabbing my purse. "Is tonight too soon to move in? I don't want to sleep in that motel if I can help it."

It seemed like he got the point and read the room. I was done playing. I needed a home before I could handle him teasing me. He stood up and towered over me. He had always been tall but he had to be almost six and a half feet tall. I had to look so far up at him that it was almost annoying.

"What motel? Did you leave your shit there?"

I grimaced. "Roadside Inn. I left a few things. The lock on that door was so flimsy that it might all be gone by now."

"The fucking Roadside Inn, Ella? I wouldn't touch that place with a ten-foot pole. We might need to get you tested before we let you move in." He put his hand on my back and eased me towards the exit. "Come on. I'll follow you back in my truck. If you have anything left, we should get it out of there before you get roaches."

I tried to subtly shift away from his touch. His hand on my back was warm and it made my skin tingle in a way I didn't appreciate. I couldn't walk fast enough to outpace his giant legs so I just had to suck it up and deal with the tingling he caused. "You just suggested I'm diseased and that I could have roaches."

"Yeah. And?" He opened the door for me, waved a goodbye to the barista, and still kept his hand on my back. "Go straight to the motel and then I'll lead you to the house you'll be cleaning."

I shrugged away from his touch finally and frowned up at him. "Vaughn."

He smirked. "Cinderella."

I took a deep breath and opened my car door. "I definitely should've throat-punched Billy. It would've made this feel a little better."

"Billy, huh?"

Sliding behind the wheel, I ignored Vaughn. I couldn't handle much more of him. I couldn't handle much more of anything or anyone. I just needed a hot shower to cry in.

Vaughn stayed behind me in his massive truck and pulled into the lot right beside me. He was out of the truck and at my car door before I could push it open. His head swiveled from side to side before he lowered his eyes to me.

"Get in and get out, Ella." He seemed serious for a change and it was alarming. I'd known him for three years over seven years earlier and that serious tone still sent me rushing into my rented room.

He stayed just outside my door as I grabbed the few things I'd brought inside and he took them from me as soon as I stepped outside. Tossing them into his truck, he walked back and stuck his head inside the room and slammed the door shut when he saw that I'd grabbed everything.

"Thanks. I-"

He pulled open my car door and pushed me inside. "The fact that you almost stayed here tonight makes me want to find this Billy asshole and shove my foot up his ass. Lock the doors."

I winced when he slammed the door but did as he said. I looked around and saw a group of guys on the other side of the parking lot staring at my car. Vaughn stood at the back of his truck for a second, staring them down, before shaking his head and getting into his truck. My heart pounded roughly at what he'd been angry about. I hadn't even noticed the guys standing there. My situational awareness had failed me big time.

Vaughn pulled out and waited for me to do the same and follow him away from the motel. With every mile I put between me and that place, I felt a little better. I was going to be cleaning up after a guy I spent three years loathing, but anything would've been better than facing those guys with just my anger and a flimsy door lock.

Instead of heading away from campus, Vaughn led us into the center of it. I got worried when he turned onto frat row and held my breath until he turned onto Rainey Street, the street that ran perpendicular to frat row, where Billy lived. If he'd expected me to clean up a frat house, I was out. Dropping out of college and giving up my dreams out. Instead, he pulled into the circle drive of a house that could've been a small replica of the White House. Only in Florida could a house like that one exist on a college campus, next to a rowdy street of frat houses and across the street from a house that looked like it had been dropped in from Italy.

The large white house, complete with columns and a massive amount of windows and what looked like a widow's walk, was unlike anything I'd ever expected. I hadn't had a lot of time to expect much of anything but I wouldn't have guessed mini white house in a million guesses.

I slowly climbed out of my car and stared up at it. There was even an American flag blowing in the breeze. The lawn was perfectly manicured, despite the rest of the town existing in a sandbox. There were flowers blooming in the flower beds, even with it being late August and a hundred degrees.

I turned in a circle to look at the houses around us and noticed a seventies style ranch, a farmhouse the size of a Target, and the typical pink and yellow houses that existed everywhere in Florida. I felt a little bit like I'd walked onto the set of *The Truman Show*. Everything was just...pretty. It was weird. It was also quiet and...pretty. I couldn't get past how pretty it was. I'd just left a hell house and a potential roach motel. Maybe I was just feeling a bit of culture shock.

Vaughn shut his truck door and walked over to me. "Cinderella's got a lot of shit to clean."

5

Ella

I followed Vaughn through the front door and nearly ran into his back when he stopped short just inside. I grunted when the box I was holding slipped out of my hands and clipped the back of his ankles. It set off a chain reaction of everything else in my hands falling.

Vaughn turned and shot me a look before stepping aside. "Roommates, meet roommate. Roommate, meet roommates."

The guys looked more surprised than I was, which was saying a lot. Jogging guy, AKA Mr. Rowing, was standing a few feet away from me, still shirtless, still as wildly good looking as earlier. Beside him was a mountain of a guy with the prettiest brown eyes and dimples I'd ever seen. Even staring at me with a weirded out look on his face, those dimples shined.

"What? V? Why is there a pretty girl moving a lot of shit into our house?" Jogging guy bounced back quickly. He grinned at me and bent down to swipe up Constantine, my stuffed cow. "Not that I mind. Who's this little guy and does he need to be replaced with someone a little bigger, but just as cuddly? I mean, he was on the floor, after all."

Vaughn punched him in the arm. "Fuck off. This is Ella. She was my step sister back in the day."

I was still processing the fact that Jogging guy volunteered to replace my stuffed animal. I looked from him to Vaughn and back to him. "Um. Hi?"

His grin just grew more devilish, if possible. He held Connie to his chest and looked me up and down. "Little sis? That's fun."

I frowned. "I'm not his little sister. Our parents were married for three years. That's all."

Vaughn pulled me farther into the house and shut the door behind me. "She got cheated on and is homeless. I'm being a great ex-step brother and told her she could live here as long as she cleans up after us."

I crossed my arms over my chest and frowned up at him. "You don't have to just say it like that. I wasn't homeless. I could've stayed at the Roadside Inn. I just didn't think it was a long-term solution."

"The Roadside Inn? You were at the Roadside Inn?" Dimples shot Vaughn a look and shook his head. "You're more than welcome to stay here. That place is a fucking cesspool. I went there to buy weed once and saw people running a tra-"

I tilted my head when he stopped talking in the middle of his sentence. "Running a what?"

Vaughn snorted. "Yeah, Booth. What were they running?"

Booth, otherwise known as Dimples, actually blushed. "I realized mid-way through that story that it wasn't really appropriate to tell in mixed company."

Jogging guy full out laughed. "Wow, Booth. Your momma would be so proud of those manners."

"She can move into the empty room, right? Any objections?" Vaughn shook his head at his friends and turned to me. "Having our own personal Cinderella will be pretty nice, guys. Think it through."

"You seriously think I'm going to object to a pretty woman moving into the room next to mine?" Jogging guy sank his teeth into his bottom lip and winked at me. Even holding my stuffed cow and making cheesy faces, he was hot.

Booth shrugged. "Yeah, no objections here."

"Let's get one thing straight." Vaughn's voice was deeper, just as serious as it'd been in the parking lot of the Roadside Inn. "No one touches her."

I made a disgusted face at him. "Vaughn!"

He turned to me. "I'm serious. You're not my step sister anymore but you were and it counts. She's off limits. Understand me? Fisher?"

Jogging guy, Fisher, rolled his eyes. "You just want me to fall in love with her, don't you?"

Booth pulled Connie from him and held him out to me. "Sorry about him. We've asked around about getting him help but there's just nothing anyone can do."

Vaughn glared at his roommates. "I'm serious."

My face was on fire. Fisher was just playing around and Vaughn was acting like his friends were going to fall all over themselves to get to me. It was humiliating. "Vaughn. Just...stop. No one is going to touch me. Can I just go to my room and unpack now?"

He hesitated, like he wasn't sure he was done being embarrassing, and then nodded. "We'll get the rest of your shit after I show you which room is yours."

"I could show her." Fisher let out a loud laugh when Vaughn whipped his head around to glare at him. "Fine! She's all yours, big bro."

That sent a wave of heat hotter than the sun through my body. I grabbed a few things and rushed to the grand staircase. "Do you guys talk a lot to your other maid service? You don't need to feel obligated to talk to me if you didn't..."

I heard Fisher grunt, like Vaughn had punched him again, and then watched Vaughn stomp up the stairs ahead of me. I glanced back at Booth and Fisher, saw they were both watching me, and rushed upstairs after Vaughn.

He stomped down the right hallway to the last door on the left and walked in. He dropped my things on the king-sized bed and turned to me with his hands on his waist. "Stay away from them, Ella Rae."

I dropped everything but Connie on the floor and rolled my eyes at him. "Vaughn, I just broke up with the guy I've been dating for three years. I loved him. I loved him and I walked in on him going down on another woman today. The only guy I want to be close to right now is a Scrub Daddy. You have Scrub Daddys, right?"

He let out a deep sigh and walked over to me. Taking Connie in his hands, he turned him over and shook his head. "I can't believe you still have this thing. It's old enough to vote now."

I stared down at the stuffed cow that had gotten me through a lot of shitty years and suddenly I felt everything hitting me all at once. Tears filled my eyes and I could tell there was no stopping them. "I'm going to cry now, Vaughn, and neither of us wants you here for that. Just leave my stuff outside, please. I'll get it later."

His grip on Connie tightened before he let out a heavy sigh. Pushing Connie into my chest, he moved past me. "We'll bring it up. Just cry in the bathroom or something."

I almost laughed. "Thanks. That's smart planning."

Just before he left, Vaughn hesitated again. "Billy who, Ella? What's his last name?"

That time I did laugh. Tears came with it, though, and I hurried into the attached bathroom to keep them to myself. I shut the bathroom door and leaned against it, my body suddenly so heavy I didn't think I could keep it upright.

6

Vaughn

My teeth were turning to dust from all the grinding I was doing as I listened to Ella crying through the bathroom door. We'd brought her stuff up in two loads and each time we entered her room, her sobs were painful and seemed to be never-ending. I paced in front of her new bed and ran through a list of Billys in my head. I couldn't imagine her with any of them. She was...her, and they were...losers.

Booth leaned against her doorway and winced with each sob. "Should we...do something?"

I shrugged. "What the fuck are we supposed to do? What does she need? Ice cream or some shit like that? Chocolate?"

Fisher stuck his head in from the hallway. "Diamonds? I'm willing to throw a lot of cash at this problem."

The sobs stopped for a second and I felt a ray of hope that maybe she was okay finally but they started back right after. I ran my hands through my hair and pulled at it. "Jesus. How much can she cry? She can't have that much liquid in her. She's only one woman."

"Can she, like, pass out from dehydration? I mean, she's been crying for a long time. Should we get her a sports drink?" Fisher pushed past Booth and moved towards the bathroom door. I grabbed his shoulder to stop him but he shrugged me off. "Hey, Ella? When's the last time you had anything to drink?"

Booth rolled his eyes. "It's like watching an ape try to learn empathy."

I snorted. "That's good."

The bathroom door cracked open and Ella's shaky voice filled the room. "I'm okay. Really. Just leave me here for now."

I growled and pushed Fisher out of the way. Pushing the door open, I felt like I'd been punched when I saw Ella sitting behind the door, eyes swollen and red from crying. She tried wiping her eyes to hide her tears, like we hadn't been listening to her sobbing. I held my arms out to her. "Up. If you dehydrate and die, you won't be much use to me. What do you need? Water? Ice cream? Chocolate?"

"Diamonds?" Fisher stuck his head around the door and swallowed audibly when he saw her. "Big diamonds?"

Ella pulled her knees to her chest and buried her face against them. "It's fine. I'm fine."

I rubbed at my chest and looked at Fisher. I didn't know what to do. I didn't go around comforting women all over the place. I just wanted her to stop crying because it made me feel like shit. I'd never seen her cry before and I didn't fucking like it. Ella pissed? Great. Ella vengeful? Even better. Ella full of anger and snark and raging against me as a kid? Loved it. Ella crying? I wanted to break shit.

"Will you guys leave me alone if I say yes to water?" She looked up at us and the expression on her face was so pitiful that I actually growled and leaned down to pick her up. She batted my hands away, though. "What are you doing?"

"I don't know! Just stop crying, Ella Rae. What do you need to make it stop?" I tried to grab her again and frowned when she just batted me away again. "Ella!"

"Vaughn!" She pulled herself to her feet and walked to the other side of the bathroom, putting space between us. "I'm sad, okay! I loved Billy and I left my dream school like an idiot to come here with him and that's all ruined now. I'm stuck here, in *Florida*, and I'm just...sad! I'm going to cry and that's okay. The best thing you can do for me right now is-"

"Diamonds?"

"-leave me to it." Ella looked at Fisher and smiled. Even though it was a sad, watery smile, I still didn't like it. "And thank you for the offer of diamonds, Fisher, but the only thing I'd want with a diamond right now is to punch Billy with it so it left a big diamond shaped knot."

I pushed Fisher out of the bathroom and turned to Ella. "Tell me his last name and I'll leave enough knots on his face that you'll never have to cry again."

"Have you ever cried, Vaughn? Jeez. You really don't understand how it works, do you?" She gave me one of those watery smiles then and gently pressed her hands to my chest. "Get out, please."

I fought the urge to touch the spots on my chest where her hands had been. "Fine. If you die in here, though, I'm going to be pissed."

Booth stepped into the bathroom as soon as I was out of the way. I instantly grabbed his shoulder but he shrugged me off and held a bottle of water out to Ella. "Drink this. I ordered some ice cream to be delivered if you want to venture out for some later."

She took it and then moved forward and wrapped her arms around him. "Thank you, Booth."

I swore under my breath and dragged him out of the bathroom. Nodding to Ella like everything was fine, I pulled the bathroom door shut and pushed both of my best friends out of Ella's bedroom. Once we were in the hallway, I glared at both of them. "Fuck off with all of your shit. I told you she's off-limits. Out of bounds. Whatever else I need to call it to get it through your heads. She's like a little sister. Remember that."

Fisher just grinned back at me. "You sure about that?"

I shoved him. "Don't be disgusting, Fish."

Booth had a smile on his face that I didn't like. "I'm just saying... I think I helped the most. I got a hug."

I narrowed my eyes at him. We were the same height but he probably had fifty pounds on me. He would undoubtedly kick my ass if we fought, but I was sure I'd put up a damn good fight. "Booth. Leave her alone."

He held up his hands and backed away. "Relax, V. You're acting like a freak right now."

I felt like a freak. Ella had walked back into my life less than three hours earlier and I already felt like I'd aged a decade. I wasn't sure getting the house cleaned was going to be worth it.

"Maybe diamonds would make her feel better." Fisher walked down the hallway with his head tilted as he thought. "A set of diamond encrusted brass knuckles would go real nice with her feelings towards that prick."

I couldn't even be mad at that thought. "That's actually a pretty sick idea."

Booth nodded. "That fucking trumps ice cream any day."

We were all quiet as we made our way downstairs. Naturally we moved towards the kitchen and I grabbed a water from the fridge for myself. Glancing at Fisher, I frowned. "Don't actually buy her diamonds, Fisher. That's fucking weird."

He shrugged. "I do what I want, V. You know that. Shit doesn't change just because your little sister moved in."

"She's not my..." I threw up my hands. "Forget it."

7

Ella

Hours later, when my stomach made it clear that I wasn't going to be able to hide out for any longer, I washed my face and ventured out of my room. I couldn't get the thought of the ice cream Booth ordered for me out of my head. I took my time navigating down the hallway so I could look at what I was going to be cleaning. There was only one other room on my side of the hallway and I knew it was Fisher's from what he'd mentioned earlier. The door to his room was shut tight but I wasn't sure I was going to be expected to clean their actual bedrooms. I was hoping not because guys were gross in their personal spaces. I'd learned that the hard way from living with Vaughn the first time around.

I held onto the banister as I made my way downstairs, the plush runner on the steps making my descent silent. The second I stepped onto the hardwood floor and made a sound, Fisher stuck his head out of a room to the left of the entrance and grinned at me.

"We were starting to worry that you'd actually cried yourself to death." He motioned for me to follow him. "Hungry?"

Walking into a massive kitchen with an island big enough to use as a dance floor, I zoned in on the sink full of dishes right away. Bowls and plates spilled over onto the counters on either side and most of them looked disgusting with leftover food caked on. My hunger dimmed and I slowly moved my gaze to Fisher.

He looked back at me with a curious look on his face. "You're not seriously going to clean up after us, right? We have a maid service."

I took a deep breath and blew it out slowly. "I don't remember Vaughn being all that funny and I didn't get the impression he was joking. It's just more of the same stuff he pulled when we lived together before. Honestly, I'm desperate and I don't care, though. My options for housing weren't great."

"I get the impression you two weren't close."

I laughed and pointed at the fridge. "Did the ice cream come? And no, we were not close. He called me Cinderella and bullied me constantly."

"Maybe he had a crush on you. Boys aren't always all that smart." He opened the fridge and pulled out multiple tubs of ice cream. "Booth got a little excited to help you, I think. We had to put some of the flavors in the fridge in the garage."

I made a face. "We were step siblings. He was just an ass. I would say he still seems to be one, but he brought me here, so... Can I have the Moose Tracks?"

"Bowl?" He saw my facial expression and laughed. "No bowl. You're a straight from the tub girl, huh?"

Moving closer to him to get the ice cream, I smiled and nodded. "Using a bowl would only slow me down. Spoon?"

He winced and looked at the sink. "I haven't seen a clean one in a while."

"How often does your cleaning service come?"

"Once a week."

"Wow. I'm impressed. You guys did a lot of damage to this kitchen in not that much time." I joined him at the sink and we both stared down at it in silence for a bit. "This place might be the catalyst I need to lose a few pounds. I don't even want my ice cream anymore. It's like staring into the depths of hell."

Fisher turned to face me and when I looked up at him, I saw that he was running his eyes down my body. "Eat the fucking ice cream, Ella. I'll wash a spoon for you. Anything to keep you from touching those curves."

My face burned and I felt breathless as he met my gaze again. I wasn't expecting the interest I saw reflecting back from his deep green eyes. Instead of feeling flattered, I realized with a sinking feeling that I couldn't remember the last time Billy had said anything like that to me, or if he ever had. I swallowed a lump in my throat and shook my head. "I'm an idiot."

"What?"

"Nothing. Just the ramblings of a sad girl who moved states to chase a jerk. Ignore me." I turned to face the sink again and nodded. "I can do this. If I didn't throw up when I saw Billy in someone's vagina earlier, I'm not going to now. You should probably back up, though, just in case."

"I had an idea for diamond brass knuckles. On a scale of one to order them tonight, how much would those interest you and would they cheer you up?" Fisher leaned against the sink with his back to the dishes. "Also, Billy seems like a fucking idiot. I really support the idea of you letting Vaughn beat the shit out of him. I'd volunteer to do it myself but I'm a lover, not a fighter."

"Fisher." Vaughn's angry voice filled the kitchen and made me jump. As I watched, he stalked across the kitchen and grabbed Fisher's shoulder to shove him away from me. "Fuck off."

Fisher held up his hands and winked at me. "Say the word and the knuckles are yours."

I rolled my eyes at him and looked back at the dishes. "I'm at the beginning of my Cinderella story. It's too early for diamonds."

"Oh, I like that." Fisher grunted and stumbled when Vaughn shoved him. "Jesus, V, I'm leaving. Relax, big bro. I'm keeping my hands to myself."

Vaughn turned on me once Fisher was out of the room. He took Fisher's place beside me but when he looked down at me it was with a scowl on his face. "Stay away from my friends, Ella."

I looked up at him like he'd lost his mind. "Vaughn. I just broke up with Billy. You just listened to me sobbing like a baby a few hours ago. What part of me looks like I'm ready to jump on the first dick that comes my way?"

His face pinched. "Don't fucking say it like that. I'm just telling you, Ella, don't let them touch you."

"You're being weird." I bravely grabbed the top dish from the sink and set it aside. "You can rest easy, Vaughn. I'm not interested in your friends. I'm pretty sure I'm never going to date again."

"That's a little dramatic."

I turned so I was fully facing him. "Are you insane? What part of I found my boyfriend in another woman's vagina don't you get? Dramatic would've been slashing his tires and telling everyone on campus that he's got a small dick and a disease. Dramatic would be filling his frat house with rats and hoping one of them bites said small dick off. I think I'm handling this whole thing rather well, all things considered. So, don't call me dramatic. If I never want to date again, I'm never going to date again!"

Vaughn held up his hands. "Okay, okay. You're not dramatic and you're never going to date again. Great."

"And rinse the food off your dishes from now on. This is disgusting."

With a growing smile, he slowly backed away. "I don't think Cinderella got to be this bratty."

"Go away."

He patted my shoulder as he walked past. "Your ice cream is melting."

I looked back at the sweating tub and pouted. "Worst day ever."

8

Ella

I met Natalie Shawn on my first day of classes. She was in my Comparative Politics class and we'd instantly bonded when the professor made a statement that revealed his very misogynistic beliefs and we'd both groaned in perfect unison. We were both political science majors heading towards law school and we hit it off. When I wasn't studying or cleaning up after three of the grossest humans alive, I went to her campus apartment to hang out. It showed me pretty quickly what I'd been missing my freshman year at Penn. I'd been so involved in the long-distance relationship with Billy that I hadn't made time for anyone else.

The one thing I considered a flaw of Natalie's was that she was really into football. I wasn't publicizing that I was living with my ex-step brother and his two best friends so she had no idea that I was living with a good chunk of the starting line. She didn't understand why I wasn't excited about the football season starting. She was determined to turn me into a fan and her plan involved making me go to a game with her. If only she knew I saw the quarterback, the running back, and a defensive lineman every day and I didn't think I'd ever be excited about watching them throw a ball around.

The guys had been coming home from practices in various states of sweaty and exhausted. The first time I'd walked into the laundry room and stumbled upon a pile of their clothes, I'd nearly died. My nose still hadn't recovered. I didn't think I'd ever recover from a lot of things I'd seen and smelled over the three weeks I'd been living with them.

The only thing I liked about football was how much it kept the guys out of the house. I was practically living alone. I'd barely seen the guys since the day I moved in. I just saw signs of their existence, in dirty dishes and piles of discarded shoes and trash. I couldn't tell Natalie all of that, or at least, I didn't want to, so I couldn't come up with a good enough reason to get out of going with her to the first home game.

The day of the game I didn't have classes so I spent the first part of the day at home, getting ahead on class work and dreading going to the game. I was meeting Natalie outside of the arena, so I had a while to get dressed and prepared to face a crowd of screaming fans. Around lunch I made my way to the kitchen and sat at the counter, eating ice cream straight from the bucket. Booth had bought so much that I'd been mostly living off of ice cream since moving in. My curves were definitely not slipping away, that was for sure.

I was doing the thing I told myself I wouldn't do anymore while eating. Scrolling through Billy's social media, just to see what he was doing. He'd reached out to me a few times, but I was consistent in blowing him off. That didn't mean I wasn't curious, though. I wanted to know if he was dating the woman he'd cheated on me with. Had she been someone important? If she was, he wasn't showing it on his feeds. When he wasn't posting drunken selfies with his frat brothers, he was vague posting about being heartbroken.

The first time I'd seen one of those sad posts, I'd felt it all the way down to my toes. It hurt. My own broken heart wanted to forget everything and go back to the way things were, but I wasn't that person. I told myself the pain would fade with time and I was already feeling better. Day by day, it got easier. I couldn't stop looking through his profiles, though. I just needed to know what he was doing. It made me feel a little more in control.

I was studying a picture someone had tagged Billy in when a massive hand appeared from out of nowhere and grabbed my phone. I screamed and grabbed my chest. "Holy shit!"

Vaughn smirked down at me. "You were really into this picture, huh? I called your name and everything. What are you looking at so closely?"

Fear turned to panic very quickly. I didn't want anyone to know how pathetic I was being. I also didn't think it was a good idea for Vaughn to find out who my ex was. I tried to grab my phone back from him and swore when he turned away and held the phone higher. "Vaughn! Give it back!"

He spun back around so fast that I bumped into him and stumbled back into the stool I'd just gotten down from. "Billy Novak? Are you fucking kidding me?"

I felt blood rush to my face and grabbed my phone back before busying myself with putting my ice cream away. "Leave me alone, Vaughn."

"You were dating Billy Novak." He shook his head. "You've got horrible taste, Cinderella. That guy is a joke. That frat house is a step up from the Roadside Inn. And Billy Novak? He's the worst of them. The fact that you only caught him cheating once is kind of amazing."

"Vaughn." I closed my eyes and blew out a slow breath, trying my best to keep myself together. "Please stop talking."

"Shit." When I opened my eyes, Vaughn looked like he was in pain. Or like he smelled something terrible. I wasn't sure he was all that great at showing empathy. "I'm sorry."

Surprising us both, I laughed. "I've never heard you apologize before. Wow. Billy did one good thing in his miserable life. He made the great Vaughn Adler say he was sorry."

Vaughn's grin was quick. "You think I'm great? That's so sweet."

I finished putting my ice cream away and dropped my spoon in the dishwasher. "Why are you here?"

"Um. I live here. I'm the guy who told you that you could live with him in his house and this is that house."

"I mean right now, in the middle of the day. Shouldn't you be testing out your cups with the rest of the football team or something?" Like an idiot, I looked down at his crotch. When I realized what I was doing, I spun away and pretended I was busy wiping the counter down.

"Did you just look at my dick?"

9

Ella

I scoffed. "Don't be disgusting."

The sound of the door opening preceded the excited voices of Booth and Fisher growing closer. They came straight to the kitchen and they both smiled when they saw me.

Fisher came around the island and threw his arm over my shoulders. The weight of his arm and the warmth of his body reminded me how long it'd been since I'd touched another human. "Look who we found. I know that you live with us but I was starting to wonder if you'd left in the middle of the night."

I looked up at him and rolled my eyes. "Who do you think keeps kicking your shoes under the stairs?"

Booth grunted. "Do you know how hard it is for me to get those out? I'm too big to be crawling into small spaces."

Stealing a glance at his wide chest and shoulders, I made a sound of agreement. "I'm only sorry that I haven't had a chance to see it."

His mouth quirked up on one side. "You've got a mean streak, Ella. I like it."

Vaughn had reached his limit of acting like a normal person. "Knock it off. Get your arm off of her, Fish. Booth, don't flirt with her. Both of you, keep it in your fucking pants."

Embarrassment struck fast and hot. I shifted away from Fisher and crossed my arms. "Have you ever tried just being human for a minute? You're still the same little prick that you were all those years ago."

Vaughn's eyes flashed. "I knew you remembered me fondly."

My phone chimed and when I looked down at the notification, I nearly threw the thing across the room. Looking up at Vaughn with a renewed fury, I stepped closer. "What did you do?"

He actually moved back a step. "What are you talking about?"

"Billy just texted me to let me know he saw that I liked one of his posts. I didn't like any of his posts, Vaughn. I'm damn good about keeping my significantly smaller than yours fingers out of the way when I'm stealthily looking at a profile that I don't want anyone to know I'm looking at. Did one of your sausage fingers hit like on one of his pictures?"

"What? No. Why would I do that?" He winced. "On purpose."

I closed the gap between us and smacked his chest. "Dammit, Vaughn! Now he's going to think that I'm still longing for him. Gross!"

"So, you're not?" Fisher caught the death glare that Vaughn sent him and laughed. "Forget I asked."

"Let me talk to him. I'll make sure he knows you're not still interested." Vaughn's face turned darker as he stepped closer to me. "Maybe I'll pay him a visit anyway. He has it coming."

"You know which Billy he is?" Booth ignored the look I sent him.

"Novak." Vaughn's answer caused Fisher and Booth to both go quiet.

One look at them told me that they held the same views on Billy as Vaughn. I could also see the looks of pity on their faces. Shame overpowered my frustration easily. "It seems that everyone knew the real Billy except me."

"Yeah, I'm going to pay him a visit." Vaughn blew out a deep breath and lightly squeezed my shoulder. "Tell him that you were showing your new boyfriend the loser you left for him and you accidentally tapped the like button."

It was a stupid idea but I appreciated the thought. I forced a smile and shook my head. "I'm just going to keep ignoring him. And I don't want you to go talk to him. No one knows I'm living with you guys and I'd like it if it stayed that way."

"What is this feeling I'm feeling? No one has ever tried to hide me before." Fisher gestured at his body. "Why would they? Why would you, Ella?"

Vaughn groaned but I spoke over it. "I don't know if you guys have noticed but this campus is obsessed with football and the people who play it. I don't want everyone hearing about the loser living with you."

"Everyone already knows Fisher lives with us." Booth grinned, making his dimples deepen.

"Bully." Fisher walked over to me and booped the tip of my nose. "Your secret is safe with me. I don't want the rest of the team suddenly hanging out here to get a peek. It's bad enough that Booth and Vaughn are here with us."

"Dammit, Fisher." Vaughn pushed his friend away from me and frowned down at me. "He's right, though. It's already annoying as hell to make sure these two keep their hands to themselves. I'm not about to run defense with the rest of the team if they want to come ogle you, too."

I heard my phone chime again and sighed. "I hate you right now, Vaughn."

He grabbed my phone again and looked at the message. "And for no reason. It's from someone named Natalie. Apparently, she's very excited about going to the game with you tonight and thinks she can convince you to love it."

I took the phone back. "Not going to happen."

"If Natalie can't convince you to love us playing, maybe I'll put on a really good show for you tonight and maybe that'll open your heart." Fisher blocked Vaughn from hitting him again and laughed. "You're so touchy about your little sis, V. Such a great big bro."

I shuddered and beelined towards the stairs. "And on that note, I'm out of here."

"Do you know if your friend has good seats?" Vaughn followed behind me. "I could get you right on the fifty-yard line."

"Even if I knew what that meant, I'd say no. I don't want to have to explain how I got great seats to a game I didn't even want to go to. Thanks, though." I flashed him a quick smile before hurrying up the stairs.

"You've got a sticky note on your ass, by the way."

I groaned and moved faster. When I was alone in my room, I realized that I did, indeed, have a sticky note stuck to my ass. My shopping list had made it downstairs and back upstairs with me. Great.

10

Ella

Natalie did not have good seats. We were so high in the stadium that I was nervous. One misstep and I was a goner. Not knowing what to expect, I'd been beyond surprised by the amount of people pushing their way into the arena to watch a bunch of guys throw a ball around. Everyone was decked out in university gear and the amount of bare-chested guys with letters painted on their chests was staggering.

I squinted at the field and shifted away from the guy sitting next to me. "Is this what you thought it would be?"

Natalie groaned. "This isn't how you fall in love with football. You can barely see the team from here!"

I thought I could see them just fine. What would I need a better view for? There was a huge section of seating reserved for the band below us and when they started playing, the crowd erupted in cheers. I flinched and looked at Natalie with wide eyes. "What's happening?"

She pulled me to my feet. "Come on. The team is coming onto the field and I can't deal with these seats. I'm going to kick my cousin's ass for making me buy these from him. Next time, we'll get tickets for the student section."

I sidestepped an older man carrying a giant foam finger and an even bigger bucket of popcorn. I flashed him a smile and he waved his finger at me.

"Go Crocs!" His loud shout created a chain reaction of other shouts and cheers.

Between the band and the fans, I felt disoriented as Natalie pulled me after her. All the way back down to the ground level where we'd entered, she was impatient and tugged me along faster. She jumped up and down suddenly and waved her arm like crazy.

"Chris! Hey, Chris!" She had an impressive set of lungs on her and her voice carried to whoever she wanted it to. "Yes! Come on. I know this guy who takes action shots of the team from the sidelines and he'd better let us on the field after what I did for him last year."

"On the field?!" I tried to dig my feet in to stop her but she was determined. "Natalie! I don't want to go on the field!"

"It's the best way to experience your first game, Ella. Trust me." She pushed her way through a crowd of people waiting in line at a concession stand and I had no option but to tuck my elbows and stumble along with her.

There was a lanky guy waiting on the other side of the fence from us. "What's up, Nat?"

I watched as she transformed into someone softer and curled her hair around her finger. She leaned closer to the fence and grinned. "Hey, Chris. Do you need two eager assistants on the field today?"

He rolled his eyes at her. "Quit with the sweet act, Nat. I know you better than that."

She stomped her foot. "I let you touch my tits last year, Chris. This is a fair trade."

He glanced back at the field and when he looked back at her, there was something mischievous playing across his face. "Two dates."

"Are you kidding?"

"Two dates and you can come in."

She looked back at me and I could see the indecision playing across her features. With a sigh, she nodded. "Fine. Two dates. You can round a couple of bases, but don't get any big ideas. This doesn't mean anything." Chris flashed a smile. "It means something. Come on. Hurry up. I need to work."

I stared back and forth between the two of them and was so distracted by the energy flowing between them that I followed Natalie through a gate tucked away next to the stands. I'd forgotten that I didn't want to go on the field. At least I had until I stepped forward and got a view of the stands in my peripheral vision. It felt like they stretched on and on above us.

"Find a spot and park it. If you get me in trouble, it's going to be four dates." Chris winked at Natalie and nodded to where a bunch of men with giant cameras were positioned. "If you wedge your way in there, you'll get a hell of a view. Run when they run or you'll get plowed over."

"Not a chance in hell on those extra dates, buddy. But thanks for the heads up. Bye!" Natalie resumed her game of tugging me somewhere I didn't want to go but then we were on the sidelines, positioned way too close to the team. "Okay, they're doing the coin toss now. We didn't miss anything."

I furrowed my brows as I studied two equally giant guys in the center of the field. If the energy in the stands had been a lot, standing on the sidelines was going to kill me. A ref held up his hand and pointed to the left side of the field, causing the cheers to grow louder on our side of the stadium.

"We're kicking off first. Okay, so that guy running back this way? That's Fisher Hayes. He's the quarterback. He's got an arm like Peyton Manning with the accuracy of a seasoned sniper. Also, he's hot as hell." She squeezed my arm as she rushed out facts about what was happening. "This is our special team. They're going to..."

I tuned her out as I watched Fisher stand next to one of the couches. His hair looked like it was already soaked with sweat and I could see black paint smeared across his cheeks like war paint. In his uniform, he looked even bigger. The way the pants clung to his strong thighs wasn't terrible, either. Natalie jumped up and down and screamed. "Yes! The offense is going in on our thirty-yard line! This is going to be a piece of cake for Fisher and Vaughn!"

I cringed. I didn't want to run into Vaughn or even see him, but judging by the way Natalie was losing her mind, I didn't have a choice about seeing him. At least in the helmets, I couldn't tell most of the guys apart. I watched the two teams line up and squat facing each other and had to cover my mouth to cover up a giggle. It just looked silly to me.

"Watch Fisher. Number twelve. Vaughn Adler is number sixty-three." She held her breath as she watched the field. "We're going to the championship this year. I can feel it."

A random man walking past heard Natalie and high-fived her. "Hell, yeah! Go Crocs!"

On the field, I could hear Fisher shouting something about Denver and then a sound filled the air that sent a shiver down my spine. Men grunting, helmets knocking against other helmets, and a sharp intake of breath all around me. I didn't understand what was happening on the field but a ball went soaring over the heads of the guys hitting each other and then another guy in our colors ran past us and caught it. Screams went up all around and the energy turned pure electric when the guy with the ball crossed over a white line.

"Touchdown! Hell yes!" Natalie grabbed my shoulders and shook me. "Touchdown!"

I would've liked to say that I left that game just as I'd gone in. Instead, I left hoarse and full of excitement that I'd never felt before. I hadn't been able to stay detached when Natalie was screaming her head off and our team kept scoring. It was a rush, I realized quickly. By the time I got back to the house that night, I already had plans with Natalie to go to the next home game and I was thinking about buying a team shirt. I'd been infected by the football bug.

I just couldn't let my roommates know.

11

Ella

My throat still hurt the next day when I walked through the library, looking for a private place to study. Despite it being a Saturday, there were enough people spread out that I ended up on the third floor where the private study rooms were. Each of them had half glass walls but they were so frosted that it was impossible to see if anyone was in the room unless you walked in. The first two I tried were full and I was getting fed up with all of the studious people working on the weekend, despite being one of them.

I quietly knocked and opened the third door, feeling like I was on a bad game show, just to find the surprise behind the door was not one I wanted. It was the equivalent of a year's worth of jello being delivered to your door in one go.

Vaughn sat at the table, facing me. He sighed when he saw me and dropped his pencil. Leaning back in his chair, he tilted his head to stare at me. "Living with me isn't enough? Now you're following me to the library?"

"Forget it. I'll just go back to the house to study."

"Stay, Ella. I'm just fucking with you." He pulled his notebooks closer to his side of the table and gestured for me to sit down. "Just try not to be annoying and we won't have any issues."

I hesitated in the doorway. "Are *you* going to try not to be annoying?"

He smirked. "Just close the door and get your books out, nerd."

I found myself doing what he said and frowned. Once we were enclosed in the small room together, I thought I'd made a mistake. I couldn't exist in the same room as Vaughn without wanting to strangle him. I wasn't going to get anything done. My stubborn refusal to let Vaughn think he got to me was the only thing keeping me there.

"You sound like shit, by the way." He twirled his pencil around his fingers and then tucked it behind his ear. "Do a lot of screaming lately?"

My mouth popped open in shock. "Excuse me?"

"At the game, Ella. Jesus." He pulled his notebook closer and shook his head. "Get your mind out of the gutter."

I almost would've preferred he thought I was screaming for other reasons than admit that I'd loved my first football game. I opened my American Politics book and grabbed a highlighter. "What game?"

He snorted. "You think I didn't see you and your friend screaming and cheering on the sidelines? You didn't exactly blend in with the rest of the team, Ella Rae. It's okay. You can admit that you loved watching us."

Cutting him a stern look, I chose to ignore him. Thankfully, he didn't fight it. I was able to make it through my weekly reading material for class before his presence drew me out of my zone.

His energy had shifted into something darker since I came in and he looked frustrated as he stared down at a section of notes. I watched as he dropped his pencil on the table and reached up to rub his eyes. His jaw was clenched but when he noticed me staring at him, he relaxed his face and smirked at me. I could tell it wasn't real, though.

Against my better judgment, I decided to offer help. "Stuck on something?"

His mouth pinched and his eyebrows drew together in a deep frown. "It's fine."

Sighing, I stood up. "You look constipated right now and your energy is cramping up the room. Just tell me what you're stuck on. It helps to have someone else look at a problem you can't solve sometimes. What class is this?"

He made a grumpy sound as I pulled out the chair next to him and sat down. Staring at me, he took a few seconds to tell me. "Statistics. I need it to graduate but I put it off for so long. I haven't had to do math since the first semester of freshman year."

I smiled as a flash of memory came back. "I don't remember you loving math back in the day, either."

"I'll figure it out, Ella. Go back to your side."

I picked up his notebook and looked over his notes while he scowled at me. "I took a stats class last year. Let me help."

He raised his hand to his mouth and started to bite one of his nails before he stopped himself. Growling out his frustration, he ran his hands through his hair and nodded. "Fine."

Putting his book down between us, I leaned in and smiled what I hoped was a reassuring smile. "What's your assignment this week?"

He begrudgingly shrugged and then sighed. "I'm making up last week's work. With football, it can-"

"Relax, Vaughn. I'm not going to judge you. Not in here, anyway. This is a safe space." I looked up at him and we both laughed. "You know what I mean. You don't need to explain yourself to me. Let's just get it done. Okay?"

He studied my face until I felt it go warm. Leaning towards the book, I looked away from him and dismissed his lingering stare.

"Okay." Vaughn cracked his knuckles and grabbed his pencil. "The sooner this is over, the sooner I can get out of here. Libraries are for nerds."

Rolling my eyes at him, I had him pull up his syllabus and then I dove into working through what he did and didn't understand. It was tricky because I could feel him grow defensive with each thing he didn't understand. I'd worked as a tutor through high school, though, and I did my best to work around his discomfort like I was still getting paid for it. We worked together, heads down, until finally he sat back with a laugh.

I grinned at him. "You got it?"

He nodded and grinned back at me. "You made it make sense. Are you going to be a teacher when you grow up?"

"Nope. When I grow up, I'm going to be a lawyer." I looked down at his notebook and shrugged. "I had it all planned out. Graduate from Penn, get into law school, and go on to save the world. And then I lost my mind and followed Billy here."

Vaughn was quiet for a few seconds and then cleared his throat. "You're smart, Ella. You'll get what you want."

I lifted my head and met his warm gaze. He was being nice and we were having a normal interaction. It was so unexpected that I wasn't sure what to do with myself. We'd moved closer together while working and neither of us had moved back into our own space. I watched as his eyes flicked down to my lips and rabid butterflies erupted in my stomach. My eyes dropped to his mouth and I stopped breathing. He was so close. If I tilted my head back, he could-

A knock on the door scared me and broke whatever kind of moment we'd been having. I sucked in oxygen and stood up just as a guy opened the door to our little room.

"Sorry. I was just-"

I hurried around to my side of the table and gathered my things. "I was just leaving, actually."

"Same. Take the room, man." Vaughn grabbed his stuff and shoved it roughly into his backpack before following me out. He was silent until we were standing in front of the library with several feet of space between us. "Thanks for helping, Cinderella."

Acting like nothing had happened, because nothing had, I rolled my eyes. "Don't call me Cinderella."

"Sure thing, Cinderella." He backed away and lifted a hand in a wave.

I gasped as an idea came to me, though. "Wait! I have an idea."

He looked cautious as he moved closer again. "I'm not sure I want to know."

"Shut up, Vaughn." Just like that, we were back to normal. "I'm sick of cleaning your beard hair out of your sink. I want to change the deal. You let Fisher bring back his maids and I'll shift my services to making sure you pass statistics."

He glanced up at the library and I hoped he wasn't thinking about what I wasn't thinking about. "I'm going to need concrete plans before I agree to it. I'm not going to let you out of our deal just for you to flake on me."

"Get a life, Vaughn. I'm not going to flake on you. We live in the same house. I wouldn't get very far if you wanted to find me." I added a sweet smile at the end. "What I meant to say is I'll tutor you once a week. We can meet wherever you want."

"Two times a week." He saw my surprise and shrugged. "You saw how much I struggled, Ella. We meet here, two times a week. Third floor. I'm free on Wednesday nights and some Saturdays. Sundays work on the weeks Saturdays don't.."

I bit my lip and considered my options. It *had* been my idea. Anything would be better than doing their dishes, surely. "Fine. Two times a week. And you agree that I'm no longer cleaning up after you?"

He sighed. "Cinderella can retire for now."

Scowling at him, I slowly backed away. "I'm leaving now. I feel like I sold my soul to the devil and I need to go enjoy my last few days as a free woman."

"Grow up, Ella. I'm a joy."

12

Ella

That Wednesday's study session was perfectly normal. I made sure to keep a good amount of space between me and Vaughn. It was almost like our tense moment hadn't happened. He was the same pain in the ass at home, though. With my chore list cut down to just cleaning up after myself, I had a lot more free time to hang out in the common spaces of the house. A few times Vaughn had come home and spotted me sitting on the couch with Fisher or Booth. Somehow, he saw us talking as a gateway connection. He made a big fuss about his friends keeping their hands to themselves because apparently, talking led to screwing. It was just as embarrassing each time he did it.

He didn't seem to understand that his friends were just being nice to me and that his over the top reactions just encouraged them to continue teasing him. How he didn't see that they didn't want me was a mystery. Fisher was a shameless flirt, but it was obvious that it was just how he acted. Booth never even got close enough to touch me. Vaughn was just an idiot.

I'd even apologized to Fisher when we were alone in the living room watching TV together one afternoon. While we sat there, an awkward tension settled over us as a couple on TV began making out. I finally looked over at him and winced. "This is weird."

He laughed and nodded. "Yep."

Since I couldn't look back at the TV without blushing, I decided that was the right time to bring up Vaughn's behavior. "Hey, I just wanted to apologize for the way Vaughn's been acting. I feel like I moved in and immediately became a thorn in your side."

"You're apologizing for Vaughn?"

I groaned. "No. Maybe. I don't know. I just hate that he acts like such an idiot. He's like someone's uptight puritan father when it comes to us existing in the same space. I don't want it to become an issue between you guys."

He leaned forward and rested his elbows on his knees. "Vaughn's going to be Vaughn, love it or hate it. I've known he's an ass since the first day I met him and still I chose to become his best friend. You don't have to apologize for him. He's just being protective."

I scoffed. "There's nothing to protect me from! You and Booth are probably the least threatening guys on campus. You've been nothing but kind to me. He acts like you're pulling your dick out when he's not looking."

Fisher raised his eyebrows and stared at me. He looked like he was going to say something and stopped himself. Instead, he shook his head and smirked at me. "Maybe he's just used to guys pulling their dicks out around him."

I grinned. "That's good. I liked that."

We'd watched TV together for a while longer, until I realized I was late meeting Natalie and had to run out. It'd been nice, hanging out with Fisher. He was funny and playful in a way that didn't allow me to feel so tense all the time. Hanging out with Booth was like hanging out with a teddy bear. He was so sweet and I felt safest when it was just us together. They were both so nice to me, but it didn't stop Vaughn from being Vaughn, just like Fisher said.

Their game that week was on Saturday morning at a college two hours away. I had the house to myself on Friday night and then I watched the game with Natalie in The Swamp, the massive hang out area under the cafeteria. The dozen or so couches were all full as we cheered on the team from afar. When I was just as excited to watch the second game as I'd been after the first, I knew I'd found a new guilty pleasure.

The excitement bled over into the rest of my day, even after I was back at the house alone. The guys had played so well and it was so cool to hear all three of them being called out on national television for how good they were. The entire campus was energized by another win. I could hear the parties on frat row like they were happening in our backyard.

When the guys got home that night, looking proud with their gym bags slung over their shoulders, it was that chaotic energy that made me forget myself. I rushed out of the living room and pumped my fists in the air. "You guys did so good!"

Booth was closest and he grunted as I bounced into his chest and hugged him. Before he could react, I moved to Vaughn and hugged him. Fisher was waiting for me when I got to him. He wrapped his arms around my lower back and hugged me back. His warm body pressed against mine from chest to thighs and I felt a different type of electricity.

Vaughn growled and pulled me out of Fisher's arms. "Fuck off, Fisher. Jesus."

"What's that smell?" Booth sniffed the air and licked his lips. "Did you bake something?"

Still reeling from feeling Fisher's body against mine, I nodded and pointed to the kitchen. "Cookies. As a congratulations for winning."

Booth pulled me into another hug and lifted me off my feet. "I could get used to this."

I laughed and stumbled back a step when he put me down and vanished on his way to the kitchen. Looking up at Vaughn, I did my best to ignore the way my body was reacting to them. "Natalie said you were amazing today. Good job."

Booth reappeared with two cookies in his big hands and a smile on his face like a little kid. "They say our names! You're perfect, Ella. How did you even do this?"

Fisher took one of the cookies and whistled. "Damn, Ella. If it tastes as good as it looks, I might have to marry you."

I blushed and waved them off. "It was nothing. Anyway... I just wanted to say congrats and tell you guys thanks for making watching football fun. If you weren't very good, I don't think I'd like it. That'd just feel sad."

Vaughn still hadn't taken his eyes off of me. I braced for him to make a comment about me keeping my hands to myself, but he surprised me. "You were a great baker as a kid, too. That's what you wanted to do back then, right?"

I softened towards him so much after those words. I looked up at him with a stupid grin on my face and nodded. "Yeah, I did. I can't believe you remember that."

Fisher and Booth were groaning behind him as they ate their cookies and Vaughn blinked a few times before looking away from me. When he looked back, there was a smirk on his face and a coldness that was much more of what I expected. "I have a good memory. Thanks for the cookies."

Taking a deep breath, I slowly backed towards the stairs. I was feeling a lot of things and I wanted to get away from them. The feelings and the guys. "I'm glad you guys are home safe. I'm calling it a night."

"Boo. Stay down here with us and watch us devour these cookies." Fisher spoke around a big bite and lost a few crumbs in the process. "Damn."

"We're going out. Right?" Vaughn's annoyance was just getting worse.

"Have fun!" I turned and sped up the stairs. I was breathing hard when I got to my room but the second I was closed inside my locked room, I couldn't think about my breathing. I could just think about the way my body felt after hugging them. It still felt tingly and warm. My mind flashed with a giant danger sign.

I did my best to brush it off. I knew better. So much better.

13

Fisher

Campus was always fun the week after a win. Being the star of the show didn't hurt, either. I couldn't go more than twenty feet without someone stopping me to talk about the game. I welcomed the chats and had made more than my fair share of friends through those meetings. As I tossed a football in the air that Monday morning, though, I didn't want to be stopped. I had something else in mind. Someone else, really.

I searched the students leaving the English building and spotted Ella and her high ponytail right away. She had a natural bounce to her walk that made that ponytail sway from side to side and did things to her body that made my mouth water. She was talking to a guy I recognized from the games and the way she was smiling up at him made me feel a little like Vaughn. Especially the punchy part.

Moving towards them, I nodded at someone who tossed out a 'good game'. Feeling a lot like a heat seeking missile, I closed in on Ella. She glanced away from the guy and did a double take when she saw me. Her smile grew even brighter somehow and I watched in awe as her cheeks turned pink.

"Fisher! What are you doing here?" She rolled her eyes and kept talking. "I mean, you go to school here, so it makes sense that you would be here. Duh. I'm just surprised to see you. Nice football."

The guy she'd been talking with nodded at me and laughed. "That's my cue. See you, Ella. Tell Nat I said she's a chicken."

Ella groaned after he walked away and looked up at me through her lashes. "You know how sometimes you forget how to people? That just happened to me. Let's not talk about it."

I held my ball out to her. "But what about my nice football?"

She laughed and pushed it away. "Why are you here, making me embarrass myself?"

"I was in the neighborhood?" I fell into step with her as we walked towards the quad. "Did you have a good class? Who's the guy?"

She stopped walking and stared up at me with her hands on her hips. "I had a good class, yes. The guy is Chris, someone who is interested in my friend, Natalie. Were you waiting on me?"

I shrugged. "Maybe. Maybe not."

"Why were you waiting on me?" She didn't budge as people walked around us.

I couldn't pull my attention from her as people threw out congrats. They were just white noise. "Can't a guy just want to walk a girl around campus?"

Her big green eyes widened. "Like a dog?"

I choked as I tried to rush to correct her but then I realized she was laughing. Frowning at her, I shook my head. "Now I'm seeing the connection to Vaughn."

She gasped and slapped my football out of my hands. "Take it back."

I moved closer to her. "What are you going to do if I don't?"

"Murder seems like a fair punishment." She smirked up at me then and I felt a chill go down my back at how sneaky she looked. "Also, I happen to know that you are one of the only people left in the world that still gets their porn magazines mailed to them."

I gaped down at her and floundered for a second before I took her elbow and pulled her off the sidewalk. I could feel my face burning and tried to find some semblance of cool. "What the hell, Ella?"

Her eyes danced with laughter. "I cleaned your bathroom, Fisher. I honestly thought you were leaving them out as a conversation piece or something."

"A conversation piece? Jesus."

"It's not a big deal. I'm not really going to tell anyone. Even if I wanted to, no one would believe that those magazines still exist. Do you not know about internet porn, Fisher?" She was having fun, I could tell.

I stepped closer to her, determined to save some face. "What do you know about internet porn, Ella?"

Both of our faces were red and we'd landed ourselves in uncharted territory but I wasn't ready to back down. I hoped she wasn't, either. Spending time with her alone was my favorite thing to do those days.

She inched closer. "I know that your magazine interests are very dirty. Such a wide variety of interests you have."

"Did you sit and take your time going through them? That's questionable, Ella. And not at all appropriate behavior for Vaughn's little sis."

"You did not go there." She went up on her tiptoes to really glare at me. "I'm pretty sure, by law, I could bite you for calling me his little sister."

I grinned. "By law, huh?"

"Ella?"

Ella's playfulness vanished in less than a second. Coming towards us was her ex, Billy Novak, with a curious look on his face. I tensed and rested my hand on Ella's back without a second thought. I told myself I was being protective, the same way Vaughn would've been.

"Ella. Hey. I've been trying to call you." He looked her over and smiled. "You look really good."

Ella wrapped her arms around herself and leaned closer to me. "I've been busy."

"Do you think we could talk? I have a lot I need to say." He was doing his best to look earnest and innocent, I could tell. "A lot to apologize for."

Ella looked up at me and I could see the panic swirling behind her eyes. I was getting ready to step in and tell Billy to get fucked when Ella turned back to him. "I have a boyfriend now so I don't think that's a good idea. Sorry."

Billy looked up at me and then back at Ella. "You're dating Fisher."

I didn't like the incredulous tone in his voice. I also didn't like the way Ella's entire body had tensed. I didn't need to think about what I did next to know it was right. I wrapped my arm around Ella and pulled her into my chest. Sending my cockiest smirk towards Billy, I pressed my lips to the side of Ella's head. She smelled so damn good that I almost got distracted.

"She's dating Fisher."

14

Fisher

I reveled in how stupid he looked, standing there, unsure of what to do with himself. "Who are you?"

Ella tipped her face up to mine. "Just an ex. We should go."

Her full mouth was rosy and looked so plush that I didn't want to deny myself the chance to taste her. I didn't even bother lying to myself to say that I was doing it to hurt her cheating ex. Cupping her face, I slid my hand into her hair and held her gaze as I lowered my mouth towards hers. When I saw that she wasn't going to pull back, I softly kissed her, still worried about scaring her. With the way she could banter back and forth with me, I should've known she wasn't going to faint from a simple kiss.

Ella fisted my shirt and pulled me closer. She parted her lips and caught my bottom lip between hers before pulling back just enough for our breath to rush out. That second of space felt cavernous and I gripped her hair to pull her back. That time, I knew what she could handle and I felt her body soften into mine when I kissed her deeper. The feel of her tongue against my lips set fire to any sense and control I might've had left.

Sliding my hand down her back, I cupped her ass and pulled her against my body as flush as I could get her. I slid my tongue over hers and groaned when she gripped my sides and shifted her hips against mine. I gripped her ass harder and felt her moan against my lips.

"Get a room!"

Ella pulled back with a gasp but I wrapped my arms around her and held her steady before she could jerk away and give away the fact that we'd just had our first kiss.

"We're good. All good, Ella." I glanced around and saw that we'd gotten some attention but Billy had fucked off. I leaned down so I could whisper against her ear. "He's gone."

She groaned against my chest. "Um. We put on a great show, right? Good job acting, Fisher. If football doesn't work out, you can fall back on being the next heartthrob in Hollywood. Me, too. I mean, I wouldn't be a heartthrob, of course. Wow. Good job."

I studied her swollen lips and blown out pupils and knew that she'd been just as into that kiss as me. I was just thrown off enough to not deny that it was all an act. "I don't think he's going to bother you again."

She untangled herself from my hold and took a step back. Glancing around, she noticed that we'd had an audience and palmed her face. "Oh, my god. I just announced that we're dating. I'm so sorry, Fisher. People saw us and… Do you think people are going to talk about this?"

I nodded. "Yeah. Big time."

"Oh, no. I'm really, really sorry. I didn't mean to make people think we were dating, Fisher. I just panicked."

I took her hand and walked with her towards the cafeteria. When she shot a curious look my way, I winked at her. "We're dating now, doll. Didn't you hear?"

"Fisher, you don't actually have to do this. I don't care if Billy finds out I was lying. I don't care about him at all." She tried to pull her hand away but I tightened my grip. "I'm serious, Fisher. I don't want to cramp your style around campus."

"My style around campus?"

"You know… With the ladies?"

I laughed out loud and had to stop walking while I regained my composure. "With the ladies? Really?"

Her cheeks flamed. "You know what I mean. If people think you're dating me, you won't be able to...you know. Unless you would cheat on your fake girlfriend. If you're that type of fake boyfriend, we should end it now, though. Being cheated on once this year was enough. Fake, or not."

I turned to face her and leaned down so we were eye to eye. "I'm not a cheater. I'm also not really a dater. You're the first girl to call me boyfriend on campus."

"Why?" I could see a cluster of freckles across her nose and when it crinkled in confusion, I watched them disappear like a cute magic trick.

"Why, what?"

"Why haven't you dated anyone?"

I shrugged as I straightened. "I was having too much fun, I guess."

Her mouth turned down as she studied me. "A good relationship can be fun."

I raised my eyebrows at her.

"Okay, so I guess I don't have a lot of personal experience, but I've heard that." She ducked her head and the expression on her face when she looked back up at me made my chest tighten. "Thank you for going along with that, Fisher. You didn't owe me anything and you could've really embarrassed me, but you didn't. I just didn't want to look like a loser in front of Billy. It's just... It's embarrassing, but he knows he was my first. Everything. I don't want him thinking he's still my only. Even if he is."

Volunteering to make it real was on the tip of my tongue but a mental image of Vaughn's head exploding stopped me from saying the words. Instead, I stepped closer to her and cupped the side of her neck. "After that kiss, I'm pretty sure he's going to think he's been thoroughly replaced, Ella."

"Thank you."

I should've been the one thanking her for that kiss. I smiled and took a deep breath that made our chests brush against each other. Her quick intake of breath was more proof that she was as attracted to me as I was to her. "We're doing this. I'm your boyfriend, Ella. I'm committed."

Her bubbling laughter was almost enough to make me kiss her again. "This is crazy. You don't need to do this. What if you meet your dream girl tomorrow?"

Crazy was the quiet voice in my head trying to tell me that I already had. I ignored it. "It's fine, Ella. I'm in. I'll keep my dick in my pants until you're ready to dump me."

Ella shook her head and backed out of my hold. Planting her hands on her hips, she blew out a big breath. "No. That's ridiculous."

"Well, I'm not a cheater, Ella. So...?" I smirked and tilted my head at her while I waited for her to get my joke and punch me.

She laughed like I'd told the best joke in the world. She even reached out and gently slapped my arm. "Oh, my god. Vaughn would've hated that joke. You're really going to give him a complex. I keep trying to tell him that you aren't trying to make moves on me but he's nuts."

I didn't think I could say a thing without bursting her bubble. If she thought I wasn't making moves, the moves I made could be played off as just filling the fake boyfriend role. I was an asshole.

"Oh, no. He's going to hate this, isn't he?" She let her head fall back and groaned. "This is just the kind of thing to piss him off."

"I'd be surprised if he hasn't already heard that I was trying to dry hump you in the middle of campus." Seeing her shocked face, I couldn't help laughing. "I'll handle him."

"Oh, yeah... I think I was too surprised at hearing I'd been dry humped to even think about him." Her eyes narrowed as she looked off in the distance. "Maybe we can make this work for everyone, though. Vaughn seems to think everyone is going to try to screw me, for whatever insane reason. If I'm publicly dating you, no one's going to make a move on me. Vaughn will have one less thing to worry about."

A sick sense of happiness settled over me. Even if it wasn't for real, everyone on campus would know that Ella was mine. That would be enough to keep most assholes away from her. I felt like Vaughn in that moment, but I liked knowing Ella was going to be seen as mine and that no one would mess with her.

"You're right. I'll make sure to explain it to him in that way." I wrapped my arms around her waist and pulled her close. Dropping my mouth to her ear, I smiled as I felt her shiver. "We've got to keep up appearances if we're going to do this. Is that okay with you?"

She brought her arms up around my neck. "You know, not all couples are so touchy."

The clean scent of her skin drew my lips closer to her neck. "That's not my couple style, Ella."

"You don't have a couple style."

I ran my nose along the curve of her shoulder before forcing myself to raise my head. "I know how I'd act as half of a couple with you, Ella."

"Yo, Fish! You dropped your ball, man. That's not how you get us to the championship game!"

Ella pulled herself free. "You dropped your nice football?"

I grinned. "And got my hands on something much nicer."

15

Ella

The fact that Fisher had never had a girlfriend was mind-boggling because he was a great fake boyfriend. Better than great. He made my relationship with Billy look like nothing. That first day he walked me to class and then was there to pick me up afterwards. He opened doors for me and carried my backpack, like a perfect gentleman. The only place he dropped the gentleman act was when he touched me. His touches didn't feel gentlemanly, or fake. His large hands touched my body like it was his. And that kiss… That kiss played across my brain a thousand times. It was the best kiss I'd ever had. I'd been in love with Billy and his kisses had never felt like that.

Of course, with all the fake relationship fun came Vaughn's wrath. I was in my room, trying to get some work done when all I could think about was the kiss, when I heard him shouting. I knew right away that he was yelling at Fisher. Since it was my fault that Fisher was cast in the role of my fake boyfriend, I rushed out of my room and found them inside Fisher's room.

"Imagine if your ex-step sister showed up here, Fish! It's fucking weird! There are thousands of women on this campus, asshole! Go fuck one of them." Vaughn growled out a frustrated breath. "If there are any you haven't fucked already since I know you don't normally do seconds. And you're shocked that I wouldn't want you touching Ella!"

"Vaughn!" I crossed my arms over my chest as both of them turned to me. "You're being an asshole to your best friend for no reason. It's my fault that Fisher ended up in this position."

"How the fuck is it your fault?"

"He was there and Billy showed up and I panicked. I just said that Fisher was my boyfriend. He was nice enough not to humiliate me in front of my ex. You should be thanking him for being there for me, not screaming at him." I looked at Fisher. "I'm sorry. You don't deserve to be yelled at."

Vaughn turned his glare back to Fisher. "It's not real? Are you fucking serious, Fisher? Why didn't you just say that?"

Fisher smirked. "You didn't give me the chance, dickhead."

"You should apologize to him."

Vaughn gaped at me. "What?"

I nodded. "Yeah, you should apologize for shouting at him like that. You've been a jerk to your friends since I got here and it's not fair. They've been nothing but nice to me. Fisher saved me today. Instead of doing whatever you're doing to keep me single and sex-starved, you should be thanking him for not letting me fall flat on my face earlier. Now apologize."

His jaw muscles worked as he clenched his teeth. "Ella Rae..."

I dropped my hands to my hips and narrowed my eyes. "I'm not moving from this spot until you do."

He growled. "You think I can't move you?"

"And have me experience the male touch? Oh, no! That's too scandalous."

"God, you're still a pain in the ass." He turned to Fisher. "I'm sorry. I should've given you a chance to explain. I still don't fucking like it, though."

I flashed a grin at Fisher and dusted my hands together. "My work here is done. Now, keep it down. I'm trying to work."

"You're working? What are you doing?" Vaughn's strangled voice matched Fisher's startled expression. "What kind of work are you doing in your room at this time of night?"

I sent them both a blank stare. They couldn't be serious. "I'm selling myself through the world wide web, of course."

Vaughn's face turned a shade of red so dark that I worried for his health. Fisher wasn't much better.

I rolled my eyes. "I'm doing homework, idiots."

Fisher sat down on his bed and patted his chest. "Don't scare us like that."

"I would've called your mother so fast." Vaughn shook his head. "I'm not going to be responsible for your downfall."

"Although, I would consider selling my feet pics if it meant not taking on so much debt." I left them with that.

After understanding that it was fake, Vaughn seemed to relax the tiniest bit. For the next week, when Fisher drove me to campus and walked me to class, Vaughn kept his mouth shut. He put his foot down about Fisher bringing me to the library for our tutoring sessions, though. I figured he was sensitive about having me tutor him so I went with it. I also figured Fisher might want a break from me.

They had another home game that weekend and since the entire campus thought I was dating Fisher, he insisted that Natalie and I sit in the seats he chose for us. We ended up being front and center, right behind the fifty-yard line. I even knew what that meant after spending so much time with Natalie.

Natalie was so excited about the seats that she barely grilled me about my sudden relationship with Fisher. She was also too busy glaring at Chris. He was busy taking photos and she huffed at his back so much that I finally asked about it.

"Did you go on your dates?"

She shot me a look that could've melted steel. "Don't even mention those stupid dates."

I held up my hands. "Sure."

She crossed her arms over her chest. "Do you know that he took me to a candlelit dinner? He planned the whole stupid thing with some friends and it was all romantic and shit."

I rolled my lips into my mouth and raised my eyebrows. I was confused about which way I was supposed to react so I just waited.

"He said all this mushy crap about wanting to date me and he didn't even try to feel me up. What the hell is that about?" She flipped off his back and turned her glare towards the play on the field. "He doesn't even know me. It's honestly so dumb."

I saw Chris turn towards the stands and watched him lift his camera in our direction. He looked through his lens for a moment and then looked up at Natalie. Despite how angry Natalie was towards him, his smile wasn't the smile of a man ready to give up. I waved at him and he waved back before going back to work.

"Was he just looking over here? What did he do?" She sat up straighter and adjusted her clothes.

"Okay, Natalie. I don't want to be rude but what the hell is wrong with you? You're primping for him right now! While telling me how he took you on a really nice date and was a gentleman the whole time. Why are you mad? I don't get it."

I heard the announcer call out Booth's name and watched as his teammates slapped him on the back. Frustrated that I'd missed his big play, I frowned. He got called out less often than Fisher or Vaughn, because of his position. I stood up and cheered, forgetting that no one else knew why I'd be so happy for Booth. It didn't matter when I saw him glance up at me. His helmet and face guard couldn't hide his grin as he waved to me.

"When did you become besties with half the football team?" Natalie sighed. "And I'm not mad. I'm just... I'm too young for a serious relationship and Chris is a serious relationship guy. Last year, I was going to let him fuck me but he wanted to take me out first. He *likes* me, Ella, and he won't just tell me to jump off a cliff, no matter what I do."

"I gave up my dream college to follow my boyfriend here so I don't really understand the hesitation. Who cares about the timing? Yeah, you're young, but it's not like dating someone ends your entire life." I shrugged. "He's really nice, Natalie. If you just don't like him, though, tell him."

She bit her lip. "I do like him. It's just too fast."

We spent the rest of the game splitting our attention between the game and each other. It was clear that our team was going to win by a landslide but it was still electric. After the last play of the game, I stood up, prepared to join the mass of people leaving the stadium.

"Whoa." Natalie's surprised voice had me turning to see what she was looking at.

My breath caught in my throat as I saw what she, and a lot of other people, were seeing. Fisher had jumped up and pulled himself over the railing. Big, sweaty, and hotter than anything I'd ever seen, he was laser focused on me. He jumped over a row of seats to go around a group of people and then he stepped back down right in front of me.

His skin was flushed and his war paint was streaking down his cheeks but his deep green eyes were narrowed on my mouth in a way that made me forget how dirty he was. He picked me up with two handfuls of my ass and took my mouth in a heated kiss that was somehow even better than the first one.

As cheers went up around us, I pulled away from his kiss and buried my face in his neck. My body hadn't got the memo about the relationship being fake. It was throbbing with need in a way I'd never felt. The suddenness of his attention had my brain spinning.

He patted my ass as he put me down. Pressing his forehead to mine, he grinned. "I like this girlfriend thing. Turns out I'm a celebratory kiss kind of guy."

I patted his chest and tried to level out my breathing. "Yeah, you are. I... Wow."

He cupped my face and tilted it up to his so he could kiss my mouth with light, teasing touches that somehow turned me on just as much as the intense kisses. "You're going to smell like me now."

I blinked up at him and then swallowed. "Oh?"

"I like it." Dropping one more kiss on my mouth, he slowly backed away, nearly running Natalie over. "I'll see you at home?"

I smiled like an idiot and nodded. "Yeah, of course."

With a final wink, he turned and jogged away. I watched him until he ran past Vaughn and then Vaughn's dark expression stole my attention. My stomach sank as he shook his head and turned away.

"Home?" Natalie patted her chest. "God, that was hot."

Shit.

16

Ella

"That sure as hell didn't look fake." Vaughn scowled at me as he leaned over and thrust his passenger door open. "Get in, Ella." I'd been walking home in the dark to cool off after that kiss but after creeping myself out, a ride sounded great. Even if it was with Vaughn. I climbed in and he waited until I had my seatbelt on to pull away from the curb. "I don't know what to tell you, Vaughn. It *was* fake."

"Bullshit. I know Fisher. He's not *that* nice. Billy was nowhere around tonight and he still had to put on that giant show? I asked you for one thing. Don't fuck my friends. Is it that hard to do?"

I was getting sick of his terrible moods. "Vaughn, I don't know how many times I can tell you this, but I'm not sleeping with your friends. Fisher is putting on a good show, that's all. You're in the same house as us. Don't you think you'd notice if we were having sex?"

He shot me a look. "I'm not an idiot. I saw that kiss tonight. He grabbed you like he fucking owned you."

My face heated but I shifted to face him more fully. "What is your problem? Even if I was sleeping with Fisher, it wouldn't be any of your business! I cleaned up after you for weeks, like we agreed on. I tutor you twice a week, like we agreed on. You act like I signed a freaking contract to be the next virgin Mary, though. You're not my dad, Vaughn! You're not my stepbrother anymore, either. You don't get to control me."

"If I was your dad, I wouldn't give a shit who you fucked."

The words were heavy and they cut deep, just the way he wanted. I snapped my mouth shut and turned to look out the window. He'd been cruel to me as a kid but he'd never said anything that hurt quite like that.

"Jesus, Ella. I'm just trying to keep the house from exploding. No matter what Fisher says, he's not a relationship kind of guy. What's going to happen when he leaves you crying in your bathroom? Am I supposed to kick his ass for you? When I told you to stay away from him?"

"Shut up, Vaughn." I wrapped my arms around myself and pressed my forehead into the warm glass. "Just shut up."

He swore. "I didn't mean to say that, Ella. I'm just-"

"You're just an asshole. You always have been. That was messed up, even for you, though. But, it's fine. We're not friends. I don't need you to be nice to me. I just want you to leave me alone. I'm not sleeping with anyone. I don't know how many more ways I can say it."

"I'm the asshole who let you move into his house, Ella."

I turned to him and waited until he looked back at me to speak. "Do you want me to leave? I could probably find something else now. Just say the words and I'll go."

He pulled into the driveway and shut the truck off. "Dammit, Ella, I'm not trying to kick you out."

"Are you trying to run me out? Because you're doing a pretty good job of it. I don't deserve you snapping at me all the time for something I'm not doing. I definitely didn't deserve that crack about my absentee father." I shoved open the door and got out. "I don't want to talk to you anymore tonight."

I slammed the door and marched towards the house, just to hear his truck start up again and him speeding out of the driveway. I glared after his truck and wanted to throw a handful of rocks at it. Jerk.

After letting myself into the house, I went upstairs and took a shower so I could change into my pajamas and go straight to bed. I wanted to call Mom and bitch about Vaughn but she was on a date and I didn't want to bother her. Instead, I punched my pillows a few times to fluff them and then I slumped into them and glared at my ceiling. I held Connie to my chest and tried to calm down. What a way to end a great night. Vaughn should've been majoring in how to be a major buzz kill.

I heard the alarm ding to signal the front door opening downstairs and heard heavy footsteps coming up the stairs a few seconds later. I sat up and braced myself for it to be Vaughn, coming to hurt my feelings some more. I was so ready for it to be him that when someone knocked, I just blurted out my real feelings. "Get fucked, Vaughn!"

The door creaked open and Fisher stuck his head in. "Not Vaughn. It sounds like that's a good thing, though."

After the kiss at the game, my body was still wired so seeing Fisher was a jolt to my system. "Hey. What are you doing here? Shouldn't you be out partying? You played a good game, after all."

He walked closer and stopped at the foot of my bed. "I wanted to check on you. I saw Vaughn after the game and he wasn't in the best of moods. I had a feeling he might take it out on you."

I clutched Connie tighter. "Well, he made a crack about my dad not caring about me, so that was nice."

"What the fuck?" Fisher came around the bed and sat down next to me. "Are you okay?"

"I don't know." I rolled my eyes. "I mean, yes. I'm okay. It was a low blow, even for him. My dad left me and my mom right after I was born.

Vaughn knows that. I shouldn't let him bother me, but I can only let so much crap go before it starts to hurt."

He frowned. "Vaughn knows better than that shit. I can talk to him. He can't treat you like that."

"No, don't. He's already convinced that we're sleeping together and lying to him about it." I pushed my hair behind my ears. "I don't know why he cares."

"I have my suspicions." He reached out and tapped Connie. "Want me to cheer you up?"

I laughed and shook my head. "You don't have to do that, Fisher. You should go out and celebrate."

"I don't do anything I don't want to do, Ella. Tonight, I'd like to cheer you up. Meet me in my room in ten minutes. You can bring your friend if you want." He stood up and backed away. "Action or comedy?"

"Action." I smiled. "Thank you."

"Hey, I'm doing this for me, too. I remember what it's like to hear you crying and this is me trying to practice some self-preservation. I almost pulled the trigger on those diamond knuckles last time."

As soon as he was out of my room, I did what I shouldn't have. I rushed to the bathroom and brushed my teeth, dabbed a bit of perfume behind my ears, and rubbed lotion into my legs since I was wearing shorts. I primped. The voice in the back of my head was throwing up warnings right and left but I ignored them all and headed to Fisher's room.

17

Ella

Fisher was in the middle of kicking a pile of clothes under his bed when I stepped into his open doorway. He looked back at me and grinned. Standing up straight and making sweeping arm motions towards his bed, he laid out his vision. "I stole some of the couch cushions to transform my bed into movie quality seating. I brought up your favorite ice cream, popcorn, and drinks. There's a list of action movies for you to pick from. Oh, and you can change the thermostat to whatever temperature suits you best. It's Ella's night at the movies in Fisher's room. Welcome."

I tried to fight a stupid grin but it was useless. All of my anger vanished instantly. Walking over to him, I hugged him briefly and then pointed to the bed. "Which side?"

He walked over to the door and looked back at me. "Is it okay if I close this? And whatever side you want. I usually stretch out in the middle, but I'll keep to myself for movie night."

I nodded for him to close the door but as soon as he did, my pulse jumped. I was alone in Fisher's room with him and we were closed in. Those danger bells kept ringing in my head.

"Do you want it warmer in here? I keep the AC turned down low so it might freeze you out. Lucky for you, the bedding was all changed today, so if you need, you can curl up under the blanket." He stopped. "The bedding wasn't disgusting before it was changed, or anything. I promise."

Laughing, I climbed onto the side farthest from the door. "I like it colder, too."

He passed me ice cream and popcorn before turning off the lights and hopping in the bed next to me. "Okay. Pick whatever movie you want. It's your night."

"Are there any you haven't seen but want to? I'm not picky." I saw him hesitate over one and nodded. "That one."

"Do you need anything else before it starts?" He saw me shake my head and hit play. "Popcorn me."

I shifted closer to the middle and put the bucket between us. "There. Do you want some ice cream, too?"

For the first half of the movie, we shared snacks, even eating from the same spoon, and watched the movie in a comfortable silence. When we'd finished everything, Fisher cleared off his bed and stretched out next to me. I stayed upright until Fisher noticed me shiver and grunted.

"Get under the blanket. I'll do it if you do it. I can't be the first one to admit they're cold."

I laughed and we both got under the covers. We were closer somehow, but we kept watching the movie without issue. After a few minutes, Fisher turned his head to watch me.

"Still cold?"

I wasn't freezing but I wasn't exactly toasty. "I'm fine."

He lifted the blanket and nodded at his body. "Come here. I'm a great furnace once I'm in bed."

Hesitating for just a moment, I glanced at the door and back at his face. After adamantly denying that I was doing anything with Fisher, it felt a whole lot like I was doing something with him. "Do you offer all your fake girlfriends cuddles for warmth?"

He rolled his eyes. "Since you're my first, I guess the answer is yes."

Throwing caution to the wind, I scooted across the bed and right up against his side. He was right. He was so warm, especially when he wrapped his arm around me and held me closer.

"Okay?"

I wanted to laugh. I was a whole lot better than okay. It would've been a slippery slope if he'd been interested in me. "Yeah, I'm okay. This is really nice. Thank you, Fisher."

"Don't thank me too much. I have a few ulterior motives." His hand moved up and down my arm, gently stroking me. "I knew you'd be a great cuddler, for one. Another is that I wanted to watch this movie, of course. And..."

I glanced up at him and saw that he was staring down at me with a serious expression on his face. "And?"

He smiled. "I wanted to spend more time alone with you."

My stomach erupted in butterflies. "Because I'm your fake girlfriend?"

He shook his head. "No. I have a confession to make, Ella."

I went up on my elbow to see his face more clearly. "What is it?"

"I didn't kiss you to play a part." His eyes moved back and forth between mine. "I played the part to kiss you."

Nerves unlike anything I'd ever felt threatened to squeeze my throat closed. I swallowed around a lump in my throat. "You wanted to kiss me?"

"You didn't know? Ella, I *want* to kiss you. There's no past tense to it. I'm an asshole for not telling Vaughn the truth, but selfishly, I didn't want him getting in the way."

"You want to kiss me." I sat up and stared down at him, trying to decide if he was serious. "I thought you didn't find me attractive."

He sat up and shook his head. "What the hell gave you that idea?"

I shrugged. "I don't know! I just assumed."

"You assumed wrong. That first day when I saw you, I blew off the rest of my run to circle back to you. I was so focused on your car that I nearly ran you over.'"

I scooted closer. "I thought you were just finishing your run. I made an ass of myself!"

"I guess I just have one question, Ella." Fisher reached up and pushed my hair over my shoulders. "Do you want to kiss me?"

I nodded fast enough that I was worried he would think I was desperate. "Yeah. Like, a lot."

His slow grin turned my blood to lava. Slowly closing the distance between us, he pressed his lips to the side of my mouth. "This isn't why I asked you to come over, though, Ella. I don't want you to think that so I'm going to lay back down and finish this movie."

I let out the breath I'd been holding and nodded. "Yeah, that's fine. I really wanted to finish the movie, too."

I didn't. I laid back down next to Fisher, not quite touching him. I wasn't sure about the rules of what we were doing so I kept my distance. Nerves had already settled in and I shivered.

"Come back over here." Fisher assumed I was cold and tugged me into his side again. "Good?"

My pulse could've replaced the drums in the school's band. My palms were sweaty. I wasn't sure I was good, but I wasn't moving. "Yep."

He wrapped his arm around me and let his hand hang over my shoulder. His fingertips came so close to grazing my chest with each breath I took in. I was painfully aware of each almost touch. I gingerly rested my hand on top of his stomach and felt his sharp intake of breath. Knowing he was as affected as I was gave me a sense of boldness. Not a very big one, but still. It was enough for me to relax into his hold and lightly rub my thumb over his abs.

I didn't have a clue what was happening in the movie. I was too aware of Fisher's body and every place it touched mine. The warmth and strength I felt under my hand was alluring and I let my strokes grow wider as I waited for him to react or stop me. I rested my head on his chest and let the sound of his pounding heart encourage me as I trailed my hand lower, until my fingertips bumped into the waistband of his jogging pants.

18

Ella

I raised my head so I could look up at Fisher. "I don't think you invited me over for nefarious reasons. Can that be good enough?"

He rolled me onto my back and wedged one of his thighs between mine. "Fuck, yes."

I lifted my mouth as he lowered his and I learned quickly that knowing Fisher was kissing me because he wanted to changed things. My body was on fire as I waited for more of his touch. Wrapping my arms around his neck, I gasped when one of his hands ran down my side, grazing my breast as it went. His tongue swirled over mine and his thigh rubbed against my core.

When I pressed my head into the pillow behind me, he took advantage of my exposed neck and dragged his teeth over it. I cried out and then slapped my hand over my mouth. "Sorry."

He tugged my hand away and flashed me a hungry smile. "I like it."

He sat up and yanked his shirt over his head. He hooked his fingers under the hem of my top and slowly raised it. "Okay?"

I nodded and held my breath as he pulled the shirt off and sat back to stare at me. I covered my stomach with my hands and felt a tidal wave of self-doubt. Billy was the only person I'd ever gotten naked for.

"Don't stop breathing, Ella. I like that, too." He smoothed his hands over my stomach, brushing my hands aside, and bent his head to kiss it. His tongue dipped into my navel before he sat back up and held my gaze. "You're fucking stunning."

I shivered and tried to pull him back down on top of me but he just smiled. I watched as he lightly flicked the front snap of my bralette and raised his eyebrows in a silent question. I nodded and sank my teeth into my bottom lip as he slowly peeled the thin lace from my chest.

"Fuck, Ella." He shook his head before locking eyes with me as he lowered his mouth. I watched his pupils blow out when he brushed his lips over my nipples and felt his groan through my chest.

Running my hands over his shoulders and across his back, I touched every part of him I could reach. He was solid and so warm. I wanted more of him, though. I ran my hand down his stomach and dipped my fingers into his pants. Feeling a hitch in his breath, I reached inside his jogging pants and cupped him through his briefs. He growled and leaned back to watch.

I stroked him like that for a few seconds before I slid my hand into his briefs and gripped his bare cock. It was girthier than I'd expected and much larger than Billy's. A moment of panic filled my brain but when Fisher thrust his hips into my grip, I forgot why I'd been worried. I worked my fist up and down his shaft, watching his expressions to see what he liked.

He groaned as he watched me. "*Ella.*"

He slid his fingers up my thighs and hooked them into my shorts. He could only get them down so far before he had to move to the bed beside me. Tugging my shorts down my legs, he leaned over and kissed me. His tongue teased mine as he stroked his fingers over my inner thighs, moving higher until he was tracing the seam of my panties. I sucked in a sharp breath as he stroked me through the thin material.

"You're so wet for me, Ella. I want to taste you." Fisher kissed me again and then moved his kisses down my chest and stomach. If he noticed how stiff I'd gotten, he didn't say anything. He knelt between my thighs, the blanket thrown to the end of the bed, and lowered his mouth to my core without a moment's hesitation. He licked me through my panties and groaned. "New favorite snack."

I reached down and caught his hand when he started tugging my panties down. "Fisher... I..."

"Too fast?" He sat up. "Shit. I'm sorry, Ella."

"No, no. I just... You don't have to do that. I can do you... Or we could just...you know?" I felt my face flame. "If that's what you want."

He growled. "I want everything. I want to fuck you, Ella. I also want to eat you out and watch you squirm as you come."

Wetness pooled at my core at his words. "I've never... Billy didn't..."

"That fucker didn't go down on you?" Fisher stood up and tugged me to the edge of the bed. "Whatever he said or didn't say? Fuck that. I'm about to enjoy myself thoroughly, Ella. Now spread these thighs for me."

I watched with wide eyes as he pulled my panties off and knelt on the ground in front of me. I sat up and watched as he pushed my thighs open. Holding my breath, I fought the urge to hide myself from him. I was so exposed.

Fisher kissed my inner thighs and then smirked up at me. Without another word, he lowered his mouth and I felt his breath ghost over my lower lips first. His lips came next and then his tongue. I gasped as I felt him lick me, the feeling so overwhelming that I tried to close my legs. He braced his shoulders against my thighs and kept them open, though.

"Fisher?" I sucked in more air as he dipped into my sex and then closed his lips over my clit. The feeling of his mouth sucking at me was enough to make me moan. I braced my feet on the bed and pressed my hips up without thinking twice. I wanted more.

He groaned into me and then lifted his face while teasing one of his fingers into me. "I want you to come on my face, Ella. I want to hear you moaning my name."

The feeling of his finger thrusting into me was intense as he flicked his tongue over my clit. My entire body buzzed. "Fisher!"

I grabbed fistfuls of the sheets and made noises that I'd never made during sex. His tongue was hot and wet against my core and the way he moved it around my clit shot pleasure out to each of my limbs. His finger was thick inside me and it would've been enough for me but he pulled it out and then slowly pushed two inside. My walls stretched for him and I let out a guttural moan from somewhere deep inside me.

Fisher wasn't finished torturing me. He reached up with his other hand and cupped my breast. His fingers teased my nipple and then clamped down harder as I cried out his name. His fingers had curled and rubbed something amazing in me. The pressure built in me until I couldn't catch my breath. I gripped his hair and held on tight as he closed his lips around my clit and sucked.

An orgasm that proved all my others to be pathetic erupted out from my core and through the rest of my body. It pulsed through me and my sex clamped down on Fisher's fingers. My vision darkened until I sucked in a much needed breath of air and called out his name again and again.

I went limp before Fisher was through with me. He nuzzled my clit with his nose and pressed kisses all over my sex and up my thighs. I shivered with aftershocks of the most powerful orgasm I'd ever had. Moaning, I untangled my fingers from his hair and let my arm fall over my face.

Fisher slowly pulled his fingers out of me and I glanced down to see him licking them clean. He watched me hide my face and growled. "You taste like a fucking dream, Ella. I could eat your pussy all day long. Your ex is a goddamn idiot."

I bit my lip and watched him crawl over me until his mouth was just over mine. His face was wet from my juices and my cheeks burned, because no matter what he said, I wasn't sure I could trust that he liked it as much as he was saying. Billy had made it seem so gross and hadn't even been willing to try. For me.

19

Fisher

Ella's hair was splayed out on the bed around her as she looked up at me with a touch of sadness in her eyes. I knew I needed to stop talking about her ex but I was pissed off that he hadn't done that for her but he'd let her catch him doing it to someone else. I wanted her to know how perfect she was more than I wanted to get off. She was so fucking beautiful beneath me, so open and willing for me.

I lowered my mouth to hers and took my time kissing her. I let her taste herself on my tongue and kissed away any thoughts of anyone else. I didn't pull back until we were both breathless. The green of her eyes was barely visible from how dilated her pupils were as she watched me.

"Your pussy is perfect, Ella." I leaned on one arm so I could reach between us and run my fingers through her wetness. "It's pretty like a flower, but it also gets so wet for me and it comes so well."

She stroked her hands down my back and held her breath as she pushed them into my pants and cupped my ass. "Do you have protection? I have a box in my room that I can get if I need to."

My cock jumped and I held my breath as she pushed my pants down as far as she could get them. In a move that gave me ideas about her flexibility, she used her feet to hook them and tug them the rest of the way down. I watched her face pinch in concentration as she reached down to grip my dick. Her small hand barely wrapped around me but she didn't let that stop her. She stroked me, her lip caught between her teeth, until my tip brushed over her lower lips.

"Oh." Her little surprised sound had her jerking her gaze to mine.

I dropped my mouth to hers and kissed her deep. I pushed my fingers deep inside her again, loving the feeling of her pussy pulsing around me. I was dying to get my dick in her but I wasn't done showing her just how magical her body was.

"I've got protection, Ella, but we're not there yet." Stroking my thumb over her clit, I grinned at the way her mouth went slack. "I want you to be as wet and relaxed as I can get you before I fuck you."

"I think I'm there." She stroked me faster. "I want you, Fisher. I've never been more ready."

"That doesn't mean I can't do more." I caught one of her nipples in my mouth and sucked. "Roll over, Ella."

She shot me a confused face but moved to her hands and knees. "This is very exposi-"

I buried my face into her from behind and groaned at the sound of her moaning my name. I fucked her with my tongue before replacing it with my fingers. I lazily flicked my tongue over her clit as I fucked her faster with two fingers. When her juices were flowing down my wrist, I pushed a third finger in and watched her pussy stretch for me. Her clit was deep red and her lips were shiny as they dragged against my knuckles.

"Oh, Fisher!" She rocked her hips back into me and threw her head back as she came again. She tightened around my fingers and collapsed forward from her hands. "Fisher, god. I can't. I can't come again."

I covered her ass in kisses and slowly shifted backwards so I could stand up and get protection. She rolled over to her back and watched me with heavily lidded eyes. When I put my first knee on the bed to climb in, she moved higher up the bed. When I got my second knee on, she had herself planted in the middle, her long legs crossed, hiding her sex from me. Her face flushed as she watched my cock swing between my thighs as I moved closer.

"Open up for me, Ella." I knelt between her knees when she opened them and slowly rolled on the condom. "Still want this?"

She narrowed her eyes and nodded. "I'm not scared."

I braced myself on my elbow next to her head and pressed my lips to hers. "Pull me in."

She bent her knees so she was cradling my hips between her thighs. Reaching down, she stroked me a few times before lining our bodies up. My blunt tip pressed against her core and I reached down to tease her clit. I watched her expressions and practiced my self-control to make sure I didn't hurt her as she grunted and took my head inside.

Her wide eyes flashed to mine and her tongue stole out to wet her lips. "God, Fisher. You're so big."

I smirked and did my best to hide just how much she was affecting me. I was supposed to be experienced but I felt like I was going to come with just an inch inside her tight little body. "If it's too much, we can stop, Ella."

Those eyes narrowed and she gripped my ass in both hands. Tugging me forward, I growled as half of my length surged inside of her. Wet, tight heat squeezed down on me, the pulsing of her heartbeat milking my cock for all it was worth.

Ella pressed her head into the bed and gasped her breath. "Oh, god. Oh, fuck, Fisher!"

I thrust the rest as deep inside her as I could get and lowered my head to suck her nipples. I was hanging on by a thread and I needed Ella to come again before I did. I wanted her to obsess over my cock and come back for more and more.

Ella thrust her hands into my hair and dragged my mouth to hers. She locked an arm around my neck to hold me in place and nipped my bottom lip. "I won't break. Fuck me the way you want to, Fisher."

I rested my weight on her and ran my hand down her side and over her hips. I gripped the soft curve of her ass and wrapped my other arm under her to hold her where I wanted her. Still careful not to hurt her, I pulled out and thrust deep again. Her breath came out in a puff against my lips but she nodded, telling me to give her more.

Holding her tight, I began slow and deep, fucking her in a way that left us both panting into each other's mouths. Her hands moved over my back and gripped my ass again. Her blunt nails bit into my skin as I sank inside her faster. Her body took me like she was built for me. Her curves took my weight, her tight pussy opened so perfectly for me, and her mouth accepted my kisses, my groans, and my curses.

"Fisher! Yes! Don't stop. God, don't stop." Ella locked her ankles behind my back and rocked her hips in time with mine. She bit and sucked at my lips between cries. "I'm going to come again. Fisher, I'm going to-"

Her words broke off as I thrust faster. She locked her arms around my neck and she whimpered. I squeezed her ass as I drove into her. The bed rocked into the wall but I didn't hear it. I was consumed with her moans and cries. I needed more.

"I want to feel you coming on my cock, Ella. Come for me."

She dropped her head to my shoulder and curled around me even tighter. "I'm close, Fisher. I'm-"

I growled as she cried out and buried her nails in my shoulders. Fucking her faster and harder, I could feel her pussy pulsing faster. I was desperate for her to come before me but I was on the edge.

Ella's body tightened around me and her core clamped down on my dick like a vise. She cried my name until even that was too much. Her teeth sank into my shoulder and her muffled scream filled my ears with just how strong her orgasm was.

I thrust a few more times and then buried myself as deep as I could get and came so hard and long that my vision blurred. I gasped her name as I filled the condom, wishing it wasn't there. I wanted to paint her walls with my come.

Collapsing fully on top of Ella, I struggled to catch my breath after coming so hard. She shivered and let out muffled moans under me. I didn't want to pull out of her but I had to throw the condom away. I kissed the side of her head and groaned as I slowly extracted myself from her embrace.

"Be right back." I walked on shaky legs to the bathroom and tossed the condom. I glanced up at myself in the mirror and almost laughed. I'd never looked more thoroughly fucked. My hair was a wreck from her hands and shining in the crook of my neck was a quickly forming bruise from her teeth.

Walking back into the bedroom, I had a big smile on my face. "Hey, little vampire. Do you- What are you doing?"

She tugged on her shirt the rest of the way before looking at me. She was flushed and looked as fucked as I did. I liked it even better on her. "I just thought I should go back to my room. Is that not...? I don't know how this works."

I closed the distance between us and pulled the shirt back over her head. Tossing it to the other side of the room, I searched her face. "Stay."

She licked her lips and slowly nodded. "Okay."

I nodded for her to get in my bed and pulled the blanket back up from where it had been kicked to the floor. I crawled into bed next to her and pulled her into my chest. "I want you here tonight."

Wrapping her arm over my chest, she curled her leg over mine and let out a happy sigh. "My ex wasn't a cuddler. This is good."

I wasn't usually a cuddler, either. If the other women I slept with tried to leave as fast as Ella had, I would've gladly let them go. It was different with Ella, though. I wanted her in my bed. I wanted her again already. The idea of not having seconds or thirds with her wasn't a pleasant one.

"If tonight showed you anything, I hope it's that you're way too good for a man with a small dick and selfish desires."

She tilted her head to look up at me and smiled. "Tonight showed me a lot of things. Like what a real orgasm feels like. And what multiple orgasms feel like. And how good it feels to be held by someone so much bigger than me."

I tugged her fully on top of my chest and cupped her ass. "I'm happy to continue these valuable lessons."

She yawned and rested her cheek over my heart. "Maybe after a nap. Orgasming multiple times is tiring. Just a little nap. A kitten nap."

I felt her body go limp and smiled into her hair. It occurred to me that I was wide awake and holding a knocked out Ella with zero plans of moving an inch. I just closed my eyes and enjoyed the weight of her body on top of mine. Each time thoughts of Vaughn threatened to come up, I shoved them down and focused on Ella.

20

Ella

I could hear someone in the weight room as I hovered just outside of the door. I wanted to take advantage of there being a workout room in the house but I was nervous to face Vaughn, or Fisher, after what I'd done the night before. I'd snuck out that morning while Fisher was still asleep and did everything I could to avoid him during the rest of the day. I didn't know the normal etiquette around sleeping with your roommate. Vaughn had said Fisher didn't do seconds and I didn't want him to think I was being desperate and needy.

A growled curse sifted through the door and I let out a sigh of relief as I placed the voice as Booth's. I didn't have a reason to avoid him, thankfully. I pushed into the room and froze in the doorway. Booth was bare-chested on the weight bench, lifting a wild amount of weight. The muscles in his arms and chest stood out and I saw just how built he really was for the first time. It was only the sound of the weights settling back in place that snapped me out of my stupor.

I closed the door behind me and licked my lips. "Hey! Sorry if I interrupted your workout. I just figured I should pretend to take care of myself."

Booth grunted but didn't say anything as he moved to another piece of equipment and started doing squats with another crap ton of weight on his shoulders. His thighs strained his gym shorts and I felt sweat pebble along my spine at the sight of his back muscles flexing. I'd known Booth was a mountain with enough strength to take down multiple men his size at the same time but seeing it undressed was another thing.

I reached up to make sure I wasn't drooling before forcing my eyes away from his body. Unfortunately, the wall in front of him was fully mirrored. I could not only see his body once, I could see it twice. I patted my cheeks at the warmth flooding them and blew out a shaky breath.

"If I walk at a snail's pace on the treadmill and call that a workout, don't judge me, okay?" I smiled and shrugged out of my oversized t-shirt as I climbed onto the giant machine. I looked at the dozens of buttons and winced. "It's been a long time since I spent time in a gym. Do all the machines feel like a sci-fi movie now?"

Booth sighed and dropped his weights before closing the distance between us. He stopped next to the treadmill and I saw that he was glistening with sweat. His scent should've been illegal. Or sold as an aphrodisiac. "How fast do you want to go?"

"Fast." I swallowed and sank my teeth as his muscles came even closer as he reached to hit a button. Then I realized what he'd asked and how I'd answered. "No! Sorry! I want to go slow. Slow. Very slow."

He lifted his eyes to mine and I saw that they were pinched. With his eyebrows furrowed, he looked grumpier than Vaughn usually did. "Are you sure?"

I nodded. "You okay?"

He rolled his lips into his mouth and nodded. "Yep."

I wanted to say more but he hit another button that started the machine and I discovered fairly quickly that our version of slow wasn't the same. I nearly stumbled off the machine and only stayed upright because of Booth's grip on my arm. "Thanks. I think-"

He was already turned away from me and back at his machine, working out those strong thighs. I watched him through the mirror and tried to imagine what had gotten him so cranky. He usually had a smile for me every time I saw him.

I stumbled again and heard Booth growl. "Pay attention to or you're going to lose some skin to that track, Ella."

I jerked my eyes back to my reflection in the mirror and told myself the flush was because of the workout. My workout set felt obscenely cheery next to his mood. The hot pink set showed off more skin than I ever would've showed out of the house. It hugged my body and left nothing to the imagination. The color made me happy but Booth's mood was working hard against it.

My eyes naturally found Booth in the mirror again and I watched him drop to the ground to do push-ups. I should've felt some shame over gawking at him after sleeping with Fisher but I didn't feel anything like it. I felt plenty of other things, but not anything remotely resembling guilt.

My feet got tangled and I went down hard. I landed in a heap a few feet in front of Booth. He moved faster than should've been possible for a man his size as he hit a button to stop the treadmill and helped me unravel myself. I laid flat on my back and groaned as he checked me for injuries.

"Well, that was embarrassing." I hated how annoyed Booth looked and just wanted him to smile at me again. "What's wrong, Booth?"

"I told you to pay attention, Ella. You could've hurt yourself. You're going to have bruises." He stood up and grabbed a towel to wipe his face. "I'll just finish my workout later. Be careful in here."

I struggled to my feet and reached out to grab his arm. "Booth, wait. Did I do something?"

His eyes narrowed as he shook his head. "No."

"Then what's wrong? I've been your roommate for over a month. I may not know you through and through but I can tell that you're upset about something." I slowly dropped my grip on his arm. "Just tell me. If I left something out or made a mess, or something, I'll take care of it. Just tell me."

He threw the towel to the floor and shook his head. "I saw you sneaking out of Fisher's room this morning."

Oh, there was that shame. I took a step back and nodded, never one to lie about things I did. Unless Vaughn asked about Fisher, because that lie would save everyone a headache. "Okay."

He groaned. "It's nothing, Ella. I'm just in a shit mood. Ignore it."

"No. Why are you upset about that? I promise I won't turn into a crazy person over Fisher. I'm not going to mess up things in the house."

"I'm not upset with you, Ella. Not really. I'm just... I was hoping you wouldn't fall for Fisher's charm." He locked his hands behind his neck and I nearly swooned over the muscles, despite our conversation. "He's my best friend and I love him but... It's shitty in his shadow sometimes."

I snorted at the thought of Booth in anyone's shadow but cut myself off at the dark look he sent me. "I'm not laughing at you, Booth. I just think it's crazy that you think you're in his shadow."

He stepped closer to me. "Am I not?"

"No! How could you be, Booth? You're a completely different person and you're each great for your own reasons." I smiled to try to lighten the mood. "Plus, you create shadows, Booth. You're too tall to stand in other people's."

He turned to walk away but I grabbed his arm again. When he turned back to me, he let out a laugh. "It's fine. I'll get over it."

"Get over what, Booth?"

"That he gets to touch you, Ella!" He walked me backwards until my back hit the mirror. Coming as close as he could while still not touching me, he dropped his voice as he spoke next to my ear. "I usually don't give a fuck that people fall for Fisher's charm. This time is different, though. I'm jealous. I'm jealous and I hate it."

"You're jealous?" I leaned into his heat and nearly whined when he moved with me to keep our bodies apart.

"I wanted it to be my room you were sneaking out of this morning."

My jaw loosened and I couldn't come up with words to make a reasonable response. I opened and shut my lips a few times before Booth gave up on me.

"It's not a big deal. I shouldn't have said anything. I should've just handled my emotions like a fucking adult." Booth took a step back and grunted when I basically threw myself into his arms. I wrapped my arms around his neck and held on tight so he couldn't push me away. "What are you doing, Ella?"

"I didn't know you were interested." I breathed him in and shuddered. "I'm sorry. I'd only ever slept with one person before last night and I don't know what's happening, but I want to kiss you, Booth. And you should tell me to go fuck myself after what you saw, but-"

He grabbed my thighs and lifted me off the ground. I gasped and leaned back so I could see his face, but I still couldn't read his expression. "The things I want... I can't, though. Not when you're confused."

I gasped when he pressed me into the mirror and trailed his nose up the side of my neck. I could feel him stiffen against my center and I tightened my hold on him. "Booth..."

He brushed his lips over my ear as he spoke in a gravel-filled voice. "I'm going to put you down and walk out of here before I do something we both regret."

"I'm not going-"

Booth rocked his hips into me and then swore. He unwrapped my arms from around his neck and put me down on my own two feet. Backing away, his eyes were all over me. "If I slid my hand inside those tempting shorts, would you be wet for me, Ella?"

I leaned heavily against the mirror and bit my lip hard. Nodding, I silently begged him to come back and continue touching me.

He looked pained as he rubbed his hands down his face and stole one more glance at me before turning around and leaving the room. Without his presence in the room, it felt a lot bigger and a lot cooler. I fanned myself and sank down on the weight bench.

I stared down at my vagina and held up my hands like it would see the question and be able to answer it. "What the hell? Is this how you handle being cheated on? You can't have two men. You can't have any men. You need to relax. Jesus."

"I'll come back later." A middle-aged woman with a look on her face that said she'd heard every word I said, backed out of the open doorway of the gym. "It's not even that dirty."

"I'm sorry that-" I was talking to an empty room. She was gone. I recognized her as one of the cleaning staff Fisher brought in. I thought her name was Mallory, but I wasn't sure. What I did know was that I could never see her again.

21

Vaughn

I needed to call off the study sessions. I was caught up on everything in the class and had a good enough handle on everything that I didn't really need tutoring until we hit a harder concept. Each time I thought about telling Ella that we didn't need to meet anymore, I couldn't follow through, though. The two times a week that we were alone in the library felt like a relief and an act of self-torture.

Watching her from across the table, I twirled my pencil in my hand faster and faster. She had her hair in another one of her high ponytails and she was wearing another sundress. Instead of giving me the break of wearing her cardigan, her arms were bare and the neckline of her dress dipped lower than ever.

She bit the tip of her pencil and mine went flying across the room. She looked up at me and frowned. "You're supposed to be reading."

I got up to get my pencil and shrugged. "It's boring."

"I don't care." She was still pissed at me. She shut her own book and crossed her arms. "If you're all caught up, we don't need to stay here."

She had every right to be pissed at me. I'd been a bigger asshole than normal. Bringing up her dad was a low blow. Seeing her kissing Fisher had fucked with my head, though. "I'm not caught up. I was just taking a break."

She sighed and stared off in the distance. "Whatever. Just let me know when you're ready for my help."

"I get it. You're pissed at me. Can we just move on? It's hard to study when you're picturing me with a book slamming into my head."

"I'm not picturing you with a book slamming into your head. I'm picturing you with your head caught in my car door as I close it over and over again." Her mouth quirked up like she was fighting a smile. "You should apologize for what you said, Vaughn. We both know it was a shitty thing to say."

She was a lot bossier as an adult than she'd been as a kid. I worked my jaw back and forth and finally nodded. "I'm sorry, Ella. I was a dick."

"Yeah, you were. A giant dick." Deciding she was over her anger, she moved to the chair next to me and smiled. "Show me what you're working on."

"You forgive me that easily?" I turned to face her and felt a wave of butterflies when my knee brushed her thigh. I should've moved it but I didn't. I wanted to touch her, even though I shouldn't.

Ella looked up at me and sighed. "It's hard to stay mad at you when you gave me a place to live. Besides freaking out over your friends, you've been a lot nicer this time around. Almost suspiciously nicer."

I turned to face her completely and turned her chair so she was facing me with her legs trapped between mine. "I'm a nice guy, Ella Rae."

She laughed and play slapped my leg. "Bullshit. You're a menace in real life and you're a menace on the field."

I caught her hand. "I'm nice to you. Most of the time."

"Like I said. It's suspicious." She glanced down at where I was holding her hand and then glanced back up at me. "Vaughn?"

I forced myself to let go of her and turn back to my work. "Alright. Don't let me fuck off anymore. I need to get this done."

With a groan, she pulled my book closer to her and leaned in, giving me a view straight down her dress. I could see the curves of her tits and the soft swell of her stomach. I leaned back but the damage was already done. I was half hard and on my way to fully hard.

"These don't seem so hard. You were doing them last week without a problem. Do you need a refresher?" She frowned when she looked over at me. "You okay? You're all red. If you're coming down with something and you locked me in this tiny room with you, I'll kick your ass."

I was going to kick my own ass. I held my breath as Ella leaned into me and pressed her hand to my forehead. She studied my face as she leaned back. She was still too close. Her sweet scent lingered in my space and I could still feel her body heat against mine. "I'm good."

"You don't seem good." She started closing the books in front of us. "I'm making an executive decision. You should take a break. Between football, football practices, classes, hovering over me to make sure no one touches me, and studying, I don't know how you haven't fallen apart yet. You need a day off."

I relaxed into my chair at the idea of getting a day off. I would've taken one anyway if it wasn't for our tutoring session. School and stress talk helped relax my dick, too. "Well, since this is my time, what should I require you to do with me?"

She scoffed. "That's not how this works."

I noticed she didn't automatically get up and leave. "Sure, it is."

"Fine. If you pick something weird, though, I'm not doing it."

I didn't have a clue what I wanted to do but I wasn't ready to part ways with Ella. It was hard to get her by herself. "Want to grab some diner food with me? I know a place."

Her eyes lit up. "Yes! I'm starving."

I stood up and picked up both of our bags. "This place has the best cheeseburgers in the world."

"What about milkshakes?"

I opened the door for her and followed her out. "Best ever."

Nearly two hours later, we were sitting across from each other in a red vinyl booth and we were both rubbing our stomachs from eating so much. She'd forgot her cardigan in the library so she was still a temptation but I'd had fun with her, despite my dick's desires. She was funnier than I remembered. She was also sweet. I didn't get to see that side much usually but watching her talk to our waitress about the woman's sick dog had proven just how kind she was to other people.

I was feeling jealous. I wasn't sure she even liked me and that was eating at me. I never cared if people liked me. I didn't give a shit. Sitting there, wondering whether or not Ella could stand me was like a thorn in my side. "Ella?"

She looked up at me from her milkshake. "Yeah?"

What was I thinking? Was I going to ask her if she liked me? Jesus. "You've got some shit on your cheek."

She rolled her eyes and wiped her face. "Thanks for not letting me walk around with whipped cream on my face. We live next to a row of frat houses and something as innocent as evidence of my milkshake could so easily be turned into something horrific."

I smirked. "Oh? What would that be?"

She met my gaze and for a second I thought she was going to say it. Then she shook her head and looked away. "Jerk."

I rubbed at my chest and cleared my throat. "Let's head back to campus. I've got shit to do tonight. People to see."

"What if I followed you around and hissed at any woman who came near? It feels fair." She laughed and grabbed her phone from the table. "Payback's a bitch."

"I can't suck my own dick, Ella." Even as I said the words, I cringed. What the fuck was wrong with me?

Leveling a blank stare at me, Ella blew out a long sigh. "Here I was, thinking you were a normal human being. My bad."

22

Ella

Booth was sitting on the couch watching TV after Vaughn dropped me off and left to get his dick sucked. I was still reeling from how much those words had pissed me off. I wanted to stab him in the penis with a fork. I was even reeling from why I felt so pissed off. For a second, the dinner with Vaughn had felt almost like a date, which was crazy. But it had. And then he said that and I felt betrayed. It was all so screwed up that I didn't want to think about it for another second. Seeing Booth was a relief so I didn't have to be alone with my own thoughts. I didn't care if Booth and I had our own awkwardness going on. It had to be better than feeling like my ex-step brother was cheating on me.

I sat on the opposite side of the couch as Booth and stared at the TV. "How was your day?"

Booth grunted. "Long."

I swallowed. Maybe sitting with Booth hadn't been a good idea after all. Something was seriously wrong with me. I felt like a bunny rabbit in heat. Everything felt more than what it was.

"How was tutoring Vaughn?"

"He's still a jerk."

Booth laughed and as tense as the room had been, it lightened up at that sound. He looked over at me and smiled. "Vaughn will always be Vaughn."

I pulled my feet under me and turned to face him. "I think he was put on this earth to make me crazy."

"I've felt like that at times, too." He muted the TV. "There's ice cream in the fridge if you want some."

"Booth! You don't have to keep buying me ice cream." I patted my stomach. "I've been eating way too much of it. If I don't stop, I'm going to have to actually work out."

"Your body is perfect the way it is, Ella. Eat all the ice cream you want." His eyes heated as they moved over my body. "Is that a new dress?"

For some reason, I went up on my knees to show him the full dress. "No. I just don't have my cardigan on over it. I left it at the library."

He reached out and lightly tugged on the bottom hem. His knuckles brushed my thigh and he smiled at my quick intake of breath. "You look really pretty."

I blushed and inched closer to him. Sitting back on my heels, I took in his deep brown eyes and his ever present dimples. He was beyond handsome. "You do, too."

He grinned and I groaned. His laugh was deep and velvety as he pretended to fluff his hair. "I feel pretty today, too. Thank you."

I rolled my eyes. "Shut up."

Shrugging, he smiled and unmuted the TV. "We don't have to talk."

We didn't have to, but I wanted to. I crawled across the couch until I was kneeling right next to him, leaning over so I blocked his view of the TV with my head. "Pay attention to me."

His laughter filled my stomach with butterflies. "What if I don't want to?"

Pouting, I sat back and sighed. "Then I guess I should go."

He wrapped his arm around my waist and pulled me into his lap. I forgot to breathe when he searched my face from that close. After a few seconds, he turned his eyes back to the TV. "I don't feel like either of us can handle my full attention on you, Ella."

"I could." I wiggled to get his attention on me again. "In the gym...I liked your full attention."

His dimples faded as he made his face as neutral as possible. "Has anything changed since then?"

"My sanity has gotten more and more questionable." I leaned closer and pressed my lips to his cheek, where his dimple should've been. "Don't hide your dimples from me."

"What are you doing, Ella?"

I kissed the other side of his mouth. "I don't know. I just want to know what it would feel like to have you touch me again."

His eyes flickered with a heat he quickly masked, a muscle in his jaw ticking as he pulled back, just out of reach. "How do you feel about playing a game, Ella?"

I perked up. The tone of his voice promised more fun than any game had ever brought me. "Pretty good."

He put me aside, stood up, and brought out two controllers for a game station. The look on my face made him laugh.. He sat on the floor in front of me and glanced back at me. "You've got a dirty mind, Ella."

I blew out a sigh and settled on the couch behind him. "Yeah, yeah. Just set up the game, Booth."

The first couple of rounds we kept it civil. After Booth cheated and beat me on the third round, the gloves came off. I reached forward and covered his eyes with my hands. He reached back and tickled my sides. I put my feet on his shoulders and pushed him around. He grabbed my feet and tickled them. I was laughing so hard my abs hurt.

Everything was normal until it was Booth's turn to play and my normal tactics weren't distracting him enough. He was closing in on my high score and I panicked. I went up on my knees behind him and used my dress as a blindfold over his eyes. What I didn't think through was that I'd just pulled my dress over a grown man's head while I was wearing it. Booth reached up to uncover his eyes and I was rethinking my life choices when a throat clearing in the doorway made us both freeze. Only my dress was still over Booth's head.

I yanked it off and back down while flashing a smile at Fisher. He stood in the doorway with a scowl on his face to rival Vaughn's. I was mortified and I did the only thing I knew to do while mortified. I made it worse. "It wasn't weird. I pulled my dress over his head so he couldn't see the screen and beat me."

"You pulled your dress over my head?" Booth looked back at me with an incredulous look on his face.

"Not in a weird way!" I covered my face with my hands and groaned. "It didn't feel weird at the moment!"

Fisher walked farther into the room and stared at us with his hands on his hips. He frowned down at Booth and then took a big breath. After a second, he loosened his shoulders and shook his head at me. "You're nuts."

I nodded. "Yeah. I'm aware. Can you believe I'm going to be a lawyer someday?"

Booth stood up and moved towards the door. "You can take over my spot in the game, Fish."

"No, stay." I got up and grabbed his hand to pull him back. "We can all play. No cheating this time."

Booth and Fisher exchanged a look that I couldn't decipher but they each sat on the couch, leaving just enough space for me between them. Fisher patted my thigh and then took the controller from me. "I'm going first."

I sighed and leaned into him. "This isn't going to turn into Booth and Fisher play games together time. I refuse to be left out."

"You don't have to be left out. You could always be a team player by making us dinner." Fisher grunted when I elbowed him in the side. "Shit. You're strong for such a tiny thing."

I scowled at him. "First of all, I'm not little. Second of all, because of that comment, you and Booth can make *me* dinner. I'm craving pasta."

Booth raised his eyebrows at me. "You want food poisoning? Because asking me and Fish to cook for you is how you get food poisoning."

Acting more put out than I felt, I groaned and stood up. Putting my hands on my hips, I frowned at them. "Up. Both of you should know how to make pasta. Come on. I'll help you."

"Will you make more cookies?" Fisher waited for Booth to stand up and then pushed him back down.

Booth grabbed Fisher's leg and dropped him to the floor. "Cookies would be amazing."

Rolling my eyes, I stepped out of the way as they both ended up on the floor, wrestling with each other. "If you both get up and act even remotely like adults, I'll make cookies."

Booth caught my leg and pulled me down on top of them. He laughed until I bit his leg. "Shit! You can't bite me."

"Little Vampire is back." Fisher didn't think his comment was so cute when I elbowed him in the thigh. "Whoa! Watch the family jewels."

I climbed back to my feet and hurriedly got out of their arm's reach. "I'm going to make cookies and save them just for Vaughn. That'll show you."

A chorus of complaining went up as I blew a very mature raspberry at them and walked out of the room. I was just pulling butter from the fridge when Fisher appeared in the kitchen, a serious look on his face.

"You two seem cozy." He saw me start to say something and held up his hands. "I'm not going to stop you if you want something with him. I just can't promise I'm not going to keep trying for myself."

"I don't know what I'm doing, Fisher."

His smile was full of dark promises. "You're sampling. I'm okay with it. I have faith in my skills. You'll be back."

Booth walked in and shoved Fisher out of the way. "Okay, wise one. Teach us your pasta ways."

I swallowed down my nerves and nodded. "Yep. My pasta ways. No problem."

23

Booth

"We're going to Larry's to celebrate. You coming?" Vaughn ran a towel through his hair to dry it. "After the work you put in tonight, you should."

I looked down at my duffel bag and pretended to search through it. I couldn't look him in the eye while lying. "I think I'm just going to head home. My head is killing me."

Fisher slapped my back. "Shit, man. A beer might help."

"I'm good. Celebrate for me." I zipped my bag shut and threw it over my shoulder. "Are y'all going out to that party at Big Bill's after?"

Vaughn nodded. "I think so. Fish won't commit to anything yet but if he thinks I'm leaving him home alone with Ella, he's crazy."

"You're leaving Booth alone with her. How's that fair?" Fisher made himself busy adjusting his watch. It seemed that he, too, was having trouble facing our best friend while hiding things.

"Booth's harmless." Rethinking his statement, Vaughn grunted. "Harmless isn't the right word. I've just never seen you go after anyone, Booth."

"As much as I love this conversation, I'm going home." I bumped fists with both of them. "Good game."

I had to make nice and talk with a few more guys on the team before I escaped the locker room and made it to my truck. I tossed my bag in the passenger seat and drove home in silence. My thoughts were loud enough.

I knew what I was doing was wrong. I wasn't normally the type to go against his friends' wishes. There was something about Ella that fucked with my head. I didn't care that she'd slept with Fisher. I didn't care enough that it would infuriate Vaughn if he found out. I hadn't slept a full night since she moved in without being interrupted by filthy dreams of her. Almost losing my control in the gym had shown me just how much I wanted to go for what I wanted. Consequences be damned.

Ella hadn't gone to the game that night because her friend was sick and she said she had a lot of homework. I'd missed seeing her in the stands but I was glad that she was already home and waiting for me. Even if she didn't realize that she was waiting for me.

I let myself in and locked the door behind me. Taking the stairs two at a time, I raised my fist to knock on her door as she pulled it open. She gasped when she saw me and then grinned. I caught her as she threw herself into my arms.

"You did amazing! I was coming out to see which one of you was home. I'm glad it's you, though. I saw that play you made where you hit the other quarterback. It was so good! Everyone was freaking out about it. The announcers read off all of your stats and everything!"

I moved us farther into her room and closed the door behind me. "Ella."

She went still as she pulled back and met my gaze. "Booth?"

"There's only one thing I want to celebrate with tonight."

Her eyes dropped to my mouth and I felt her tighten her arms and legs around me. "What do you want?"

"A kiss." I licked my lips as her sweet scent flooded my head. "One kiss, Ella."

Her lips stretched in a wide smile as she watched me. "Just one kiss?"

"That's all I need."

She lowered her mouth to mine and gave me a gentle kiss. "Just that, huh?"

I walked to her bed and sat on the edge with her straddling my lap. "That could be a kiss you gave to your grandparents, Ella. I want a real kiss."

Running her hands through my hair, she nodded. "Me too."

I cupped the back of her head and pulled her mouth closer. Her breath smelled like one of the chocolate cupcakes she'd made us and I felt a low rumble in my chest before I closed the distance between our mouths. Unlike the first kiss, she didn't move away. She kept her face tilted up to mine and offered me more. If I was only going to get one kiss from her, I was going to make it count. Tightening my hold in her hair, I sucked in a shaky breath and stroked my tongue over her bottom lip.

Ella shuddered in my lap and opened her mouth for me. She tasted like chocolate. It was enough to make me kiss her deeper and throw caution to the wind. Whatever plan I'd had was out the window. I stroked my tongue against hers and growled when she pressed her hips down on mine. I couldn't get enough of her. She bit my bottom lip and then stroked it with her tongue, pushing me even closer to my control snapping.

I kissed down her jaw and rubbed my beard over her throat, loving the way she whined and rocked her hips more. I sucked at her neck and soothed stinging bites with swirling strokes of my tongue. Kissing back up to her mouth, I swallowed her moans and gripped her ass. I pulled her even tighter against me and rocked my hips forward to meet her movements.

Hard as steel, my cock tented my shorts and Ella rubbed herself against it, using it to get herself off. She let her head fall back and I buried my face in her chest. The thin t-shirt she wore did nothing to hide her hard nipples. Like a man possessed, I took one and then the other in my mouth and sucked. Ella gasped and grabbed two handfuls of my hair.

I groaned against her chest as her movements made precum leak from the tip of my dick. I was too close to coming in my shorts but I wasn't going to stop Ella when it sounded like she was close to her own release. I tugged her head back, forcing her body to arch and present more of her perfect tits to me. Sucking and biting at her nipples, I shifted my hand on her ass and slid it halfway down her leggings. Just as my fingertips connected with the warm skin of her ass, a sound other than her moaning accosted my ears.

The alarm sound that announced the front door opening.

Ella froze against me and when our gazes connected, her eyes widened. "Oh, shit."

I stood up and gently put her down on the bed. She locked eyes with my tented pants and her mouth popped open. I groaned and moved towards the door. "Stop looking at me like that, Ella."

She cleared her throat and nodded. "Yeah, sure. That thing isn't going to be on my mind for weeks, at all."

I could hear footsteps pounding up the stairs and swore. "Someone's coming."

She shook her head and pointed to the bathroom. "Hide!"

I rushed into the bathroom and hid in the shower. A laugh threatened to choke me but I forced it down. It didn't matter that I was an adult hiding to avoid being caught making out. I couldn't laugh and give away my presence. If whoever was home came into Ella's room, I was fucked. Especially if it was Vaughn.

A loud knock sent my stomach careening straight to hell. As I listened, Ella opened the door for Vaughn. I couldn't hear what he said but I could hear the annoyance in Ella's voice.

"Go away, Vaughn. I'm in for the night. Not that it would be any of your business if I did go out to party." She coughed and I winced, hoping she wouldn't say she was feeling sick since that was the excuse I'd used. "Besides, I'm not feeling the best."

I tipped my head back to stare at the ceiling. If Vaughn went to check my room and saw that it was empty, he would know exactly where I was. I was in the middle of trying to figure out if I could climb out of Ella's bathroom window and scale down to my room when her voice caught my attention.

"Will you do me a favor before you leave and go downstairs to get me some crackers?"

"You serious?" Vaughn groaned. "Fine. Just get in bed. You look all red and blotchy."

As soon as Ella whispered to me that I could leave, I tiptoed down the hallway to my room, making sure Vaughn didn't look up the stairs and spot me. Once I was in my room, I leaned against my door and blew out a shaky breath. I'd lost control and we'd almost gotten caught. Despite that, I was still hard as a rock and tempted to go back to her room as soon as we were alone again.

I knew I wasn't going to get anywhere until I took care of my dick. At least I had the feeling of Ella fresh in my mind to get me there.

24

Ella

As soon as I was sure Vaughn was gone I rushed down to Booth's door. I knocked and shifted on my feet. I was full of adrenaline, turned on, and I wanted to explore the feelings Booth created in me. He'd just wanted one kiss but I wanted more. Unable to wait, I quietly opened the door and stepped into his room. He wasn't in the room but I could hear the shower running. A true sign of how much I was lusting after him was how I walked over to the partially open bathroom door and looked in.

Booth was standing under a stream of hot water, one hand fisted against the wall as he leaned forward and stroked himself with the other. Everything I'd felt through his shorts was on full display and it was mesmerizing. He was as gifted as I'd imagined. Maybe too gifted.

Booth's eyes were closed as he worked his fist up and down his length. His lip was caught between his teeth and his eyebrows were pinched together. I could hear his rough breathing as he got closer.

I knew what I was doing was risky but I wanted him. Instead of leaving him to his privacy, I pushed the door open enough to slip inside. I shut the door behind me and the sound of it clicking shut snapped Booth's eyes open. He froze and stared at me with a slightly horrified look on his face.

I pushed my leggings down and watched his face shift into something hungry and impatient. I shot a look up at the lights, knowing I couldn't turn them off, and took a deep breath before pulling my shirt off. Standing in front of him with nothing on was both exhilarating and terrifying. Booth's expression encouraged me, though. I moved closer to him and nodded to where he was still fisting his cock. "Don't stop."

After a moment's hesitation he did as I said. His eyes never left my body as I opened the shower door and stepped inside. Steam warmed my skin and left me flushed instantly.

Booth turned and watched me, his shaft pointed at me. "What are you doing, Ella?"

Sinking to my knees in front of him, I looked up and swallowed. "Let me help."

He groaned and tightened his hold on himself. "Ella... I'm never going to last with you like this."

"That's okay. No one should be home for a while." I licked my lips. "Booth."

He swore and stepped closer. His heavy cock was deep red and had veins running the length of it. I'd seen sex toys like it and had been intimidated. Seeing it as Booth's cock just made me feel determined.

"Open your mouth, Ella." His voice turned gruff when he spoke to me sexually. It was a tone I'd never heard him use anywhere else. It was like sweet, gentle Booth stepped back and made room for a different Booth, one who knew what he wanted and planned on getting it.

I held onto his thighs and held his gaze with my mouth open. His nostrils flared as he brushed the tip over my lips. I pushed my tongue out and tasted him before leaning forward to take more of him inside. He was hot and velvety against my tongue. Booth's eyes burned as he watched me take more of his length. He still fisted himself but I didn't want him to have to do any of the work. I pushed his hand away and wrapped both of my hands around him so I could stroke every inch I couldn't take in.

"Fucking hell, Ella. I'm not going to last." Booth fisted my hair and held me steady. "Keep those eyes on me, baby."

I sucked him harder and felt his body stiffen. I moaned as I watched his expression twist in pleasure and that was all it took for him. He growled as my mouth was flooded with his come. Pressing my thighs together as he continued coming, I swallowed for the first time in my life. I was so turned on that I couldn't sit still. The look on Booth's face was nearly feral as I stroked the last of his come into my mouth. His shaft only softened slightly and I was busy appreciating it when the water shut off and he grabbed me under my arms to pick me up.

I wrapped my arms and legs around him and felt his shaft wedged against my core. Moaning, I stroked his wet hair out of his face and kissed his neck. "*Booth.*"

He carried me to his bedroom and climbed on top of his bedding, even though we were both wet. "Ella, you're so fucking beautiful."

I gasped when he settled the lower half of his body over mine and ground his shaft into me. "I want you inside me, Booth."

He cupped my breast and focused on my nipple with his fingers and mouth before coming back to my mouth and kissing me hard. "Not yet. Let me make sure you're ready first."

"I'm ready, Booth. Please. I want to feel you." I felt his hesitation and stiffened. "I'm sorry. You don't want this, do you?"

"Are you fucking crazy, Ella? Do you feel my dick? I want this more than I want to breathe." He dropped his head to press his forehead to my shoulder. "I just want to make sure I take care of you."

"I'm pretty sure that won't be an issue."

"There are some things I'm good at. And other things I haven't...done." He lifted his head and studied my expression. "I haven't had sex before."

When my eyes widened I felt him start to pull away and locked my limbs around him tighter. "How? You're...you. Are you saving yourself? I don't want to pressure you, Booth. No matter how much I want you, I-"

"I just never felt like it. I was fine getting off other ways. I want you, though, Ella. I just don't want to disappoint you. I can get you off with my mouth and fingers. Let me-"

"Booth, fuck me."

25

Ella

"If you want to, do it. I'm not going to be disappointed." I moaned when Booth shifted and rubbed against my clit. "I want your mouth and fingers, too, but right now, I want your cock inside me."

He ground his teeth and nodded. I could see the nerves playing behind his eyes and pushed him onto his back. He tugged me on top and reached over to his bedside table to grab a brand new box of condoms. His big hands slightly shook as he ripped open a condom and looked up at me.

I took it from him and smiled before I rolled it over his shaft. "I've never been on top so we're both pushing boundaries tonight."

"You look fucking good on top of me, Ella." He watched as I braced my hands on his stomach and lifted my hips until I could use one of my hands to guide him to my core. He held his breath when I let my weight push his tip inside me. "*Fuck.*"

I gasped and sank down an inch when Booth stroked my clit with his thumb. There was a mixture of pleasure and pain as I dropped lower and his cock stretched me. Moaning and digging my fingertips into his stomach, I took a deep breath and forced the rest of his length inside. A wild cry tore past my lips as an orgasm hit me fast and hard.

Booth gripped my hips in his hands and held me still. "Shit, Ella. Fuck, you feel good. You feel too good."

I struggled to find my voice. "You... Oh, my god... So big, Booth. So good."

He sat up and took my mouth in a deep kiss. His cock throbbed inside me and his hands were rough as he grabbed my ass. "Are you okay?"

I let out a broken laugh. "I will be."

"Tell me if it's too much, Ella. I want to fuck you but I don't want to hurt you." Even as he said the words, he slowly lifted me off his cock and pulled me back down on it. The feeling made my eyes roll.

I locked my arms around his neck and held on as he repeated the motion. I was being stimulated from the outside and inside and I could feel a bigger orgasm growing already. He was touching parts of me that felt magical. He worked me up and down his shaft, getting himself off with my body. The sounds of pleasure he made filled my head.

He rolled us over and watched my body move with his every thrust. He experimented with the strength, groaning when my chest swayed with the stronger moves. He wrapped his hand around the back of my neck and settled into a slower, deeper thrust that stole my breath and left me thrusting my hips up to meet his.

"You feel so good around me. So hot and wet. I'm so deep inside you, Ella. You feel like mine right now." Booth covered my throat in open-mouthed kisses. "I want to feel you come on my dick again."

I ran my hands down his back and nodded at him. "You're going to make me come again, Booth."

He sat back on his heels and held my legs against his chest. Thrusting faster, he reached down and played with my clit. "I want to watch you come. I want to see your face when your pussy squeezes my cock."

I gripped the bedding and cried out as he fucked me fast and hard. I could feel my body tensing and my orgasm teetered just a breath away.

"Say my name, Ella. Fucking scream *my* name as you come on *my* cock."

"Booth!" I screamed his name as my orgasm crested and slammed through me. My muscles locked up and my breath caught in my chest. My fingers ached from where they dug into his bed.

With a shout, Booth came and my body shook with pleasure. My muscles released and I cried out as I felt my core flooding. I tried to scramble away from the feeling but Booth held me tight as he finished coming. Gasping and shaking, I came harder than I could ever remember.

Booth pulled out and I felt him staring down at my core. I tried to close my legs but he reached down and rubbed my clit in quick, almost rough movements. I screamed as that flooding feeling came back. Jerking as my orgasm grew giant again, all I could do was hold onto Booth's sides as my body stiffened and my come soaked his bed.

He dropped his mouth to mine and kissed me as he pushed me into one more orgasm. Finally I twisted my hips away from his touch and shook my head as I gasped for breath.

"No more. No more." I felt him pull me on top of his chest and wrap his arms around me but I was floating outside of my body for a few minutes after that. I wasn't even sure what day it was when I could open my eyes and breathe normally again.

Booth was watching me with a smirk on his handsome face. His hair was a wreck and his lips were swollen and red but he looked like a god. "I no longer have any fears about my cock not getting the job done."

I let out a weak laugh. "I tried to tell you."

"I'm glad I waited." He stroked his hand over my hair and watched me with a soft look on his face, the cockiness gone for the moment. "You're so beautiful, Ella. I don't know how I got you here, but I'm fucking glad I did."

I pressed a kiss to his chest. "You don't know how you got me here?"

"You're so fucking far out of my league." He said it like it was a fact, like there was no room for argument.

"Are you out of your mind?" I sat up, straddling him, and scowled. "You really believe that?"

He laughed easily and rubbed my thighs. "Yeah, because it's true."

"It's not. You're so hot, Booth. You have the most bedroom of all the bedroom eyes. And those dimples? I can't even talk about your muscles because I've already made a mess of your bed and I don't want to make it worse." I rubbed my hands up his chest. "You went from never having been inside a woman to making me...do that...tonight. Hot and skilled? You're the full package."

His eyes were serious as he watched me. "You really believe that."

"That was my line." I smiled. "But, yeah, I do. Why else do you think I came to bed with you, Booth? I know my track record in this house isn't great, but I'm not that easy."

"I didn't think you were." Booth looked like he was thinking over everything I'd said. "You're amazing for a guy's confidence."

I leaned down and kissed him. What I meant as a light kiss quickly turned into something heated. He expertly rolled us over and kissed down my throat. "Are you sure you were a virgin before tonight?"

He cupped my breasts and looked up at me with a wicked look on his face. "I'm absolutely positive. I'm going to remember sliding into your pussy for the rest of my life, Ella."

I licked my lips as he sat up and straddled my stomach. I watched him rub his thumbs over my nipples and then grip his shaft. I blew out a shaky breath as arousal drenched me. "You can have a first of mine, too, Booth."

He watched as I cupped my breasts and pushed them together. With a low growl he slid the first half of his cock between my breasts. "Fuck, Ella. Never leave my bed."

I held on as he found a rhythm and writhed under him until he stopped what he was doing to settle between my thighs and make me come even more with his mouth. He was right. He made getting me off with his mouth and fingers an art form. When I limped back to bed that night, I admitted to myself that I didn't know what I was doing, but it was fun.

26

Ella

I walked out of class and right into Billy's chest. An apology was on the tip of my tongue until I saw that it was him. I tried to sidestep him and avoid a conversation but he quickly spun around and fell into step with me.

"Just give me five minutes, Ella."

I adjusted the strap of my backpack as it dug into my shoulder. Everything was making me uncomfortable that morning, especially Billy. "No."

"I don't want anything from it. I just need to apologize. I know I fucked up, Ella, and I hate that I hurt you." He caught my arm and pulled me to a stop. "Please, Ella. I know I don't deserve a chance to talk to you after what I did but I need it. It's eating me up to know that I hurt you. I just need a few minutes. Two minutes, even."

I looked down at the ground, doing my best not to be swayed by the sad puppy show he was putting on. Billy had no idea how far his cheating was from my mind. I had other messes to think about.

"I'm begging you here, Ella. Please. You know me. Give me two minutes and I won't bother you again if you decide that's what you want." He grasped my shoulders and blew out a ragged breath. "Please."

I stepped out of his reach and shook my head. "No."

Leaving him behind, I walked blindly through campus. I didn't have another class for a few hours but I had to get away from Billy. I felt mean. Logically, I knew I had every right to turn him away. I didn't owe him anything. It wasn't easy for me to hurt people, even if they deserved it. I was arguing with myself in my head about whether or not I was cruel when a big hand covered my eyes from behind.

"Guess who."

I pushed Fisher's hand away and turned to smile at him. "How old are you?"

He shrugged. "Old enough."

A heavy feeling made my stomach sink like lead. Guilt ate at me. "Hey, do you have a minute to talk?"

He winced. "You're picking Booth over me?"

Rolling my eyes at him, I shook my head. "And chance breaking the star quarterback's heart before he plays in the big game? The whole school would come after me if we lost."

He wrapped his arm around me and grunted. "I see this conversation isn't going to be about you losing the ability to be dramatic."

I let Fisher lead me to a bench in the middle of the quad. Once we were both sitting, I squeezed my hands together and forced myself to look him in the eye. "I slept with Booth."

His eyes widened and his cheeks took on a pink hue. Sitting back, he shifted so he wasn't touching me at all. "Okay. I wasn't expecting that. Don't people usually ease into the bad news?"

"I just wanted to get it out." I bit my lip and tried to read his emotions. "I don't know the rules of what we're doing here but I know that I would never want to upset you in any way."

"We're not doing anything here." He rubbed his hands down his face and shook his head. "Sorry. I don't know what we're doing, either. I guess it doesn't matter, though. Are you and Booth dating now? Damn. I really thought my skills would pull through for me."

I reached up and tightened my ponytail. "No. I'm not ready to date anyone right now. I'm attracted to both of you but I just broke up with Billy and I should take some time to be single. At least, that's what everyone says."

Fisher visibly relaxed. "Okay. What does that mean for...*this*?"

Watching him gesture between the two of us, I slowly lifted my shoulders. "I don't have a clue."

"Do you still want to come to my room and watch action movies?" His slow grin was as charming as it was sexy.

"I feel like such a bad person, but yes." I groaned and covered my face with my hands. "What does that say about me?"

Closing the distance between us, Fisher wrapped his arms around me and kissed my shoulder. "It says you're a lot wilder than I expected you to be."

I gently punched his thigh. "Not funny."

He caught my hand and laced his fingers through mine. "You're talking to the wrong guy if you think I'm going to think less of you because you slept with Booth. My first three years on this campus were spent sleeping with-"

"That's okay, Fisher. I don't need to hear that."

"Well, well, well. Feeling territorial, Ella?" He laughed at the sour look I gave him. "My point is that sleeping with two guys doesn't make you a bad person. You're making up for lost time while you were dating that dickhead Billy. Or maybe Booth and I have just mastered the art of seduction and you can't handle us."

Wincing, I rolled my lips into my mouth.

"What?"

"I seriously think you both cast a spell on me, or something. I've never been like this. With Billy, I could go weeks without caring about sex."

"I don't want to think about you having sex with him." Fisher read my expression and cut me off. "Yes, Ella, I am feeling territorial."

I raised my eyebrows and searched his face for any sign that he was messing with me. "You are?"

He gripped the back of my neck and pulled my face close to his. "Yes, I am. And before you ask, I still don't know what any of this means. For now, that doesn't matter. You're my girlfriend and everyone on this campus knows it."

"Fake girlfriend."

"Whatever you say." Kissing me, he ran his hand down my neck and over my shoulder. His fingers were rough against my sensitive skin and when his lips followed his fingers, I tipped my head for him and let out a small moan. He sat back and groaned. "You have no idea how much those little sounds drive me crazy."

The campus bell began to ring, signaling the start of a new hour. It was enough to drag me out of my Fisher haze. I moved a safe distance away from him, so I wouldn't be lured back into his arms, and glanced around. The quad had filled up with students enjoying the pretty weather. I blushed when I realized that I'd just moaned for Fisher in public, where a lot of people could hear. Vaughn would have a field day with that little bit of information.

Thinking of him made my heart beat faster. I looked up and saw that Fisher was still watching me. "What about Vaughn?"

His face twisted in annoyance. "You're a grown woman, Ella. He's pretending to do the big brother thing but I know that's not the real reason he's trying to keep everyone away from you. I wouldn't normally do anything that could hurt our friendship, but I like you."

"You like me?" I grinned. That was so sweet. "Wait. Why do you think he's doing it?"

Fisher stood up and offered me his hand. "You're a smart girl, Ella. I think you know."

27

Ella

"Watch out! You're going to ruin our streak!" I leaned forward on the couch and slapped Fisher's shoulder. "Go!"

"You're stressing me out! If I lose, it's your fault!" He jammed at the controller for all he was worth. "My fingers are too damn big for this!"

Booth scoffed. "Fuck off with that. If I can do it, so can you."

I jumped off the couch when Fisher died in the game and stood in front of him with a disappointed look on my face. "You had one job. How the hell did you manage to lose? Now we have to start over and you saw how hard that first boss was."

He tugged me to the floor next to him and covered my mouth with his hand. "Do you hear anything, Booth?"

I bit his hand and laughed when he let me go. "You're stronger but I'm smarter."

"Or mouthier." Fisher saw my hand coming his way and caught it. "Definitely mouthier."

"I'm going to get another drink. You should spend some time thinking about what you did." I stood up and nodded at Booth. "Make sure he's feeling guilty for killing us."

Their laughter followed me to the kitchen as I pulled out the pitcher of sangria we'd made earlier. It was all for me since the guys thought wine was gross. They were sticking to beer. They'd won another game that morning and we were celebrating their win. Vaughn thought they were crazy for staying in since he was going to what he called 'the biggest party of the year'. Crazy, or not, they'd stayed in with me and we were having a blast. We'd played a bunch of games and even watched a few episodes of a show Booth liked. Dinner was pizza ordered in and dessert was a pie I'd baked for their win. I'd even put their numbers on the crust and I'd made it the day before since I knew they'd win.

I grabbed them two more beers and made my way back into the living room. They'd apparently made an executive decision and the game had been turned off for a football game. I settled on the couch between them and huffed. "That'll teach me to be a good errand girl."

"This is supposed to be a good game. We play Georgia in three weeks. Consider this homework." Fisher took his beer from me and tapped it against Booth's. "Go Crocs."

I tried to pay attention to the game but I just didn't care about it if I wasn't watching the guys play. I decided it was a good time to call Mom. "I'll be upstairs. I'm going to call my mom."

Booth booed me. "Don't leave us. If it's just the two of us here, it really is sad that we stayed home."

"What the hell? It's not sad. I like hanging with you, asshole." Fisher turned his attention to me. "But, seriously, we stayed home for you. You could always talk to your mom here."

I made a horrified face as I shook my head hard enough to send my ponytail flying. "Nope. Not a chance in hell. My mom isn't a speakerphone mom. She's more of a hide in a closet and turn your phone volume as low as it'll go mom. I'll be back, though. Just watch your football and keep each other entertained."

I didn't give them a chance to object. Rushing upstairs, I flopped out on my bed and dialed Mom. As soon as she answered, I knew it was going to be a doozy of a conversation. I could hear her shouting at someone before greeting me in a kind tone. "Mom? Are you okay?"

"Yeah, and your brother had a bigger dick, asshole! Don't come back!" She cleared her throat. "Oh, yeah, sweetie. I'm great. How are you?"

"What's going on there?"

"Oh, I was just asking my date to leave. That's all." She grunted. "Men are so sensitive these days."

"Where are you? Did you bring a random guy home? What did I say about not handling becoming an adult orphan very well?"

"He wasn't a stranger. I slept with his brother a few weeks ago. Nice family." I could practically see her waving my concerns off. "Anyway. You didn't answer me. How are you?"

"I'm fine, Mom."

"Why aren't you out celebrating? Your team won today. You should be getting drunk by now."

I smiled. "I stayed home with Fisher and Booth. I made your famous sangrias."

"Wait a minute. You stayed home with Fisher and Booth? Where's Vaughn?" She knew all about my roommates. Just not that I'd slept with two of them. No one needed to know that.

"Out." I clutched Connie to my chest. "I hardly see him if it's not our tutoring time."

"And how does he feel about you staying home alone with his two roommates?"

"Fine." Even I could hear how my voice had gone higher with the lie. "Everything's fine."

"Which one did you fool around with?" She listened to my silence for fifteen whole seconds before she cackled. "I was just teasing! I never thought you had that in you. Good for you, Ella Rae. It's about time you had sex with someone besides that Billy asshole."

"Mom! I'm not talking to you about this."

"Why not? I want to know. Which one did you sleep with? Let me pull up that picture you sent me." She sighed dreamily. "The one with the dimples reminds me of this guy I knew from my first job. He was a giant. Everywhere. I walked like someone had kicked me in the vagina for a week after that."

"Mom! Oh, my god. This is so wrong for me to hear!" I pulled Connie over my face and screamed into him. "When I come back home this summer, we're going to family therapy."

"Great. We can work on your prudish ways. You didn't get those from me. Maybe it was a dormant trait from your grandmother. God knows she had a stick up her ass the size of a telephone pole." Mom seemed to realize what she'd said. "May she rest in peace."

"She's going to haunt you one of these days." Wanting to change the subject, I brought up baked goods. "I made her recipe for apple pie yesterday. It was delicious."

"You're not cheating me out of this information today, Ella. Which one did you sleep with?"

I groaned. "Mom!"

"Ella!"

"Both!" I gasped and slapped my hand over my mouth. Betrayed by my own mouth wasn't the way I thought I'd go out, but there wasn't a chance in hell that I wasn't dying of embarrassment after blurting that out.

"Ella Rae. I can not tell you just how deeply impressed I am. Of course, my daughter bagged two complete hotties. I'm so proud!" The sound of her clapping her hands together showed just how genuinely happy she was.

"You're not a normal mother. You know that, right?"

"Thank god for that. Is it good sex? I know you weren't having good sex with your ex. I hope these two were better."

I sat straight up. "How did you know that?"

"Well, for starters, how uptight you were. Also, I accidentally read the journal you keep on your computer." She rushed to explain herself. "I was looking for something else! It was open and before I knew it, I'd already read all about Billy not being the best at sex. You were so sweet, though! Too sweet. You have to make sure you find a man who can make you orgasm. So? Do these guys?"

"Mom. If I didn't think you'd get on the first plane here, I'd tell you that I'm cutting you out of my life. Why would you read that?! And why would you talk to me about it now?" I stood up and paced. "None of my other friends have ever mentioned their moms talking to them about orgasms. You know that, right?"

"I'm sorry that I'm a cool mom. I'm just not sexually constipated, Ella." She sniffed. "My mom read me bible verses while telling me that sex was a horrible sin. The first time I had sex I cried like a baby and told my boyfriend that I was going to burn in a lake of fire. He dumped me right then and there. I didn't want that for you. I wanted you to be free to do whatever you wanted."

I sighed. "I don't really want to cut you out of my life."

"You'd be lost without me. I keep you on your toes. When you're a fancy lawyer and someone tries to throw you a curveball, you'll be so prepared for it because of the way I raised you."

"You're right. I'm not saying thank you, though." I laid face down on my bed and groaned before turning my face to the side so I could talk. "They were amazing. That's all I'm saying."

She screamed in my ear. "Yes! You deserve a good dicking do-"

"Mom?"

"Yeah?"

"I'm going to hang up now. I love you."

She laughed. "That's fine. I have a meeting with a doctor in an hour."

"What? Is everything okay? Why are you meeting a doctor this late?"

Before she spoke, I realized I'd walked into another sex story. "Clive is a gynecologist. After I kicked my date out a few minutes ago, I texted Clive. Clive knows where the g-spot is and how to work it."

"When did you have time to text Clive?" I cringed. "You set up a booty call while you were talking to me, didn't you?"

"Don't ask questions you don't want the answers to, honey. I love you! Go have sex!"

I ended the call and groaned into my bed.

"Clive sounds nice." Booth sounded like he was holding back a laugh.

I shook my head and spoke into my bedding. "Go away!"

Fisher didn't bother hiding his laugh. "Your mom sounds like a blast."

"I hate you."

28

Ella

I sat on Booth's bed and pouted. They'd been teasing me nonstop about the conversation with my mom. I wasn't even sure why I'd followed them to Booth's room. I should've punched them both and locked myself in my room, all alone. It wasn't fair; I hadn't even had Mom on speaker. Her voice just carried. They'd heard so much of our conversation.

"Come on, Ella. Don't be mad." Fisher knelt in front of me and clasped his hands together like he was praying. "We'll stop. Promise."

Booth was at his record player, choosing a record to play. He looked at me over his shoulder and smirked. "I've got a record just for this occasion. I think your mom would love it."

When the scratchy sound gave way to a singer's voice, I groaned. Of course, I recognized the song as one Mom had played all the time when I was a kid. *"Cherry Pie"* by the artist Warrant wasn't exactly a lullaby, but it'd put me to sleep when Mom sang it to me. Hearing it come out of Booth's speakers brought a blush to my cheeks. "Why do you have this? This is from about a hundred years ago."

"I stole my mom's record collection when I moved out. She had all the classics." Booth moved towards me, moving his hips to the music. "Up, Ella."

Fisher sat on the bed next to me and grinned. "And now we see why Booth has a mile long list of women trying to get his attention."

Booth pulled me to my feet and into his arms. Spinning me around, he proved that his dance moves were as good as his moves on the field. His singing voice was like warm, melty chocolate, too, and I might've swooned a bit. Until he sang one of the most famous lines in the song. Then it went from swooning to full out collapsing in a pile of goo.

"Tastes so good, makes a grown man cry." He purred the lyrics against my ear and snaked his hand lower on my back.

I was breathless and standing on shaky knees by the time the song ended. When Fisher caught me by my waist and lowered me to the bed next to him, I sank like an anchor.

"Okay?" Fisher ran his hand up and down my thigh. "Booth's song choices are always immaculate. And accurate."

Booth turned off the record player and tapped a few buttons on his phone. A more modern rock song played from the speakers around his room. The beat was hard and slow and it made my heart race even more than it already was.

We'd left Booth's bedroom door open but Booth walked over and shut it. "In case Vaughn comes home, we won't have to hear him complain about my music. He doesn't seem to think my playlists are as great as Fish does."

I swallowed and nodded. The music was loud enough that Booth had to shout so I could hear him. When he sat next to me on the bed, though, and asked me if I wanted him to turn it down, I shook my head.

We sat there, just listening to music for a few minutes. I felt like screaming. The tension was suffocating but I didn't understand it. I mean, I understood it, but I didn't understand why it was as thick as it was when both of them were sitting on the bed with me. It wasn't like-

Booth turned my face to him and lowered his mouth to mine. He held my head and deepened the kiss while I sat there, torn between kissing him back and stopping because Fisher was there. His tongue teasing mine made me forget why I'd been hesitating. As soon as I started really kissing him back, though, he pulled back.

I looked up at him, confused, and then heard Fisher clear his throat behind me. I spun around to him and held my breath. I expected him to look pissed off. What had I been thinking? What had Booth been thinking?

Fisher pulled me onto his lap and growled before taking my mouth in a fierce kiss. I clutched his shoulders and felt the world shifting around me. I didn't know what was happening. The music drowned out the part of my brain that put up blockades against me doing the sort of thing I was doing. Not that it was a common situation I ended up in.

When Fisher eased back, I opened my eyes and saw that both of them were watching me. I pressed my fingertips to my mouth, feeling both of their kisses still. "Whoa."

They looked at each other before looking back at me. Fisher spoke first. "If this is too much, we can fuck off."

"Say the word and it's finished, Ella."

I licked my lips and swallowed a lump of nerves. I felt nervous about how it would work and if they would look at my body with all of the lights still on. I realized I didn't feel nervous about what was happening, though. I trusted both of them. I still wasn't sure I could say the words, though. I didn't think I could ask them for something I didn't know how to describe.

"Do you want to leave?" Booth caught my chin and held my gaze. "A nod is all you need to do."

I shook my head.

Fisher pressed kisses down my throat. "It stops at any time you want it to."

Seeing that I wasn't running away, Booth pulled me from Fisher's lap to the space between them. He smiled before kissing me, his hand resting on my throat as he did. I gasped when I felt Fisher's lips on my shoulder. Booth pulled back and searched my eyes. Whatever he saw made him groan before kissing me again. His teeth raked over my bottom lip just as Fisher sucked harder at the crook of my neck. I pressed my thighs together and whimpered into Booth's mouth.

Fisher tugged the loose neck of my shirt off my shoulder and claimed the exposed skin with his teeth and tongue. Somehow they knew when to shift and Fisher pulled my mouth to his while Booth seamlessly focused on my neck. They went back and forth like we'd been doing it for years.

I rubbed my thighs together, so turned on after so much of their attention that I ached. Still, I was unwilling to make the first move, in case I still didn't understand what was happening. I gasped when Fisher's hand rested on my thigh and when he went to pull it away, I grabbed it and put it back on my thigh, higher than he'd been. I felt Booth's hand next, slowly stroking my inner thigh. It was heaven and hell.

My hands were in the way and I was unsure of where to put them until Booth let out a low laugh and brought my hand down to his thigh. I nipped his lip a little for laughing at me but he shifted his hand higher and moaned. Putting my hand on Fisher's thigh, too, I held them there, feeling the differences in their size and the material of their clothes.

Fisher pulled my mouth back to his and swallowed my cry when Booth cupped my sex over my shorts. His big hand forced my thighs open wider and the heat of his palm drove me to rock my hips into it.

Fisher shifted his hand higher, moving it slowly so I could stop him if I wanted. When I didn't, he cupped my breast and I felt his breath hitch against my lips. I felt like I was soaring through outer space with both of them touching me. The only thing anchoring me was the feel of their strong thighs beneath my hands. Wanting more of that, I stroked my hands higher. Fisher's growled curse came against my mouth before Booth turned my face to his. His kiss was hungrier as my hand crept higher. He pressed his palm into my clit through my shorts and underwear and held it steady while I rocked against it.

Kissing across my shoulder, Fisher grunted and shifted back. He grabbed the bottom of my shirt and pulled it over my head, dislodging my hands and breaking my mouth away from Booth's. The black bralette I had on drew both of their mouths to my chest. Fisher stayed while Booth came back to my mouth.

Moving my hands back to their thighs, I started higher that time. I brushed against two very hard erections at the same time and shuddered. Fisher sucked my nipple through my bralette and Booth's hand disappeared, just for me to feel it sliding inside my shorts. He pulled my underwear to the side and the first stroke of his finger through my lower lips created a newer level of need.

Booth growled. "Up on the bed, Ella."

29

Ella

I scooted back and watched them watch me with matching stares, full of heat and need. Once I was in the middle of the bed, Fisher followed and quickly took my bra off. Both of them let out groans at the sight of my bare breasts but when Booth tugged both my shorts and underwear down my legs, there was silence.

I tried to close my legs, nervous that they'd changed their mind, but they each gripped the inside of the knee closest to them and held my thighs open. I gripped my hair and stared at the ceiling, too overwhelmed to see them staring at my core.

"So pretty." Booth's voice was full of awe as he trailed his hand up my thigh. He stroked my sex and spoke with a rough tone to his voice. "So wet for us."

I moaned. Wet for *us*.

Fisher grunted as he stretched out and stared down at me. He held my gaze as his fingers joined Booth's. I opened my mouth to cry out and he stole the sound with a kiss. Their fingers explored, stroking and teasing. My head swam at the sensation.

One of them circled my clit as the other pushed into my core. With the adrenaline flooding my body, I was so on edge that just that small contact had me building towards an orgasm. Gasping and scrambling to close my legs, I panicked at the idea of coming in front of both of them.

Booth wedged his body between my thighs and growled. "I can feel you squeezing my fingers, Ella. Come for us. Show us."

God, that word. *Us.* I couldn't handle it. My toes curled and I tried my best to stay silent as I came by biting down on my lip. It was useless, though. With both of them touching me, I had no chance of staying quiet.

Before I was over that orgasm Booth buried his face in my sex. He took long licks and looked up at me. "Can you handle more?"

I wasn't sure what he meant at first, not until I saw Fisher yanking off his shirt and shorts next to me. Despite everything, seeing his naked shaft made me blush. I watched as he stroked himself and moved closer to my head. I swallowed down a wave of nerves and nodded. I wanted to make them come, too.

"Tap my thigh if it gets to be too much, Ella." Fisher ran his hand through my hair and watched as I sat up enough to reach him. As his tip brushed my lips and I stuck out my tongue to taste him, he groaned and tightened his grip on my hair. "Fuck, Ella. Let me in."

Booth pushed his fingers deep in me and stroked my clit with his talented tongue and the sensation would've made me scream if Fisher hadn't filled my mouth. I closed my mouth around his girth and tried to make it good for him while I was so distracted by what Booth was doing to me.

Fisher worked his cock in and out of my mouth, slowly feeding me more of his length. When I couldn't take anymore, he groaned. "I'm never going to last with you moaning on my cock like that, Ella."

I let out a muffled cry when Booth pistoned his fingers in and out of me faster and faster. He was pushing me, forcing me to come like I had before for him. I could already feel the orgasm swelling inside me.

He lifted his mouth and out of the corner of my eye I saw him look at Fisher. "I've never loved changing my bedding so much."

"What-"

My back arched and I screamed around Fisher's dick as I came hard. I lost all control of my body and Fisher took over by thrusting into my mouth faster. Booth shifted and I opened my eyes to see him kneeling on my other side. He pulled my hand to his dick and stroked himself with it.

"Fuck!" Fisher lurched over my head as he came. His come filled my mouth and I swallowed as fast as I could to keep from choking on it. When he pulled out Booth turned my head towards himself.

Booth barely got his tip inside my mouth before he came. His deep growl of pleasure filled the room and he shifted before he was finished coming to mark my chest with his seed.

I fell back on the bed and laid there, waiting for my brain to kick on again. I felt Booth massaging his come into my chest, something I knew he liked from our night together. I groaned and looked up at them. They were both watching me like they weren't sure how I was going to react. I smiled and managed to lift a hand in to give them a thumb's up.

Fisher visibly relaxed and then shifted down the bed. He grinned at me as he pulled my body to where he wanted it, right in front of his face. "We can't leave you messy, Ella."

My new angle put my head in Booth's lap and he reached down to tease my nipples. "She's such a pretty mess, though."

I was still so sensitive but Fisher stroked me gently at first, taking his time to warm me up. Booth was hard again next to my head and I turned my head to lick his length.

A loud banging on the door made me gasp and find the energy to roll away from both of them. I was already in my shorts and t-shirt when Booth stepped out of his bed. I was mid-panic, thinking of who was at the door. Before I could climb out of a window, Fisher threw on his shorts and wrapped his arms around me. He held me with my back against his chest and walked us into the bathroom like that before slipping his hand over my mouth.

"You gotta stop mumbling 'oh, fuck', Ella. It's kind of a giveaway." He held me tight and pressed his lips to my ear. "I'm just going to tell you right now. If Vaughn murders me for defiling you, I'm good with it after what just happened. I'll die a happy man."

I elbowed him in the side and then we both went silent as Booth turned off his music. I heard him open his door but I couldn't make out what he was saying. I felt like smacking my head into the wall for getting caught in the predicament we were in. My body was still throbbing, so I couldn't be all that sorry about it, but I did regret that Vaughn might've tried to kill Booth and Fisher.

"Can you hear anything?"

I shook my head. "What are they doing out there?"

Fisher grunted and dropped one of his arms from around me. I felt him reaching between us and looked at him over my shoulder. "Sorry. My phone is vibrating in my pocket."

"Is now the best time to check your messages?"

He let me go and slapped my ass loud enough for it to echo in the tiled bathroom. I spun around, ready to murder him for giving our location away, but he was holding up his phone, a message thread between him and Booth open. "Vaughn got him to help take someone home. The coast is clear."

I blew out a giant breath and pushed my hair out of my face. "I'm going to my room before I have a heart attack."

He wrapped his arms around my waist and smiled. "Can I come?"

I batted his hands away. "You already did. We all did. And now I'm going to escape to my room to think about what the hell just happened."

"I could come again..." He saw my face and laughed. "Fine. I'll go to my own room and come to just the thought of you."

"Really?" I realized how interested I sounded and groaned. "No. No, no, no."

"Fine." He walked with me out of Booth's room. His voice grew serious as we got to his room. "Hey. Don't freak out about what just happened. Okay? It was a first for us, too."

I looked down at our feet and then up at him through my lashes. "I won't."

"I like not having to lose you to Booth if you want him, too." He let out a dramatic sigh. "Anyway. Goodnight, Ella."

I went up on my tiptoes and kissed him. "Night, Fisher."

30

Ella

I stared down at my phone, looking at the time slowly ticking by. I'd been waiting for Vaughn to show up in the library for nearly half an hour. He'd never been late for our tutoring sessions before and I was worried. I'd already texted him to ask if he was coming but I hadn't gotten anything back. My mind went straight to the worst option possible. Besides him being dead or hurt, it was him finding out about what I'd done the night before. I was still scandalized by it myself, so I could only imagine how he would react.

I tapped my fingers on the table and chewed on my bottom lip. I considered calling Mom while I waited but I felt like she'd know I did something crazy. Her sex sixth sense was remarkable. I couldn't talk to Natalie about it, though, so I was close to bursting. I wanted someone else to tell me that I wasn't out of my mind.

Giving up on waiting patiently, I called Vaughn. I was too antsy to just sit around. His phone rang and rang until the call went to voicemail. Groaning, I started shoving my things back into my backpack. Being in the library, in complete silence, was going to make me nuts. I was replaying the night before over and over again, going over every little detail. How it had happened, how Booth and Fisher felt, had it been good enough for them?

I needed to go straight to my room and journal. Except I didn't even trust my journal anymore, thanks to Mom.

I'd just stood up to leave when the door was flung open. I jumped and gasped while clutching my chest. "Jesus!"

Vaughn looked like an angry bull as he came in and slammed the door shut behind him. He was standing like he was ready to charge and I could see a vein in his neck throbbing. His nostrils were even flaring. "Ella Rae Daughton."

I dropped my backpack and took a step back. "Why do you look like you just shot up steroids?"

"I have a question for you." He stepped closer. "Why the fuck were your panties in Booth's room?"

My face felt like I'd set it on fire as I stared back at him with wide eyes. My panties? Internally, I was freaking out. I was screaming about how dumb I'd been to leave my panties and how dumb I'd been to sleep with Vaughn's friends at all. I couldn't imagine telling him the truth, though, so I went the defensive route. I twisted my face into a scowl. "How the hell do you know what my panties look like?"

He moved closer. "Tell me the truth, Ella."

Deny, deny, deny. "Answer my question, Vaughn. How do you know they were my panties?"

"Goddammit, Ella, I saw your laundry. That part doesn't matter! What matters is that they were in my best friend's room."

"What do you mean, you saw my laundry?" Denial and defensiveness were making a super combination of crazy. "Have you been looking at my panties, Vaughn? You pervert."

His eyes narrowed as he turned around and shook his head. "Jesus, Ella. Just fucking tell me the truth. Are you fucking Booth?"

Facing his back, I could admit it. Especially since he hadn't asked about Fisher, too. Still, I was quiet as I answered. "I did."

He spun back around to me. "What the hell is your problem, Ella? You couldn't find anyone else on this campus to screw? It had to be my best friend?"

I had found someone else but he didn't need to know that. "I didn't sleep with Booth just because I was looking for someone to screw, Vaughn. It just happened."

"It just happened?" He gave me a look that made me feel two inches tall. "You never could take responsibility for your fuck ups. I just thought maybe you'd grown up a little since you were thirteen."

Anger surged through me and I rounded the table to plant myself right in front of him. "You think I'm not taking responsibility? I said it happened. What more do you want? You want the details? You want to know-"

"Stop talking, Ella."

"-how he fucked me? You want to know positions and an orgasm count?"

Breathing harder, Vaughn inched even closer. "You're a brat, Ella. Someone told you not to do something and you just had to do it, didn't you?"

"Not everything is about you, Vaughn! I didn't do it to spite you. You were far, *far* from my mind while I did it." I was seeing red and I wanted to jab him where it hurt. "Booth made sure of that."

"Fuck you, Ella."

"Fuck you, too, Vaughn. I hate you!" Breathing just as hard as Vaughn, I stared up at him with a growing desire to rip his hair out. Or throat punch him. Or-

Vaughn grabbed my arms and pulled me up onto my tiptoes. His eyes flicked down to my mouth and he growled. "I mean it, Ella. Fuck you."

My blood was fire in my veins. I shoved my hands against his chest. "I mean it, too."

His eyes shifted to my mouth again and the tension shifted. Without warning, and without knowing who moved first, his mouth was on mine and his hands were on my waist, dragging me into his body. It was an eruption. I grabbed his hair and held on while he spun me around and pinned me to the door. His mouth was harsh on mine, his teeth raking over my lips, his kiss almost more bite than kiss. His hands were everywhere all at once, touching my bare thigh and then cupping my breast in a hard grip.

I tugged on his hair and panted his name when he stroked his hand down my thigh and tugged it up around his hip. Grinding into me, he gripped my ass and kissed down my throat. His bites stung but I couldn't get enough of them.

I raked my nails over his shoulders and he yanked my cardigan down my shoulders, pinning my arms until I could work them free. I moaned when he cupped my breasts and pushed them together so he could bury his face in them. I got my arms free and slipped them inside his shirt. His skin was hot under my fingers.

Vaughn sucked at my breasts, giving a little pain with every bit of pleasure. Moving his mouth back up to mine, he reached under my dress and shifted his hips so he could slip his hand inside my panties. His mouth hovered over mine as he growled at me. "You're fucking soaked, Ella. Why are you so wet for someone you hate?"

31

Ella

I bit his bottom lip and locked gazes with him. "Maybe it's not for you."

"Fuck you." He pulled his hand from my underwear and my hips tried to follow him.

I heard his zipper in the quiet of the room and buried my nails in his back. "Fuck me, Vaughn."

He yanked my underwear to the side and I heard it rip just before I felt his hot erection against my lower lips. He brought his other hand up and covered my mouth before thrusting his full length into me. I cried out into his hand and my head dropped back against the door with a hard *thud*. He gripped my thigh and kept my leg wrapped around his hip as he pulled out and thrust deep again.

Pressing his mouth to my ear, he whispered harshly. "Do you still hate me, Ella?"

I couldn't answer. He fucked me like he really did hate me. He stretched me and pushed me to my limit and never hesitated in his thrusts. My back and shoulder blades took the brunt of his power against the door but I clung to him for more. He gripped my face hard to keep me quiet and grunted against my throat.

"Are you going to come on the cock of the guy you hate? Are you going to come for me, Ella?" He fucked me even harder and the sounds of my muffled moans grew louder. "You want someone to catch me fucking you? What would Booth think?"

Breathing hard through my nose, I careened closer and closer to the edge but I tried to fight it. I didn't want to give it to him that quickly.

Vaughn moved his hand up my thigh and clutched my ass. His fingers dug into the space between my cheeks and he stroked a fingertip over my virgin hole. "You're going to come for me."

He pressed his fingertip inside and my body went up in flames. I came hard, crying out into his hand and dragging my nails down his back. I heard him growling out my name like it was a curse and then I felt him coming inside me. No one had ever come inside me before and feeling his come flooding my insides dragged out my orgasm.

"Fuck, Ella Rae." He thrust into me a few more times and then just held me there, pinned to the door. His head on my shoulder, his finger still in my ass, and what felt like an obscene amount of his seed in me. Truly fucked. "I didn't use a condom. Fuck."

I extracted my nails from his back and reached up to pull his hand away from my mouth. "Vaughn?"

He slowly lifted his head to face me. "I'm fucking sorry, Ella. I've never done that before. I don't know what-"

"*Vaughn?*"

"Yeah?"

"Can you take your finger out of my ass?"

His eyes crinkled in the corners and his lips went pale from how hard he was pressing them together. He cleared his throat as he pulled his finger free. When he met my gaze again, it was like all the tension in the room evaporated. His laugh was loud and deep and it jarred his dick that was still inside me.

I couldn't believe I was laughing with him after what we'd just done but I couldn't stop. My cheeks hurt after a few minutes of it and I started to feel the aches all over my body. "You wanna get out of me, Vaughn?"

He bit his lip and nodded. "Yep. Sorry about that."

I groaned when he stepped away from me and had to reach down to pull my mangled underwear back into place. "Sorry for staying or for being there in the first place? Or for leaving...a mess..."

He tucked himself back into his pants and shook his head. "Definitely for the last one. Are you on anything?"

I nodded. "No one's ever tested it before now, though."

His eyebrows climbed his forehead. "Oh?"

"Shut up, Vaughn."

He grinned and ran his hands through his hair, fixing it. "So you're telling me that I shouldn't feel special that I'm the only guy to ever come in you?"

I slapped his arm and tried to fix my clothes. "How did I get here? And why are you so happy with me now? You wanted to rip my head off when you first came in."

He tilted his head. "Are you seriously asking me why I'm happy after I just had a great fuck?"

Hearing him call it great made me blush. "I guess I was. That was dumb. You didn't answer my first two questions about being sorry, by the way."

"Are you going to be weird if I say I'm not sorry for it happening?" He rubbed his jaw and leaned against the table. "I mean, I know it's not going to happen again but I can't say I'm sorry. What about you?"

I nodded. "Kinda the same. I'm glad we're not yelling at each other anymore."

"Aw. I thought you liked fighting with me." He sobered up after a minute and looked around the small room we were in. "I don't know how quiet we were. I don't want people getting the wrong idea about you."

Nerves bubbled up inside me. "That I let my ex-stepbrother fuck me against a door?"

He groaned. "That you're a cheater. Everyone thinks you're with Fish."

I covered my face with my hands and groaned. "Oh, yeah. That."

"No one's going to find out about us because we're never going to do this again. Right?"

I nodded quickly. "Definitely not. There are some lines that are just out of bounds."

"Like my friends."

I winced. "Vaughn..."

"I'm serious about it, Ella Rae. I don't want you sleeping with my friends." He frowned at me. "I'm still pissed that you slept with Booth."

I shifted and felt some of his mess slowly leaking out of me. "Oh, god, Vaughn. I have to go home and take care of this. It's coming out."

He looked confused until I pointed at my crotch. "Oh. Oh! Okay, yeah, let's get you home."

"Stop smirking, asshole."

"Sorry. It's just..." He grunted. "Nothing."

I blew out a deep breath. "How do I get out of here without anyone knowing what we did in here or your mess leaking down my thighs?"

Groaning, he walked around to grab my backpack where I'd dropped it. "You have to stop talking about it, Ella. You're killing me."

I saw that his pants were bulging and gasped. "Vaughn!"

"What? I'm a man. It's in our biology to like it!"

I pulled out a chair and sank into it. "We can't go out with you like that. And we agreed this is never happening again, so you need to not like it."

He sat across from me and we both just stared at each other for a few seconds before he stood up. "Nope. I can't just sit here and not think about it. I'm going to make sure no one's watching and we're getting the fuck out of here."

"Oh, thank god."

32

Fisher

"Well." I stared across the table at Booth. We were sitting at a Mexican place we both liked off campus and it was time to talk about Ella. There'd been an elephant in the truck with us on the ride over and, no matter how awkward it felt, we had to sort it out.

Booth stared back at me and cleared his throat. "Well."

A waiter brought over chips and salsa and took our drink order. As soon as he left, I met Booth's eyes and groaned. "I don't even know what to say, man."

He nodded. "Me either. I can't say I like knowing what you sound like when you come, dude. I'm feeling awkward as hell."

I cringed. "Don't even say it. I can't think about it."

"That was crazy. How did that even happen? Were you aiming for that? Because I wasn't aiming for that. All of a sudden, it was just happening." He rubbed his face and shoved a chip into his mouth, talking around it. "She's a siren. Or a witch. I don't know how else we ended up in that position."

"Don't say position." I thanked the waiter for our drinks and we placed the same order we always did. "But, no, I wasn't aiming for that. I just went with it."

We were quiet for a few minutes, both of us lost in thought. Finally, Booth looked up from where he was breaking a chip into a dozen little pieces. "The weirdness between us aside... How was it?"

I couldn't lie. "It was the hottest fucking thing I've ever done."

He let out a deep sigh of relief. "Thank fuck. I was starting to worry that I was fucked in the head. Having her like that..."

I nodded swiftly. "Yeah, I know. It was intense knowing that we were both...you know."

"Again, I hate that I know what you sound like, but...I wouldn't say no to more." Booth gulped down half of his drink in one go and swallowed loudly. "I want her alone. Obviously. But sharing her was so hot. I can't imagine if we went all the way."

I shifted in my seat and blew out a shaky breath. I'd been thinking the same thing all night. I didn't even know how many times I'd come from the thought of both of us fucking Ella. I just knew my dick needed a break. "It would've happened last night if Vaughn hadn't come home when he did. She wanted us as much as we wanted her."

"Fucking Vaughn."

"Yep. Fucking Vaughn." I looked around the mostly empty restaurant. "I feel like he's going to pop out from behind a bush at any moment and dropkick me through a window."

"Same. I had to sit next to him in the truck last night with Ella's scent all over my face and breath. The whole drive I was debating if he'd be willing to kill himself to kill me by yanking the steering wheel and sending us into oncoming traffic." He shuddered. "I've never been happier to park my truck before."

"Part of me wants to tell him to fucking loosen up about her but another part of me realizes that if you two were trying to fuck someone in my family, I'd be pretty pissed, too."

"She's not part of his family, though. They were step-siblings a decade ago." Booth went quiet as our food was dropped off. "He doesn't talk about her or anything at all the entire time we've known him and suddenly he's trying to be the world's most protective stepbrother? It's weird."

I nodded. "I know. I've never seen him go feral like this before. It's almost enough to make me want to keep my hands to myself."

We both paused and then Booth laughed. "That ship has sailed, buddy."

"What I'm hearing you say is that the damage has already been done so we should just keep going until we can't anymore?"

He grinned. "Seems silly to try to put spilled milk back in the carton."

"I don't think that's how that saying goes."

"Fuck off."

We finished our late lunch and hung out for a while, watching an NFL game. By the time we got home it was already dark out. Neither of us admitted that we were actively avoiding having to face Vaughn but that's what was happening. Our efforts were in vain, though, because as soon as we pulled into the driveway, there he was.

"Oh, fuck. He looks pissier than usual, doesn't he?" I went ahead and got out of the truck, fully expecting to get punched once I did.

Vaughn stopped in front of my truck and glared at us. "You're screwing Ella."

Booth and I glanced at each other and I decided to take the first hit. "Vaughn, shit happened and-"

"Are you trying to excuse Booth for doing it?" Vaughn's face turned an even darker shade of red as he realized the truth. "You're not making an excuse for Booth. You're making an excuse for yourself."

I winced. "Alright, Vaughn. Let's just take a deep breath, man. You look like your blood pressure is pretty high."

"You both fucked her." He let out a dangerous sounding laugh and spun in a tight circle. "She didn't mention that."

"Vaughn,-" Booth tried to say something but Vaughn didn't want to hear from us. He just wanted to rage.

"Fuck you both. You're my best friends. I asked you for one thing. Don't touch her. One fucking thing and you both could've have cared less about what I wanted. We don't do that to each other. Or maybe we do. I don't know what the fuck is happening around here anymore, apparently." He'd shifted into something worse than rage in the middle of his rant, disappointment. "Fuck it."

I watched him turn to walk away and couldn't just let him go. "Vaughn, wait. I'm sorry."

"I'm done talking to both of you tonight. If I keep looking at you, I'm going to lose my shit. I don't want to do anything to hurt either of you, even if the feeling isn't returned." He jogged into the house and slammed the door shut behind him.

I looked over at Booth and his look of regret matched what I felt. "Shit. I thought he'd hit us and that would be enough."

"Yeah, this feels a lot worse." Booth shook his head. "I think I have to be done. I don't want to hurt Vaughn. Pissed off Vaughn, I can handle. Disappointed Vaughn? That sucked."

I nodded and let out a deep sigh. "Yeah, same. That felt fucking horrible."

We both just stood there for a while, giving Vaughn ample time to do whatever he needed to do before going to his room. Neither of us said much else. We were both trapped in our own guilt, feeling like shit for hurting Vaughn. Even if I didn't understand why he was upset, I could see that he was. That didn't feel okay.

"Well."

Booth grunted. "Well."

33

Booth

"How's it going with Ella?" I tried to sound casual as I asked, despite feeling anything but. "With being the boyfriend, I mean."

Fisher glanced around to make sure no one could hear us and shook his head. "It's brutal. I'm doing my best to keep things as friendly as possible but it's not easy."

I sat forward and rested my elbows on my knees. "I've just tried to avoid her to make it easier. Somehow, it doesn't make it easier, though. It's been two weeks and I just want her more. Vaughn's just now starting to talk to me like normal again, though."

"He's still pissy with me. Every time he sees us doing the whole couple thing, that vein in his forehead starts throbbing." Sighing, he stared out across campus. "I miss cookies after our wins."

I couldn't help grinning. "We got spoiled really fucking fast."

"How could we not? She baked for us. She put our names on those little cookies, man. She mentioned that she's been going to her friend's apartment after the games." Standing up to pace, he looked so unfamiliar in that moment. The Fisher I'd become best friends with Freshman year didn't do stressed. "I think she's baking for other people. I swear I can smell fresh cookies every time I come home."

"What's Vaughn's issue? Why's it matter so much if we sleep with her?"

I ran my hands through my hair and tugged at it. "I feel like I'm losing my mind. I can smell the cookies all the time, too, but I can also still smell *her* in my bed."

"I think-" Fisher froze. "There she is. I'm not sure I can pretend to be the boyfriend without copping a feel right now, man."

I followed his gaze and spotted Ella walking from the cafeteria to the English building. She was in another sundress, her thighs exposed a little more with each long step she took. Since it was starting to cool off outside, she had a cardigan wrapped tight around her. Her hair bounced in her high ponytail and I watched her smile at someone in passing. My fists clenched with desire as I watched her and I felt the same struggle I did every time I thought about her. I wanted her. I didn't want to hurt Vaughn. I wanted her. But Vaughn.

"Is that...?" Fisher's voice changed as Billy Novak appeared behind Ella and covered her eyes with his hands.

I was up and off the bench before I could even process what I was seeing. Billy was trying to play with Ella. I watched her stiffen and struggle to push his hands away, watched him try to hug her after she pushed him away. Seeing red, I charged towards the pair, not sure what I was going to do once I got there. Beyond murdering Billy.

As we got a little closer, I could hear Ella's raised voice. "Don't touch me, Billy!"

"Hey!" I shouted, drawing half the campus' eyes, but one look in our direction had Billy backing away. "What the fuck is your problem?"

He held up his hands and put a fake smile on his slimy face as I came chest to chest with him. Only I towered over him so it wasn't really chest to chest. He laughed a little too loudly, doing his best to save face. "What's wrong, bro? I'm just talking to Ella."

I shoved him backwards and followed his retreat, step for step. "You don't touch her."

A tiny hand on my chest was all it took for Ella to take over the situation. She looked up at me and flashed me a bright smile. "Thanks, Booth. I'm okay."

I searched her face to make sure she was telling the truth and relaxed the slightest bit when I saw that she was. I glared back at Billy, though, and practically snarled at him. "Stay away from her."

Fisher stood next to Ella and wrapped his arm around her. "I've never seen you so close to tackling someone outside of a game, man. I don't think most of the people on campus have ever heard you talk, much less raise your voice."

I looked at his arm around her and got hit with such a wave of jealousy that I had to put some space between us. I took a few steps back and nodded, doing my best to hold it together. "I'll see you both later. I need to go do something."

"Booth, wait-" Whatever Ella was going to say, I missed it. I tucked tail and jogged away. I didn't stop until I was home and breathing so hard that I had to stop at the bottom of the stairs and catch my breath before I could climb them.

Feeling frustrated, I paced my room and tried to calm down. I was fighting my attraction to Ella so hard to be a better friend to Vaughn but it was a losing battle. I wanted her. Seeing her ex touching her, seeing Fisher touch her when I couldn't, it was making me nuts. There was something about her that was just different and I felt something akin to panic at the idea of never getting to touch her again.

I checked my watch and saw that I was missing a class but I didn't care. I wouldn't have been able to focus anyway. Without knowing what else to do, I called the one person who'd always been able to calm me down.

She answered right away. "Boo? Hi, honey! You never call me during the day. What's up?"

Mom had been my entire support system growing up. She was still the person I depended on for most things.

"Hey, Mom. I just had a minute and figured I'd check in." I knew she could tell I was lying right away. She'd been a bit of a helicopter mom when I was growing up. She didn't like me having to deal with any bad emotions so she'd tried hard to save me from them. To a detriment at some points. When I was young, her solution had been to ply me with food to keep my happy. She was a young mom and hadn't known what to do. Food cheered me up, though, so that's what she leaned into. Even when I'd gotten chubbier and chubbier.

"Something's wrong. Tell me, Booth."

I blew out a rough breath and sank down on my bed. "Everything's fine, Mom. I just... I think I really like this one person who's off-limits."

"It's a professor, isn't it? Which professor? What's his name? I knew this would happen. You didn't have a dad and now you've got daddy issues. Is he using his power over you, baby? Tell me everything."

I gaped at the phone for a few seconds before I could find my voice. "Mom, what the hell? I'm not gay."

She seemed genuinely shocked. "You're not?"

"No, I'm not. Why do you think I'm gay?"

"Well, you never talked about girls. I'm very open to the idea of you being gay, Boo. Don't make any decisions right now." She sighed. "Are you sure it's not a male professor?"

"It's not a decision I'd need to make, Mom. I'm straight. Sorry, but I was just born this way." I had to laugh. "I just had to come out to my mom as straight. Wow."

"Oh, anyway. Moving on from that bit of disappointing news. Is it a female professor?"

"It's not a professor, Mom. Jeez. I don't have daddy issues. Some would argue I have mother issues, though." I rubbed my face. "I think I have feelings for Ella."

"Your roommate? Why is she off-limits? That seems stupid. You're both young and straight, I guess. Where's the harm?" She called out to her secretary. "Melissa, Booth just told me he's straight and likes a girl."

"Okay, this was a bad idea. I've got to go. I love you, Mom. Bye!" I hung up before she could argue and groaned. That hadn't gone quite as planned but I was distracted from all my jealousy over Ella, I guessed.

34

Ella

When I got home that night, I rushed upstairs and straight to Booth's room. I knocked before I could chicken out and as soon as he answered, I wrapped my arms around him in a tight hug. "Thank you. For earlier. I didn't get a chance to thank you because of...everything...so I just wanted to say it... So, thank you."

He leaned against his door frame after I slipped out of his arms and watched me. "I'm sorry I ran off. I was jealous."

I rocked back on my heels like he'd slapped me. I had to open and close my mouth a few times before I could form my thoughts into a sentence. I wasn't used to such blatant honesty. "You were jealous?"

He nodded. "I'm doing my best to be a better friend to Vaughn but it isn't easy. Seeing Fish get to touch you is hard. So, yeah, I was jealous. I wanted to be the one holding you."

My cheeks heated and I stammered. Hearing him admit it so openly was somehow both butterfly-inducing and a balm to my wounded ego. I'd been convinced that he hadn't liked what we'd done or that Vaughn had told him about what we'd done in the library. He'd pulled back from me hard and while I understood it, I didn't like it. "You were jealous."

He smiled and his dimples made it devastating. "I was jealous. *Am* jealous."

"You are jealous." I realized I was starting to sound like an idiot and shook my head. "Sorry. I just spent the last two weeks thinking that I'd done something wrong so I'm a little shocked."

"You thought you'd done something wrong?"

I smirked up at him. "Now *you're* repeating *me*."

He glanced down the hallway and his jaw muscles clenched. "You did nothing wrong."

"Vaughn found my panties in your room. If the way he came after me was anything like the way he came after you, I assume it wasn't pretty." I looked down at Vaughn's door and sighed. Things were weird.

"He was more hurt than I expected." Booth stepped forward and brushed his knuckle down my cheek. "I don't want to be a bad friend."

I nodded as a heavy weight settled over my chest. It was for the best. One of us had to be strong enough to stay away from the other. It clearly wasn't going to be me. "I get it."

"No, you don't. I don't want to be a bad friend but I'm going to be. I can't watch other guys touch you and keep my sanity, Ella." His cheeks went pink. "I called my mom and tried to talk to her about it today. That's how close I am to losing my mind. She thought I was gay and was super disappointed that I'm not. It was a whole thing that I wish I could've avoided."

I snorted. "She thought you were gay? If she only knew…"

"Really, Ella?" He shook his head. "She'll never know because I'm not going to ever tell my mother how much I like eating your-"

"Incoming." Fisher hurried our way after spotting us. "Vaughn is about two minutes behind me."

I looked at the two of them and felt my own sanity slipping away. "I have to go…"

Booth looked at Fisher and then back at me. "Vaughn has dinner with the coach and his wife tomorrow night. Those things go on for hours."

Fisher nodded. "My room?"

I nodded hard and fast. "Yep. That sounds... Yep."

Booth smirked at me, the confidence oozing off of him so damn sexy that I wanted to throw caution to the wind and jump into his arms right then and there. "Think of us, Ella."

I flushed and nearly choked on a giggle before turning and speed walking down to my room. I'd just reached my door when I heard the downstairs door slam shut. I let out a relieved breath and locked myself in my bathroom to call Mom.

I thought about Booth calling his own mom and caught my reflection grinning like an idiot in the mirror. I turned away from that version of myself and sat on the counter. As soon as Mom answered, I whispered as much as I could at her. "Mom, I need help. It's about sex. Please don't be weird."

"Oh, my god!" Her voice was so loud, even without the phone being on speaker, that when she talked to someone in the background, I was able to make out every word. "Put that thing away for a second, Carl. My daughter needs sex advice!"

I groaned. "Mom!"

"Okay. What do you need help with? I know you're not a virgin, so anal? Is it anal?"

"Mom! No!" My skin was on fire as I tried to remember why I'd thought it was a good idea to call her. "It's not about that. It's...something else."

"What? Tell me! I'm dying here."

"You're not the one with blue balls, lady." A man's voice sounded out from the background.

"Oh, my god. Mom."

She read the horror in my voice. "Oh, relax. We weren't hooking up yet. Carl's fine. Ignore him. I am."

I focused on the reason I'd called her and blew out a big breath. I knew I was insane for wanting her opinion but I wasn't sure I could trust myself. "So. You know how I slept with two of my roommates?"

"Yes! And I'm so proud of you for that."

I shook my head. "Okay, anyway. I think I just set up a date to have sex with both of them. At the same time."

Her screams were of pure joy.

Talking through her screams, I pressed on. "I just need to know. Is it okay? What I'm feeling, what I want... Am I messed up?"

"Messed up? No, you're not messed up! You're living your best life finally, baby!" I heard a door closing on her end and when she spoke again, I would've sworn her voice sounded a little watery. "Baby, this is amazing. You're coming into your sexual nature and I'm so proud of you. I know I joke a lot but the power you can feel from taking charge of your sex life is huge, Ella. Letting go of expectations that have been forced on you by one very uptight society is the best version of freedom."

I sniffed and fanned at my eyes to keep from crying. "Not all moms would be so cool with this... Thank you."

"Okay, so let's talk logistics. Taking two men isn't easy, if the men are any good. You're going to want-"

"Mom?" I cut her off. "I still don't want to talk details. I just wanted to know that it's okay, I guess."

"Oh, boo." She laughed happily. "It's more than okay, Ella Rae. Are you sure you don't want some tips?"

"Positive. I love you, Mom. Go back to your date."

"You've inspired me. I think I'll have Carl call his brother." She heard me gag and cackled. "There's my uptight baby! I love you!"

35

Ella

After the longest day of my life, I spent a solid two hours preparing for my secret meeting with Booth and Fisher. I shaved every part of my body I could reach, lotioned, curled my hair, and even put on makeup. I wore an oversized t-shirt with nothing on under it. No one was finding my panties that time. After I was ready, I paced my bedroom floor and did my best to push down whatever nerves tried to pop up. I was embracing my sexual side, like Mom said.

I was pretty sure most women didn't get pep talks from their moms before sex but Mom had really helped. I'd just needed to know that she wouldn't balk at what I was doing. If she wasn't horrified by me, then I was okay.

I'd spent two weeks sad and overrun with thoughts about sex with the guys. I'd convinced myself that it was never going to happen again and I'd tried to accept it. I'd also spent two weeks doing my best not to think about Vaughn. That was another story, though.

When someone knocked on my door, I nearly jumped out of my skin. I rushed to it and pulled it open, just to see Vaughn standing on the other side. I watched his eyes move from my head to my toes before moving back up slowly. By the time he met my gaze, I was bright red. "Um, hi."

He stared at me and I could see the wheels turning in his mind. "Going somewhere?"

I forced a laugh and pulled the hem of my shirt lower. "I'm in my pajamas."

"Your hair and makeup are done." He checked his watch and growled. "I have to go. I have this dinner thing with the coach's family. He does it with every member of the team and it's my turn. This shit goes on for hours. I won't be back until late."

I nodded. "Okay."

I could tell that he wanted to say more but he hesitated. He glanced down the hallway and shook his head. "Put some pants on if you go downstairs, Cinderella."

"Yes, *Dad*."

He narrowed his eyes at me. "I have heartburn now. I never had heartburn before you moved in."

"You're getting older, Vaughn. That kind of thing happens." I realized I was pushing him into a fight and forced myself to stop with the sass. "I'll put on pants if I go downstairs, Vaughn. Go to your dinner and have fun."

He continued to stare at me for a few more seconds before swearing and walking away. I watched him go and pushed my guilt away. As soon as the front door slammed shut, both Booth and Fisher's bedroom doors swung open. I almost laughed as both of them stuck their heads out at the same time.

I didn't wait for an invitation. I ran across the hall into Fisher's room and climbed onto his bed. I was kneeling in the middle of it before I'd even looked around to notice that he'd set up mood lighting and music. Booth was inside almost as fast as I was and then Fisher had the door shut and locked.

A wave of nerves struck me but I pushed those right down with the guilt. "So."

Booth ate up the distance between us with a few long strides and then he was tugging me off the bed and into his arms. His kiss was rough and hungry as his hands roamed my body. When he stroked one of them up my thigh and found no other material waiting to block him, he groaned and pulled back. "You're not wearing any panties."

Fisher pressed into me from behind. "You seem a little excited, Ella."

Booth cupped my sex and grinned when I moaned. "She's *very* excited. Her excitement is practically running down her thighs."

Their confidence in touching me together was through the roof. Their hesitation was gone as they did what they wanted to my body. Fisher cupped my breasts and kissed my neck while Booth gathered my wetness on his fingers and then pushed two of them inside me. I dropped my head back on Fisher's shoulder and moaned.

"Oh, god." Widening my stance, I gripped Booth's massive shoulders and held on as he began pumping his fingers faster. They'd only just started touching me and I was already lost in the pleasure.

Fisher played with my nipples and nipped my earlobe. "We're fast learners, Ella Rae. We know what we want and that you're going to give it to us this time."

Booth hooked his thumb over my clit and rubbed. "You're going to come for us so many times. We have hours before Vaughn gets back."

My core clamped down on his fingers as I came for the first time. I moaned their names and struggled to stay on my feet as the gravity of it all hit me. What we were doing was so much bigger than any of my wildest fantasies and I couldn't help reveling it in.

"We're just getting started, baby." Fisher ran his hand down my stomach and took Booth's place over my clit. He gently stroked it while turning me so we could both watch as Booth undressed and sat on the edge of the bed, his dick firmly in hand. "If it's too much, say so, Ella."

Booth nodded. "You're in charge."

I shivered and wobbled when Fisher shifted away from me to pull my shirt over my head. "What if I don't want to be in charge?"

Booth's dimples deepened as he slowly grinned at me. "That works, too."

Fisher undressed behind me and pressed his naked body against mine from behind. "You're going to bend over and suck Booth's cock, Ella. You're going to keep this perfect ass up for me and I'm going to fuck you while he watches. Sound good to you?"

I moaned and nodded. "Yes, please."

Booth crooked his finger at me. "Come here, Ella."

I was breathing hard and shaking with desire. My heart was hammering away in my chest. Before I could bend over, Fisher turned my face towards him and kissed me. I felt Booth's mouth over my nipples and whimpered. It was happening. I was the center of their focus and it was a heady experience.

When Fisher pulled back from kissing me he winked and then pressed between my shoulder blades so I'd bend at the waist. My ass pressed into his dick as I bent and I could feel how hard he was. Then Booth's cock was in front of my face and he was wrapping my hair around his fist to get it out of my face.

"Suck me, Ella."

I gripped his thighs for balance and ran my tongue over the tip. I loved the sound of his breathing stuttering and the way his fist tightened in my hair. I opened my mouth and took the head inside, running my tongue over it like it was my favorite sucker.

"Goddamn, Ella." His voice was gruff as he met my gaze and pushed my head lower. "Relax your jaw, baby. Open that mouth and let me have it."

At the same time, I felt Fisher spreading me from behind and I moaned wildly as he sank his length into me. I jolted forward and gagged as the motion forced more of Booth's cock into my mouth than I was ready for.

Fisher gripped my hips and pulled me back into him, just so he could thrust into me again.

"You're so wet, Ella. So wet and so tight." He stroked his hands over my ass and then gripped my hips again as he thrust deep. "You're taking both of us right now and I've never seen anything hotter in my life."

I sucked harder and deeper at Booth, single-mindedly determined to give as good as I got. I listened to his moans and felt the way he tugged at my hair until I was letting every deep thrust from Fisher rock me forward and farther down Booth's length.

"Jesus. This is... Holy shit." Booth grunted when his tip brushed the back of my throat. "Yes, Ella, open that throat for me."

36

Fisher

I rode Ella hard from behind, thrusting into her perfect pussy faster and harder as I watched her swallow more and more of Booth's cock. She was taking us beautifully, stuffed full at both ends. I couldn't get enough of her. I stroked her back and her ass, touching her everywhere I could. I didn't miss the way her walls tightened on me when I brushed over her asshole.

Booth swore and dropped his head back. "Fuck, Ella!"

Her muffled moans and cries of pleasure filled my room. Her body moved between us like she was made to be there. When I planted my hand on her low back and dropped my thumb to play with her ass, she bucked her hips back at me and did something to Booth that had him pulling her head up so he could regain his control.

He held her face in his hands and held her steady right in front of him, watching her intently as I fucked her. "How good do you feel right now, Ella Rae?"

She moaned loudly and spoke with a breathy voice. "So good."

I felt the way her pussy slammed down on my cock when he called her Ella Rae. "Ella Rae."

Her body responded the same way again. She cried out our names and let out a wild cry when I pressed my thumb deeper into her ass. "Fisher!"

I waited until Booth brought her mouth back down to his cock and then I gently fucked her ass with my thumb. "Seems our sweet little Ella Rae likes being called that while we're fucking her."

Booth met my eyes over Ella's body. "Isn't that what Vaughn calls her when he's pissy?"

Ella made an unhappy sound but with her mouth full, her protest was weak. Especially when I could feel her body tightening and readying to come.

"Our Ella Rae is going to come with our dicks filling her, my thumb up her ass, and to the name Vaughn calls her." I reached my other hand around and stroked her clit. "Like a fucking angel, Ella Rae."

Her response was instant. She came hard, her knees buckling almost immediately. I held her up and slowed my strokes until I was just buried deep in her, letting her walls massage my length. She lifted her head from Booth's dick and screamed as her orgasm rocked her. When she was panting and whimpering, I moved my hand from her clit and rubbed her back.

"You're so perfect, Ella Rae." I gently eased out of her body with a nod to Booth. I yanked off the condom I'd put on and threw it away before climbing on the bed.

Booth picked Ella up and put her on her hands and knees in front of me. He knelt behind her on the bed and I looked back and forth between Ella's pleasure heavy eyes and Booth's hand. He gathered her juices and smeared them across her asshole before rolling on a condom and pushing into her pussy.

Her eyes went wide as he gripped her shoulders and sank his whole length inside her. She watched me stroke myself and dropped her head to take my cock deep in her mouth. Her hair tickled my stomach as she muffled her own cries.

Booth shifted his grip so he held the back of her neck and I felt Ella suck harder as he eased a finger into her ass. He groaned and began fucking her harder. "So fucking good, Ella Rae."

I jerked my eyes up from her and saw Booth's eyes widen at the feeling of her body reacting to that name. I nodded when he looked at me and then pulled her hair out of her face so I could watch her take my dick deeper.

Booth worked a second finger into her ass and began fucking her ass the same way he was fucking her core. He rode her hard and every deep stroke sent her deeper on my cock until I was knocking against the back of her throat and fighting the urge to come from how she was sucking at me.

"Are you going to come for us again, Ella Rae?" Booth growled her name and I could tell we were all close to our ends. "Come for us before Vaughn comes in and sees you spread out like this."

The way those words triggered an instant orgasm in Ella was like magic. She was instantly shaking and letting out muffled cries around my cock. Her throat loosened enough that my tip slid inside and I lost any ounce of control I had left. I pulled back enough to not choke her and then I came hard, filling her mouth. I watched her struggle to swallow as I just kept coming and didn't stop until she was a mess with my come dripping down her chin.

Booth came with a shout and Ella shook between us as pleasure ravaged her. He held her ass up as he finished but she let her front half collapse into my lap, my dick resting just under her cheek. When Booth finished and sank back into the bed, the rest of Ella collapsed between my legs. I could feel her tongue gently lapping at the side of my dick as she continued to shake and moan.

When my dick was too sensitive I pulled her onto the bed next to me and stretched out with her in my arms. Booth crawled higher to lay on her other side and we all just tried to catch our breath as we came down. I felt like she'd sucked the life right out of me and I was struggling to keep my eyes open. If Ella's soft snores were anything to go by, she'd succumbed to her exhaustion.

"Well."

I turned my head to look at Booth and grinned. "Well."

It didn't take long for Ella to jerk herself awake and when she did, she pressed her face into my chest and her ass into Booth. "I'm dead."

I stroked her hair. "I hope not. We've still got hours."

Booth looked at his watch and groaned. "That took less than twenty minutes. I feel like we should be embarrassed."

Ella lifted her head and shot me a look. "More than that and you'd have to scrape me off this bed."

"We're not done with you, yet, Ella Rae." Booth gently slapped her ass. "I want to learn more about how fast you can come to the idea of Vaughn walking in on you."

I grinned when I saw her face go dark red. "It's hard to lie when we're buried inside your pussy, Ella. She doesn't lie."

She groaned and sat up. "Stop talking or I'm leaving."

Booth grunted. "Give my mouth something else to do then, Ella Rae."

He laid flat and smirked at her, daring her to do what he wanted. I watched as she hesitated and seemed to talk herself out of it.

"Come on, Ella Rae. Sit on my face or I'm just going to keep talking about how you come to the idea of Vaughn-"

She practically vaulted up the bed. She knelt with her knees on either side of his head and glared down at him. "If you suffocate, you'll have deserved it."

He gripped her thighs and growled. "What a way to go."

I waited until Booth was eating her out and she was moaning to kneel next to her. "What do you think he would do if he walked in right now? Do you think he'd scream and shout about us defiling you or do you think he'd see your curves and your soaked pussy and want a taste?"

She gripped my headboard and sank her teeth into her lip. Her eyes were pure fire as she looked at me but she couldn't hide how close she already was to coming again.

"Let me show you what I think he'd do, Ella Rae." I stood up and stroked my already hard dick. "Open your mouth."

She did without hesitation.

"Reach back and jerk Booth off while I show you what Vaughn would do if he walked in, Ella Rae." I watched as she did as I said and then I held the tip of my dick against her bottom lip as I pumped my fist up and down my length. "He'd want to fuck you the same way we do. He'd want to see those lips close around his dick and he'd want to feel your tongue stroking the come out of him."

Her face flushed and she had a hard time holding my gaze but she did. She watched as I jacked off for her and she held her mouth open, with her tongue slightly out, waiting for me to come for her again.

I wasn't sure we made it even ten minutes that time before we all came again. When I did, though, I wiped her mouth and pressed my mouth to her ear. "What a good girl, being so willing to take care of Vaughn, too."

37

Ella

I searched my room for my notebook until it was a disaster zone. I had class in half an hour and we were having an open notes test. Without my notebook, I was sure I'd still pass but I wanted a perfect score to take back to Penn when I went. I was getting panicked the longer I couldn't find it. I tried to remember the last time I'd had it with me and cringed when I realized it was with Vaughn in the library.

We'd continued our tutoring sessions but we'd started leaving the door open as a guarantee that we wouldn't do anything stupid. Neither of us spoke about the reason we left the door open, but it was obvious. Outside of the sessions I'd been avoiding him like the plague, though, so I wasn't excited about having to go and ask him if he'd seen my notebook.

After my adventure into adventurous sex with Booth and Fisher, I'd been avoiding all of them as best as I could. It wasn't like we could've had any alone time anyway, not with the way Vaughn had glued himself to their asses. But after coming in front of the two of them to the idea of Vaughn walking in on us, I just wanted to hide. I was mortified that they'd so easily learned my secret.

Despite us sharing several heated looks, we'd barely seen each other without a group around us since that night. Their football schedule was getting busier with their away games getting farther and farther away. My classwork wasn't as hard as it'd been at Penn but it was still challenging to make sure I was learning everything possible so I wouldn't be behind when I transferred back. I'd also started a part-time job at the coffee shop I'd met Vaughn at when I'd asked him to let me live with him. I only worked two nights a week but it was enough to leave me feeling like I didn't have much free time.

Another reason I wanted to hurry was that I knew if I timed it right, I'd catch Fisher coming home from class when I was already driving to campus. Our couple outings had dwindled because of my fear of facing him.

I bit the bullet after glancing at my phone and hurried down the hall to Vaughn's room. I knew he was in because I'd heard him stomping around. I knocked and shifted from foot to foot as I waited. When he didn't answer right away, I knocked harder. "Vaughn! I think you have my notebook!"

I tried the door and realized it was unlocked. Letting myself in, I kept my eyes on the floor so I didn't see anything and tried to find his backpack.

"I let myself in! I need to find my notebook! Please don't be in here, doing anything weird!" I bumped into his bed and blushed. "God, I need help."

"What are you doing?" Vaughn sounded surprised to see me and when I glanced up, I was surprised to see him. He was wearing just a towel around his waist and his tan skin was still dripping from his shower.

I told myself to stop staring and get the hell out but I was frozen. "I... My notebook... You have it?"

He strode over to his door and shut it before walking right up to me and holding my gaze as he bent forward and grabbed his backpack from right behind me. "Feel free to look."

His clean scent filled my nose and I swallowed loudly. He was close, too close. He was also naked. So naked, except for the towel, but it was barely doing anything. I forced myself to take the bag and turn away from him. I stood with my back to him and struggled with the backpack's zipper. My hands were shaking and I felt like my blood was racing around my body so loudly that he could probably hear it.

I gasped as I felt him press into me from behind. His body was so hot that I almost instantly melted into him. I tried to stand strong, though. "Vaughn... We said we wouldn't..."

His arms slowly wrapped around me and he splayed his hands out across my stomach. His breath teased the baby hairs that escaped my ponytail as he leaned closer. "I know what we said."

A whimper stole past my lips as his hands slowly moved higher. "We can't."

His lips brushed the skin under my ear. "We're not."

Then why was I tilting my head to the side to give him more access to my neck? Why was he trailing kisses down my neck and over my shoulder? Why was I pressing my body into his and wishing my clothes were gone?

I spun around just before he cupped my breasts and whatever plans I'd had to be strong and resist went out the window as soon as I saw the look of need on his face. I knew who closed the distance between our mouths that time. It was me. I clung to his chest and kissed him like I wouldn't survive without his lips on mine. I held his face and let him draw me tight against his body. I lost myself in his bare chest and soft lips.

He shoved my cardigan off my shoulders and had the zipper halfway down my back when I came to my senses and leaned away from him.

"Wait. Wait, I... I slept with Booth and Fisher again. I just... I have to tell you that before I kiss you again. I... Oh, god." I twisted away from him and quickly found my notebook in his bag. "I'm sorry. I shouldn't have kissed you."

He was quiet for so long that I was forced to turn back around to face him. His face was blank but his eyes were a storm of anger. "When?"

I winced. "Vaughn, I-"

"When, Ella Rae?"

My body reacted to him calling me that and I felt even worse. "The night you went to dinner with your coach."

"And the other one?"

I stared back at him for a few seconds, trying to figure out how to tell him that I'd slept with them both the same night, at the same time. The answer felt like never. I opened my mouth and shut it tight again.

"Ella Rae." He searched my face and was still confused. "What aren't you saying?"

"I slept with them the same night. Together. I know that isn't what you want to hear, Vaughn, but there it is. I have to go." I tried to leave but he caught my arm.

"You slept with both of them, at the same time?" His whole face had gone thunderous. "They fucked you together?"

Besides the whole being turned on by the idea of Vaughn catching us bit of that night, it'd made me feel empowered. I'd felt brave and sexy. But hearing Vaughn say it made me feel small and ashamed. I clutched my notebook tighter and stared at the floor. "Let me go."

He instantly released me. "You should go."

I blew out a shaky breath. "I am. I'm leaving. I have class. I'm sorry I kissed you. I shouldn't have done that. I just…"

"You just what?"

I slowly looked up at him and met his dark gaze. "I'm sorry that you're angry at me. I don't like upsetting you and causing trouble. I don't feel good knowing that I disappointed you."

He sighed and reached out to cup the side of my neck. "I'm not angry at you. Not really. I told them to stay away from you and they went about as far from that as they possibly could."

"It's my fault, too. I don't know what's wrong with me. I was fine having mediocre to bad sex with Billy for years. I'd only ever slept with him before moving in here and now I've slept with all of you and maybe I should move out. I don't want to cause trouble between the three of you." I didn't realize I was tearing up until he dragged me into his chest. "Don't comfort me. I did exactly what you asked me not to do. You should be mad at me. Even if I don't get your reasoning for telling me to stay away from them, I still should've respected your wishes."

He sighed. "You're not moving out. You're safe here and I can't trust you not to go back to the Roadside Inn. Your self-preservation skills are fucking horrible."

"They are not."

"You let me close you in here with me with nothing but a towel and your tiny panties to keep my dick out of you." He grunted. "Terrible self-preservation right there."

I wrapped my arms around him and held on tight. "I don't know what's happening, Vaughn. I'm not supposed to want you."

"But you do." It was a question, whether he phrased it like one, or not.

"Yes." I felt him stiffen against me and then hold me tighter.

"See? Absolutely zero self-preservation." He rested his chin on my head and groaned. "It'll be fine. I can't exactly explain why I don't want them touching you so I'm just going to keep my mouth shut."

I leaned back and looked up at him. "Why don't you want them touching me?"

He glared at me and stepped away. "You know."

I bent to pick my notebook up from where I'd dropped it and inched towards the door, knowing I was going to miss my test if I didn't leave. "I don't."

He just shook his head. "You're a smart woman, Ella Rae."

I wanted to stay. I wanted to demand he explain because he couldn't possibly mean what I thought he meant. I wanted to know if he didn't want them touching me because he wanted to touch me. That was too bad, though, because I had a clock hanging over my head and Vaughn had already turned away from me.

"Go, El." He looked at me over his shoulder. "Before I make you miss your class."

I hesitated until he turned back to me. Then, seeing his threat was real, I ran while I still could. I was so wired from our interaction that I didn't bother driving to campus. I just jogged the entire way, hoping it would burn up some of the crazy energy coursing through my body. Once I got to class, with minutes to spare, I remembered why I don't jog. It took an embarrassing amount of time to catch my breath and I was disheveled in a way that couldn't be passed off as cute.

38

Ella

The next week passed in a blur. There were stolen glances and tense moments but nothing ever happened. Our schedules never aligned and I was never alone with any of them. I wasn't sure what I would've done even if I was. I was confused about some of my feelings and haunted by others. I couldn't tell anyone about the ones about Vaughn and those were the ones eating me up the most. I wasn't supposed to like him. I definitely wasn't supposed to want to touch him all over.

I still went to the home games with Natalie and cheered like my life depended on it. I baked them so many cookies that their coach complained about their energy levels after eating so many sweets. I was a part of their lives without really being in their lives in any significant way.

It got harder and harder to sleep in my room, knowing they were all just a short walk away. A short walk to powerful orgasms and being held while I slept. I was ready to start chaining myself to my bed at night to keep myself in my own bed.

I knew that part of me was making it easy for us to never run into each other because I was scared. I didn't know what it meant for me to have feelings and desires for three men at the same time. I didn't know what that looked like or how it worked out. I didn't want to get hurt again. Another part of me knew that it was already October and I would be going home for break soon. After that, it was just a semester more before I went back to Penn. I felt like if I could just wait it out a bit longer, I wouldn't have to make any decisions.

I'd given up my housing secret to Natalie a while back and she'd been pissed at me at first for not telling her but she'd quickly sensed that my emotions were scattered about my roommates so she didn't push. Just like I didn't push her to date the amazing guy working so hard to get her to date him. I respected her privacy about Chris and she respected mine about my roommates. It worked out.

Everything had fallen into a sort of tense peace until Natalie begged me to go to a Halloween party with her on campus. It was massive, apparently, and I just *had* to go. She'd convinced me to dress up and we'd spent a few hours planning our costumes and buying the stuff for them, just for her to call me the night of and cancel because she'd tripped and sprained her ankle. I felt bad for her but I'd spent half the day getting dressed up for the party and I'd actually gotten excited about going.

The trouble started when I made my way downstairs to find whatever sweets were lying around. I planned on taking it all back up to my room, curling up in bed in my costume, and watching scary movies until I fell asleep. Only, instead of sweets, I found my roommates standing around the island, drinking beer.

I stopped short in the doorway and was deciding how awkward it would be if I just slowly backed away when Fisher looked up and spotted me. His eyes went wide and he choked on his beer.

Booth glanced over next and he just stared for a few seconds before shaking his head. "Shit."

I didn't even have to look at Vaughn to know he was staring at me. I cleared my throat and held my skirt out as I curtsied. "Natalie and I were going to a party but she twisted her ankle. We were going as pirates together. Looking for booty. But the booty was candy… Anyway. Now, I'm just going to find some booty here and go back upstairs."

Fisher coughed a few times before he fully recovered. "Pirates. Sure."

I looked down at myself and groaned. "I wanted to go for the male pirate costume but they didn't have my size. Apparently costume makers think that female pirates were…a little scandalous."

I felt their eyes on my costume, or the lack thereof, and blushed. The skirt I had on barely covered my ass, the corset top had my chest all but exploding out of the top, and the knee high boots made me feel less like a pirate and more like a lady of the night. It'd seemed okay when Natalie was in a matching costume next to me. We were going to be skanky pirate ladies together. Alone, I just felt like a joke.

Vaughn finally broke the silence. "We're going to a party at a house on campus. You can come with us."

I laughed because I just assumed he was joking but when I looked at him, he seemed serious. I gestured at myself and shook my head. "No. No, I can't. This outfit was acceptable when Natalie was going to look just like me but I can't go out in this without her."

"You can." Booth had recovered enough to smile. "You'll be with us."

I hesitated. "It's really okay. I'll be fine here."

Fisher clapped his hands. "You're going with us. It's final. Are you ready or do you have a bottle of rum or a chest of treasure to grab before we leave?"

I glared at him. "I hate you."

He smirked, back to himself. "Liar. Come on, pirate wench. To the booty we go!"

Vaughn smacked him in the arm but laughed. "You should get a jacket. It's cold out there."

I scoffed. "If I'm doing this, I'm doing it. No jacket is going to ruin my look. I'll be fine."

"Famous last words." He walked over to me and straightened my pirate hat while sneaking a look at my cleavage. "Cute."

I brushed his hands away and hurried to the stairs. "I do have to get one thing upstairs. I'll be right back."

When I came back down with a fake sword thrown over my shoulder, they all laughed. I pointed it at each of them as a warning before grinning and following them out of the house. I broke out in goosebumps immediately and shot a look at Vaughn to see he was staring at me with a smirk on his face.

"Want to go get a jacket now?"

I pushed my shoulders back and tipped my chin higher. "Nope. I'm great."

"You can have mine if you get cold later." Booth stopped at his truck and opened the back door for me. "Need help?"

"I'm a pirate, sir. I can do it by myself." I studied the large gap between the ground and the inside of his truck and tried to sort out a plan but he grabbed me from behind and put me inside before I could figure it out. I drew the line at him buckling me in and slapped his hands away. "Don't even try it."

Vaughn slid into the backseat next to me and scooted to the middle of the bench seat to lean forward and talk to the other guys. I felt his hand on my knee right away, though, and a surge of adrenaline flooded my body. I stared at him in the dark truck but he didn't look back at me. His hand did slide higher on my inner thigh, though.

I put my hand over his to slow his climb and he shocked me by interlacing our fingers. I was dumbfounded and sat there like an idiot, staring at our hands. Vaughn was holding my hand. I was holding his hand.

It was only Booth's eyes on mine in the rearview mirror that broke my stupor. I flashed him a smile and looked out the window at all the people on campus, walking around in their own silly costumes. I felt less like an idiot by the time Booth parked the truck. I thought I was ready to face a party with them until Vaughn let go of my hand and I missed it.

I wasn't supposed to miss his hand.

39

Vaughn

An hour into the fucking party and I was being forced to watch Fisher put his hands all over Ella. They were supposedly dating so he argued that they had to make it look real. It sure as hell looked real, with his arm over her shoulders, his hand hanging dangerously close to her full tits. If I was willing to share my pity party, I would've acknowledged that Booth looked just as pissed as me. Every guy who walked by looked at Ella, at the way her body filled her pirate costume, and Fisher was the one getting to claim her as his.

The party had already been in full swing when we arrived and we were barely tipsy to everyone else's drunk. I didn't feel like partying anymore. I wanted to go back home and drag Ella to my room to see how far she'd let me get.

Every time our eyes met, I could feel the tension that had been there between us since the day in the coffee shop. It'd grown larger and had changed into something heavier, but it never went anywhere. She caught me checking her out multiple times and instead of looking scandalized by it, she looked turned on. Her chest rose and fell a little faster, she sat with her legs pressed a little tighter together.

Of course, I saw her exchanging looks with Booth and Fisher, too, and it just drove me crazier. I was beginning to itch from how much I wanted her and it'd been a little while since I'd done anything truly stupid so when she excused herself to go to the bathroom, I followed her.

I waited until she finished and when she stepped out, I was there, waiting for her. There was a line of people waiting for the bathroom but I'd been to the house before for a different party and I knew that the basement was kept closed off during the parties. I caught her arm and pulled her after me to the basement door at the back of the house. I opened it and we slipped through it, to the other side where it was a lot quieter and a lot darker.

"Where are we?" She sounded nervous.

I pressed against her and ran my mouth up the side of her neck. "Basement. Follow me."

I led her down the carpeted stairs and left the lights off as I crossed to the other side of the basement, away from the view of the stairs if anyone came down. As soon as I knew no one would easily catch us, I braced my hands on either side of her head and blocked her in between my body and the wall behind her.

She looked up at me and smiled. "I'm supposed to be upstairs with Fisher."

I growled and pressed my hips to hers, letting her feel how hard I was for her. "I don't care where you think you're supposed to be, Ella Rae. You could've stopped and gone back to him at any point. You wanted to come down here with me."

She shivered and let her head rest on the wall behind her, knocking her hat off in the process. She let it hit the floor without blinking. "We said we wouldn't do this again."

"We lied." I rolled my hips into hers and smiled as she moaned. "Do you want to go back upstairs, Ella Rae? Or do you want to let me do what I want?"

She licked her lips and slowly lifted her arms and wrapped them around my neck. Leaning into me and tilting her mouth closer to my ear, her voice was husky as she spoke. "I want you to do what you want to me."

I gripped the back of her neck and pulled her mouth to mine. Stroking my tongue past her lips, I tasted the fruity drink she'd been sipping on since we got to the party. I wasn't expecting her hand cupping me through the front of my jeans and broke our kiss to groan. "Jesus, Ella. You don't know what you do to me."

She kissed my chin and down my throat. "Tell me then."

I hissed out a breath when she unbuttoned my pants and pulled the zipper down. She shoved both my jeans and boxer briefs down and wrapped her fingers around my base. My eyes rolled back when she dropped to her knees and ran her tongue over my tip. "Dammit, Ella Rae."

Her mouth was heaven as she took me inside. She sucked me deep and then twisted her tongue all along the underside of my shaft before letting my dick pop free. "Tell me what I do to you, Vaughn, so I know I'm not the only one losing my mind."

I gripped her hair and tilted her face up to mine before she could take me back into her mouth. "I haven't thought about anything but being inside of you again since the first time. I have to stop myself from going to your room every night. Our tutoring sessions have become an act of torture. I sit there hard the entire time and hope that some divine intervention comes along and slams the door shut so I know it's okay to fuck you against it again."

Her eyes were wide when I finished, her mouth slightly open. As soon as her lips started to tip up in a smile and I knew I hadn't freaked her out, I slid my dick into her mouth and groaned when she didn't hesitate to suck me again.

I watched her work her mouth up and down my length, watched the way her eyebrows pinched in concentration, and then saw her eyes lift to meet mine. Her cheeks went pink when she saw that I was watching her. "You're stunning with my cock in your mouth. I need to be inside you right now, though."

I pulled her up from her knees and took her mouth in a heated kiss. Her hands were already back on my cock, stroking me. I loved knowing she was as hungry for me as I was for her. I pulled away and then turned her to face the wall.

"I want to watch you take your panties off for me." I had to squeeze the base of my dick as I watched her reach under her skirt and slowly drag her simple white panties down her thighs and over her boots. I took them from her when she stepped out of them and shoved them in my shirt pocket. "Put your hands on the wall and spread your legs."

Ella moaned and did what I said. She stood there, ass sticking out, with her lip caught between her teeth. When I shoved the bottom of her skirt into the waistband, she gasped and shot a glance towards the stairs.

I stepped forward, letting my dick rest against her ass, and bit her shoulder. "If anyone comes down, we'll hear them."

She looked at me over her shoulder and nodded. "I trust you."

My chest tightened and I found myself gently stroking her cheek. I wanted her to trust me and want things from me that I had no business wanting myself. I didn't want to delve into those thoughts right then so I just nodded at her before shifting back so I could line up our bodies. It was only as I pressed my tip against her wet lower lips that I realized I wasn't wearing a condom. I hesitated and when I did, Ella arched her back and shifted her hips back so the head pushed into her.

She dropped her forehead against the wall and moaned. "Vaughn, what are you waiting for?"

Fuck, I liked her being needy. "I'm not wearing a condom and I'm trying to convince myself to do the right thing and put one on."

She went still and quiet for a moment and then looked back at me. "We didn't wear one the first time..."

I gripped her waist tight. "I should, though. It's stupid to take the risk..."

She nodded just as I thrust the rest of my length into her. A loud cry tore past her lips and her sex clamped down on my shaft. "Vaughn!"

I reached around her to tug down her top and grip her full tits. "I should but I don't want to, Ella Rae. I want to feel your walls milking my dick with nothing between us. I don't care that it's stupid."

Her voice was shaky as she agreed. "I want to feel you come inside me."

That was all it took for me to lose whatever chance I had at being safe. I pressed my body into hers and held her with my dick as deep as I could get it. "Your pussy feels so good around my dick, Ella Rae. And this ass... I want to do things to your ass that would make you slap me."

She whined and tried to rock her hips. "Fuck me, Vaughn."

I trailed one of my hands up her chest and over her throat, using my grip to bring her face back to mine. I stared into her big green eyes and smirked. "Say please."

A flash of stubbornness flashed across her face before her features softened and she licked her lips. "Please, Vaughn. Please, fuck me."

I growled and kissed her hard as I pulled out and thrust deep again. I swallowed her cries of pleasure and felt her heart hammering away at the base of her throat. She reached back and grabbed the back of my neck, holding onto my hair as I quickly settled into a rough pace. I could hear the sound of our skin slapping together in the quiet basement and the sound of her wetness fueled me. I wanted more. I wanted her to walk out of the party looking like she'd just been fucked rough. I wanted people to know it was me who'd made her so wet it dripped down her thighs.

Pounding into her, I pulled my mouth from hers and watched hers fall open as she went up on her tiptoes and clung to whatever she could. Her other hand grasped at the wall, fingernails denting the drywall. "Vaughn! Oh, god!"

I stroked my other hand over her stomach and between her thighs. Her clit was slippery with her juices as I ground my palm into it. My breath was choppy as I fucked her like I'd never fucked anyone else. "Fuck, Ella Rae. You make me fucking crazy. I want to push you down and fuck you like this in front of everyone so they know you're mine."

She cried out and I could hear that we were being loud but I didn't care. Not when her pussy was rippling with her pleasure and milking my dick. Her throat was soft under my hand and I tightened my grip just enough to make her gasp.

"I want to fucking ruin you. I want to fuck every hole you've got until you're full of my come. That's what you do to me." I saw movement out of the corner of my eye and jerked my head around in time to see Fisher and Booth standing at the base of the stairs, eyes wide as they watched us.

40

Vaughn

I froze but Ella was too far gone. She started coming on my dick with the power of a fucking industrial vacuum and I only avoiding coming in front of my two best friends by a miracle.

Ella cried out my name as she came and writhed between me and the wall. She moaned and panted, so lost in her orgasm that she didn't react to my stillness for several seconds. When she did, she followed my gaze and I swear to god, her pussy clamped down on me even harder. She was paralyzed for all of five seconds before she seemed to realize what was happening. She basically turned into a fucking cat, nearly climbing the wall to get away from me.

I narrowly avoided losing my dick as she leapt away from me, yanking at her clothing until she was mostly covered again. Then, she wrapped her arms around herself and froze, her eyes on the ground.

I shoved my still hard dick away and stood between her and the guys. "Look..."

"Actually, this explains a lot." Fisher whistled. "No wonder you were so bitchy about us touching her."

"I wasn't bitchy..." I glanced back at Ella and frowned when I saw her swipe a tear away. "Hey, don't cry. We'll talk about this and it'll be fine. Just don't cry."

Booth walked past me, shot me a look that dared me to say shit to him about what he was about to do, and wrapped his arms around Ella. "Why are you crying?"

She looked up at him and her bottom lip wobbled as she did. "You just saw... You caught... Why aren't you freaking out?"

I felt a wave of something hot wash over me as I saw for the first time how Booth touched her and how she let him. It was clear there was something between the two of them. I swallowed around an uncomfortable lump and glanced back at Fisher.

He looked from Booth and Ella to me. "She's not just yours."

"We kind of figured there was something between the two of you after you came like a fire hydrant to the thought of him walking in on us fucking you, Ella Rae." Booth let out a deep chuckle at the way her eyes snapped to me and then back down again. "Yeah, it seems like it's time all the secrets come out."

I made a strangled sound as I processed what he'd said. "What the fuck? Were you roleplaying me finding you fucking Ella?"

Fisher snorted. "She started it."

Ella gasped. "No, I didn't! I didn't. I'm not... I feel like a freak right now. I'm mortified and I think I just want to go home."

I took a deep breath and walked over to her, edging Booth out of my way. I cupped her face in my hands and waited until she looked up at me. "You're not a freak. This is fine. No one's freaking out. I'm calm. Booth and Fish are calm. Okay?"

She hesitated before melting into my chest. "I'm freaking out. Does everyone hate me?"

Booth stroked the back of her head. "Why would we hate you?"

She shot him a look that said he was nuts. "You just caught me having sex with Vaughn. After I had sex with you two. And Vaughn didn't want me sleeping with y'all again but I did and we did a lot... And I just... I think I'm going to have a heart attack."

Fisher came over and pressed a kiss to the side of her head. "No one hates you, Ella. It seems like we've got some stuff to figure out because none of us seem interested in leaving you alone."

I looked at my two best friends and the way they were surrounding Ella with the same soothing energy that I was trying to give out. We were all three just trying to comfort her. I blew out a breath that ruffled her hair. "Shit."

They all looked at me but it was Ella who hesitantly spoke up. "I'm sorry, Vaughn. I don't know what to say."

I smiled and pushed her hair behind her ears. "You don't have anything to apologize for. I was just coming to an understanding with myself. Fisher's right. We do have some shit to figure out because we all want you. We all care about you."

Ella's eyes went even wider. "You don't have to-"

Fisher cut her off. "He's right. We care about you, Ella Rae."

Booth just nodded and shrugged when she looked his way. "I thought it was obvious. The whole virginity thing?"

Fisher and I both nearly broke our necks while snapping our heads around to him. I was tongue-tied so Fisher spoke up first. "I'm sorry. Did you just say virginity?"

Booth's face went pink. "Uh, yeah..."

Ella transformed in front of our eyes. She stood up straight and planted herself in front of Booth. "If either of you think you're going to make a big deal out of this, you've got another thing coming."

"I'm not going to make a big deal out of it. I'm just going to say goddamn, because I've seen you fuck and I would not have pegged you as a recent virgin." Fisher shook his head and winced. "Not that I was admiring your skills, or anything. I'm just saying."

I raised my eyebrows. "I'm disturbed."

Booth grinned. "Thanks, I think."

Ella cleared her throat and spotted her panties in my shirt pocket. She tried to grab them but I caught her hand. "I can't walk out of here with no panties on, Vaughn."

Fisher smirked. "Sure you can. And since you're technically my girlfriend, I'll be in charge of making sure that skirt stays down. My hands will be busy but my heart will be full."

I elbowed him. "Fuck off."

"How are those blue balls, by the way? You cock blocked us for months so it's only fair that we cock blocked you tonight." He laughed when I cringed. "At least we all got to see Ella come. That's always worth it."

I found myself lifting my fist to bump his and Ella smacked both of us in the stomach. I grunted. "Hey. At least I'm not trying to punch anyone."

"Just give me my panties and take me home. I don't want to sort this out in someone's basement." She reached for her panties again and I caught her arm and spun her into my chest. With her back to my front, she stilled as I cupped her sex. "Vaughn..."

I glanced at Fisher and Booth and saw they were both watching with interest to see what I was going to do. Seeing that they weren't freaking out, I gently stroked her clit. "I want to hear more about this fantasy of me walking in on you with Booth and Fish, Ella Rae. When we get home we can figure out if your imagination is as good as my reality. But you're not getting your panties back. This way, as soon as we're in the truck, I don't have to take them off again."

Ella shuddered and let out a quiet moan. "I shouldn't..."

Booth shifted to stand in front of her. "Says who?"

"If you don't want this, that's okay. But it seems like you do. I can feel you getting wetter by the second, Ella." I inhaled the scent of her hair and smiled. "Let's go home."

Fisher pulled Ella into his arms and kissed her. His hands gripped her ass and I forced myself past the instant jealousy. I watched her press her hips into Fisher and saw the way Fisher looked at her when he pulled back. I wasn't sure if he knew it, but I could see it all over his face that he had big feelings for her. I felt some of the jealousy ease up with that realization. We were all fucked when it came to Ella. She had us in the palm of her hand and I didn't think she even understood it.

41

Ella

I wasn't sure what to expect once we were alone in the truck but it wasn't for Vaughn to pull me into his lap and spread me open for Fisher to watch from the front seat. My awareness was so heightened as I waited for someone to explode that every one of his breaths against my neck felt erotic.

"Drive safe or I'll kick your ass." Vaughn spread my lower lips open and grunted to Fisher. "Are you waiting for a fucking invitation?"

I gasped as Fisher reached over the seat and stroked his hand over my core. He held my gaze as he pushed two fingers inside me. My brain went up in flames as Vaughn shifted his hand and pushed a finger in next to Fisher's.

"Fuck, you're dripping wet, Ella."

Fisher smirked at me. "She likes when we call her Ella Rae. Just like you."

Vaughn groaned into the side of my neck. "Is that right?"

"See for yourself."

I held my breath as Vaughn spoke in a quiet growl against my ear. "You like the way I call you Ella Rae?"

They both moaned as my body reacted. Booth swore from the driver's seat. "This is bullshit. I should've forced one of you to drive."

I reached out and grabbed his shoulder, wanting to connect him to whatever the hell we were doing. I dropped my head back on Vaughn's shoulder and moaned. "This is crazy."

"Look at the way you naturally want to take care of all three of us, Ella Rae. This isn't crazy. This might just make sense." Fisher pulled his fingers out of me and sucked them clean before pushing them deep again. "I told you. I'd rather share you than not get to have you at all."

"I need to taste you as soon as we get home, Ella Rae. I need to drink straight from the source." Vaughn turned my face to his and stared into my eyes. "You can call this off at any time. Know that."

I searched his face and swallowed down my nerves. "I trust you. I trust all of you."

"What the fuck...?" Booth's annoyed and questioning voice turned into one of slight panic. "Oh, shit. Vaughn, we've got company."

Before I could see what was happening, Vaughn had already eased me off of his lap and was swearing while trying to make sure I was covered. "What? Who is it?"

"My dad." Vaughn adjusted himself in his pants and rubbed his hands down his face. "What a great fucking time for a surprise visit."

I felt all the blood drain from my face. "Oh, my god. Do you think he knows? How would he know? Oh, my god. Maybe someone saw us. Why is he here, Vaughn?"

He grabbed my hand and squeezed it. "Relax, Ella Rae. He doesn't know anything. He doesn't even know you're living here."

I frowned. "You didn't tell him I was living here?"

He opened the door as soon as Booth parked and looked back at me. "I didn't know what to say so I didn't say anything."

Booth looked back at me. "Should I just keep driving?"

Vaughn leaned back into the truck. "Not funny. Get out, Booth."

I looked down at myself and my panic went through the roof. "I can't see him like this. I'm just going to hide. Leave me here."

Booth shrugged out of his jacket and handed it back to me. "Come on. Let's get this over with."

With his jacket on I looked like I was wearing a knee-length dress so I felt a lot better. I was able to get out of the truck without running into traffic from shame at least. It'd been a decade since I'd seen Paul but he still called to check in on me every few months. He'd been the closest thing I ever had to a dad and he hadn't written me off when he and Mom divorced. I hadn't talked to him since I left Penn, though. I felt crushing shame for multiple reasons in that moment.

The sound of Paul's voice was usually comforting and welcome but right then, it was the last thing in the world I wanted to hear. He greeted Vaughn like he hadn't seen him or spoken to him in years. "Son! Looking good! I caught that last game against Auburn. You and Fisher are a killer duo."

"Hey, Dad. What are you doing here?" The sound of them hugging and slapping each other on the back was loud, even with the street being alive with Halloween fun.

"Hey, Mr. Adler. How's it going?" Booth greeted Paul just as happily as Vaughn and I wondered for a second if they weren't glad to be getting out of whatever the hell we'd been planning on doing.

"I was a few towns over for business and I decided to pop over and surprise you guys. I didn't realize it was Halloween until I got here. I was just about to leave to head to my hotel so I'm glad you three showed up."

Vaughn cleared his throat and I cringed from behind Fisher. "Actually, Dad, there's four of us now."

"Oh? You got a new roommate?"

I stepped forward and smiled what I hoped was an innocent and sweet smile, something that said I hadn't just had his son's penis in my mouth. "Hey, Paul."

His eyes went wide and he rushed over to hug me. He'd always given the best hugs. Dad hugs. He squeezed me tight and spun me around like I was still a little kid. "Ellie! What are you doing here? Look at you! You're all grown up!"

I swayed when he put me down and shrugged. "I transferred here at the beginning of the semester. It's not a permanent move, though."

"Why didn't you tell me, V? I would've come over a lot sooner." Paul ruffled my hair and grinned down at me. He was just as tall as Vaughn and had the same slim build. He hadn't changed much in the decade that had passed. Maybe there was a bit of silver at his temples but I was already telling Mom in my head that he was still the same handsome Paul. "How's your mother?"

"She's as nuts as ever." I grinned. "I can't wait to tell her that I saw you. She's going to be pissed that you still have all your hair."

He let out a rowdy laugh and threw his arm over my shoulder. "Kid, you've still got the best sense of humor. I can't tell you how happy I am to see you, Ella. I need to call you more. But this is amazing. My two kids, together again."

I choked on my next breath at his words. Oh, god. Vaughn patted me roughly on the back while Booth and Fisher snorted and gave each other looks that said everything I was freaking out about in my head. His two kids. As if we were still siblings. I was going to vomit. Or pass out. Or maybe I'd do both and they'd let me choke to death on my vomit.

"Vaughn! Really?" Paul leaned forward and touched the lacy edge of my panties that were sticking out of Vaughn's shirt pocket. "You can't be more of a gentleman with your sister around?"

Fisher picked me up and threw me over his shoulder. It was a good thing, too, because I was trapped in my body, screaming at the top of my lungs inside my head. He patted my thigh and laughed. "Vaughn? A gentleman? Unlike me, he's still a cad. I've settled down. I didn't think I'd have to meet the parents so early, but I can handle it, Mr. Adler."

"You two are dating? That's amazing. I knew it would take someone special to tie you down, Fish." Paul grunted. "And call me Paul. Both of you. I have to tell you every time I come around. You especially have to call me Paul if you're dating my daughter."

Fisher laughed too easily. "Paul, you have no idea how happy I am to have you visiting. This is just great."

42

Ella

"We'll hang out tomorrow, Ellie?" Paul tilted his head to talk to me without Fisher putting me down. "I've missed you, kid. I've got to be better at checking in on you."

"Of course. I'll clear my schedule for you." I was getting light-headed from all the blood rushing to my head but I was kind of hoping I'd just pass out and everything would be back to normal when I woke up.

"Night, everyone. Try not to have too much fun down here." Fisher grunted and took a step backwards. "Jesus, Vaughn."

"You're going to have Dad thinking that Ella isn't going to her own room for the night." Vaughn let out a forced laugh. "Don't give him a heart attack like that."

I pressed myself up enough to glare at Vaughn. "I'm sure that Paul doesn't care about my chastity, Vaughn. I'm an adult."

"Do these two still fight like they used to?" Paul sighed. "And Ellie's right, Vaughn. She's an adult. If you touch my little girl while I'm in the house, though, I'll have to kill you, Fisher."

Booth laughed. "They definitely still fight. I think it's probably changed a bit, though."

"I'm not going to touch anyone." Fisher's hand lifted from where it'd been resting on my thigh. "I'm saving myself for marriage."

Paul let out a booming laugh. "I'm just messing with you, son. Mostly."

My voice came out as a squeak when I spoke. "Okay! Goodnight, everyone!"

When Fisher finally started climbing the stairs, I was so embarrassed and horrified that I was considering running away. The irrational part of my brain was already working out the details. I could live with the crazy doll woman who wanted to watch *Buffy* and braid my hair. Or maybe those men in the Roadside Inn parking lot were actually very nice and I'd become an important member of their friend group.

"Breathe, Ella." Fisher squeezed the back of my thigh. "In and out."

I sucked in a ragged breath and blew it out so hard that his shirt ruffled. "I think I'm dying."

"I can't say I blame you." He jogged up the last few steps and carried me to my room. "That was horrible. I didn't know the step sibling thing was still a thing."

"It's not!" I stumbled when he finally put me back on my feet but he caught me. I pulled him into my room and shut the door behind him. "It's not still a thing. He hasn't talked like that since right after the divorce! I am not okay. I mean, that... I'm going to hell. Right? I just did that with Vaughn and then Paul touched my freaking panties! And he's calling us siblings! Can you just push me out of the window and put me out of my misery?"

Fisher covered his mouth to try to hide a laugh but I still saw it. He held up his hands when my face shifted from panic to anger. "I'm sorry. It's just... It's hard not to find it a little funny."

"Get out." I marched to my door and threw it open. "Or I'm going to tell *Dad* that you're touching my maidenhood."

He tried to hug me but I put my hand up and motioned for him to go away. "Aw, come on. I'm sorry. Don't be mad, Ella Rae."

I glared at him. "You suck."

"Can I come back when he leaves?"

"I'm locking my door and I don't want to see any of you. Maybe ever again." I closed the door in his face and locked it. "I'm dropping out of college and joining a traveling circus!"

I could hear him laughing on the other side of my door and growled before stomping across my room and throwing myself into bed. I grabbed Connie and hugged him tight. Things were not okay. I couldn't get the *ick* out of my head. Vaughn was *not* my sibling. We'd only been step-siblings for three years a decade earlier. That didn't count. It couldn't.

I suddenly felt disgusted at myself. I'd thrown myself at Vaughn at the party and anyone could've caught us. Did everyone think of us as siblings still? Would people think it was taboo? I couldn't go around telling everyone that I didn't think of Vaughn as a step-brother if they found out. What would Paul think if he knew? What would Mom think? Had I managed to do something that she wouldn't be okay with?

Panic sent me rushing into my bathroom to brush my teeth and take a long, hot shower. It was a confusing thing. I was so horrified by Paul acting like we were all still a big family that I scrubbed at my body until I was bright red. When I tried to clean between my thighs, though, my body still reacted to the idea of Vaughn inside it.

I was spiraling and I wasn't sure how to stop. I wished I could laugh it off like Fisher. I wondered how Vaughn was taking it. I couldn't help wondering if Booth thought I was a freak. When I tucked my raw body into bed, all I could do was lay there and stare at my ceiling. I needed to talk to someone who would reassure me that I wasn't a complete monster but I couldn't tell anyone what I'd been doing. I only had myself to talk to about it and I sucked at making myself feel better.

I felt like hours had passed when I heard the front door alarm chime. I laid in bed, waiting for them to come to my room, waiting for a knock on my door. When none came, I convinced myself it was because they'd all decided that I was some sort of pervert they didn't want anything more to do with.

That was the thought that kept me up most of the night. That they wouldn't want anything to do with me anymore. They'd become my best friends without even trying. I felt connected to them and if they cut me off, I wasn't sure if I'd be able to handle it. Even though I'd been in a cycle of avoiding them or sneaking around to sleep with them the entire time I'd lived in their house, I'd gotten comfortable with knowing they'd be there.

I was still awake when the sun came up. My eyes felt awful, like there was sandpaper behind my eyelids, and my stomach hurt from how much I'd been stressing. I wanted to go downstairs and get a cold bottle of water, or some ice cream, but I was too afraid of running into anyone.

It was that fear of running into someone that finally got me up and rushing around to get out of the house before anyone else was awake. I was a giant chicken but I'd worked myself into a true panic. I snuck out of the house like I'd robbed the place and took off at a jog once I was outside. I didn't stop until I was downstairs in the cafeteria, tucked away in the corner of the big open space.

I hadn't brought any of the books I'd need to study so I just sat there and tried to busy myself with my phone for hours. When the rest of the campus started coming to life and the cafeteria filled up, I sank lower in my little corner and did my best to look like I wasn't melting down inside. Judging by some of the looks I got, I was pretty sure I was failing.

43

Ella

"Ella?"

I jerked awake and looked up to see Billy standing over me. Before I could tell him to go away, he'd already pulled a chair up close and was sitting down.

"Are you okay?" He looked me over and frowned. "Did you sleep here last night?"

I sat up and rubbed my eyes. Looking around, I saw that The Swamp was packed. I wasn't sure how long I'd been asleep but I could see a couple of people nearby shooting judgmental glances my way. I wiped my mouth to make sure I hadn't been drooling and finally turned back to Billy. "What'd you say?"

He scooted even closer and rested his hand on my knee. "Are you okay?"

I cleared my throat and nodded while moving back in my chair so his hand fell away. "Yeah, I'm okay. I must've nodded off."

"Long night?" He shot me an almost embarrassed look. "I saw you at the party with Fisher last night. You looked great, Ella."

My face burned at the mention of that party. "Um, thanks. Do you need something, Billy?"

He dropped his head and blew out a long breath. "I deserve that. I know you don't owe me anything, Ella, but can I talk to you? I just need five minutes."

"Billy..."

"Five minutes, Ella. Please."

I looked around the room and considered my options. If I left, I'd need to go home and that could mean facing the guys. I couldn't very well stay without talking to Billy unless I planned on being the world's largest dick. I chose to be a chicken again. "Five minutes."

He moved even closer and grabbed my hands. "Thank you. I just have some things I need to say."

I shot him a look and tugged my hands free. "It's not going to change anything, Billy."

"Just listen to me first. Please." He saw that I wasn't going to say anything else and nodded. "Thank you. I just can't stop thinking about what I did. I don't know what happened to me once I got here, Ella. The frat, the parties, it all just went to my head. I never stopped loving you. I need you to know that. I still love you and I think a part of me always will."

I shifted in my seat, feeling uncomfortable. It was hard for me to remember that he was the guy I'd sobbed over when I first got to campus. Things had changed so much.

"I hate myself for what I did to you. I know how much you gave me, Ella. Beyond your first time, you gave me your love and your trust. You gave up Penn for me and I know how much that meant to you. I'm an idiot. I'm sorry for everything." He let out a bitter laugh and grabbed my hands again. "It's not an excuse but I just lost myself here. I wanted to be cool and having a serious girlfriend back home just didn't work. I know I should've broken up with you before I did the things I did. I should've been fair to you. I was too busy wanting it all to think of you, though."

Staring across at him, I was too surprised by his honesty to take my hands back. "Wow."

"I think I just wanted to have my fun and be able to go to you at the end of the year. It's crazy, Ella, but I still think about our future. I still have hope that you'll forgive me in a few years and we'll end up together. Me, you, Connie, and maybe a few dogs living near Penn while you study for the bar and pass it with ease, despite stressing over it for months." He squeezed my hands. "Do you ever think of me and our future?"

I swallowed down the people pleasing need to placate him. "I'm sorry, Billy, but no."

He sat back and nodded while blinking quickly, like he was stopping tears. "I deserve that."

"What you did really hurt me. It made me feel like the biggest fool in the world. I gave up so much for you." I took a deep breath and met his eyes. "That's all behind me now, though. There's nothing between us anymore. I could never trust you again. Not in a million years. I hope you grow from this and treat your next girlfriend better. I just don't feel any interest in being around to find out."

"You don't even think we could be friends?"

I shook my head. "I don't want to sound harsh, Billy, but no. I don't want to be your friend. I'm not angry anymore and I don't want anything bad for you. I'm just...done."

He looked down at where he was still clinging to my hands. "Okay. I get it. It's what I deserve, even if I hoped for a different outcome."

I gently pulled my hands free. "Thank you. For apologizing."

"Even if we aren't friends, I still feel like I need to tell you something, Ella." He sighed. "I still care about you and don't want to see you hurt."

"What is it?"

"Fisher. I don't know how serious things are between you and him but I've been on campus with him for long enough to know him, Ella. He's a player. Worse than I ever could've been." He saw my face scrunch up in annoyance and rushed on. "I'm not being an asshole here, Ella. I'm just trying to look out for you. I've heard shit around campus, recently, about him getting caught with random girls."

I looked away and took a few moments before clearing my throat and facing him again. "I don't know what you expect me to say, Billy."

"Nothing. I'm not trying to gain anything here. I just need to know that I at least tried to warn you. Even if you don't believe me. He's using you. There are rumors, rumors that you live with him, rumors that you're sleeping with him *and* his roommates."

My gut-deep reaction to deny that made me open my mouth a little too much. "Vaughn was my stepbrother, Billy! Jesus."

"Vaughn Adler's your stepbrother?"

I tightened my ponytail until it hurt and shook my head. "He was. A decade ago. Only for three years. It barely counted. The reason I'm living with them is because I was homeless after you fucked me over. Vaughn gave me a place to stay out of obligation, I'm pretty sure."

"Wow. I had no idea." Billy shook his head. "Okay, but you still need to watch out for Fisher."

I stood up and sighed. "Thank you for warning me, Billy. Consider your good deed of the day done."

He stood up and wrapped me in a tight hug. "I love you, Ella. Even if you don't feel anything for me, I still love you. You deserve someone who treats you right. That's all I'll say."

I gently pushed him away and nodded. "Thanks."

He stayed where he was, close to me, and rested his hands on my shoulders. It was an intimate pose and I would've backed away if the chair I'd just vacated wasn't pressing into the backs of my knees. "I'll always look out for you."

"Okay, Billy. You can let me go now." I sighed a breath a relief when he stepped away but all that relief was short-lived because Vaughn decided to grace us with his presence at that exact moment, booming anger his weapon of choice.

"Get the fuck away from her, asshole."

44

Ella

Billy, to his credit, didn't pee his pants and run away crying. He faced Vaughn with a frown and a sense of confidence that he had no right displaying. "What's your problem, Adler? We're just talking."

Vaughn stepped up to Billy and stared down at him. "And now you're not."

"Seriously? I was apologizing to her. We're good. You don't need to act like a giant dick."

Laughing like a villain in a movie, Vaughn shook his head. "You're not good. You need to stay the fuck away from Ella. Consider her off-limits. You don't talk to her. You don't look at her. And you sure as hell don't touch her."

I grabbed his hand. "Vaughn, come on. He was just leaving."

"Why are you acting like a jealous boyfriend? Aren't you her stepbrother? You're a little outside your bounds here, dude." Billy clearly had a death wish. "Are you fighting for your buddy or for yourself?"

"Enough!" I glared at Billy. "You need to stop talking and go."

Vaughn had gone silent, something that worried me a lot more than his villain laugh. I tugged at his hand, desperate to get away from the stares that were turning on us.

"You should watch out for stepbro here, Ella. If I didn't know any better, I'd say he wants a lot more than a family connection."

"Come on. Let's go." I was able to pull Vaughn a few feet away but I realized I'd left my phone on the arm of the chair. I let go of him to go back and grab it but then all hell broke loose.

Billy grabbed my arm. "There's something wrong with him, Ella. That's not how a step-"

I stumbled back as Vaughn hit Billy. It wasn't pretty. Billy tried to hit Vaughn back but Vaughn was bigger and pissed enough that he didn't even notice the one punch Billy landed. If there were any people who hadn't already been watching, they were definitely looking then as Vaughn knocked Billy to the floor and then dragged him back to his feet to hit him again.

I watched in shocked silence as Vaughn was finally pulled off Billy by a few guys I recognized from the team. He was red-faced and he didn't look like the guy I knew. His face was twisted in fury and he was still struggling to get back to Billy. Three guys were holding him back, shouting for him to calm down, and it was like he couldn't hear a word they were saying.

Billy managed to pick himself up off the ground and looked past Vaughn, at me. "He's a fucking lunatic, Ella! Bullshit that he's just your stepbrother!"

I wanted to run away and hide but instead I moved to stand in front of Vaughn and placed my hands on his chest. "Hey. Stop. I want to leave. Please get me out of here, Vaughn."

He glanced down at me and after a few seconds he blinked a few times and nodded. He shrugged out of the holds the guys had him in. "I'm good. I'm done. I got my point across."

"That's not how a stepbrother acts over his sister, Ella!"

I ignored Billy and pushed Vaughn towards the exit. "Please get me out of here. I want to go. Now."

Vaughn searched my face. "Are you okay?"

I glanced around and saw the way people were staring at us. They were all thinking about what Billy was shouting. I could see it all over their faces. There were multiple phones pointed at us and I could already feel the rumors spreading. "No. I'm not."

Turning away from him, I all but sprinted to the exit. Vaughn caught me on the stairs and pulled me to a stop. "Hey. Look at me. It's okay. I'm fine."

I slapped his chest and let out a bitter laugh. "Of course, you're okay! You just lost your mind and tried to kill someone! He didn't stand a chance against you."

He frowned. "Wait. Are you worried about him? After all the shit he just said?"

"No, I'm not worried about him, Vaughn! I was quietly and efficiently cutting him out of my life for good when you showed up and started acting like a jealous boyfriend!" I snapped my mouth shut when someone walked past us. As soon as we were alone again, I shook my head and lowered my voice. "Vaughn, you can't act like that. You can't beat your chest and scare men away from me. It doesn't look right."

"What the fuck, Ella Rae? He grabbed you. What was I supposed to do?" He shook his head hard and laughed. "You didn't say shit when Booth and Fisher acted the same way. Why the fuck is it okay for them to get angry and scare that asshole away from you, but it's not for me?"

I threw my hands up. "You're not my boyfriend, Vaughn! You're not supposed to act like that over me."

"I know I'm not your goddamn boyfriend, Ella. I've had you shoving Fisher down my throat for months. I know who everyone thinks is your boyfriend."

"You're still acting like a jealous boyfriend, Vaughn."

"Maybe that's how I fucking feel? Have you ever considered that?" He tugged at his hair and leaned closer. "Let's just go home. We should talk about last night."

"No." I swallowed my next words as a group of people walked past us on the stairs. They shot us looks that made me cringe. They were all thinking about me and Vaughn sleeping together, about me and my stepbrother sleeping together. After they passed us, I stared down at my feet and let my panic talk for me. "This was a mistake, Vaughn. What we did... It was wrong. With your dad showing up and now this... The world is sending us plenty of hints. We can't do this again."

He grabbed my hand. "Ella, just-"

I pulled my hand free and shook my head. "No. It was a mistake. That's all. I have to go."

I turned and ran up the last of the stairs, leaving him standing there. I saw people glance my way when I charged out of the cafeteria and not knowing the reason they were looking at me made me think it was because they were all thinking about me being a disgusting person who slept with their stepbrother and cheated on her boyfriend. With a rising sense of panic I ducked my head and got out of there as fast as I could.

45

Vaughn

I entered the house like a tornado, slamming open the door and banging around the kitchen with enough force to send a few of the barstools to the ground. I grabbed an ice pack from the freezer and slammed more doors open and shut as I looked for a towel to wrap around it. I wanted to break shit. I wanted to rip the cabinet doors off and build a fucking bonfire with them.

"Whoa. What's going on, Vaughn?" Fisher stepped into the kitchen and raised his hands when I spun around to face him. "Shit, man. What happened?"

She wouldn't cut him off. She wouldn't tell him or Booth that they were a mistake. She would carry on with them. All because they hadn't been a part of her family for a second in time a decade earlier. It was bullshit.

"Jesus, Vaughn. Talk to me. What's wrong?" Fisher looked up as Booth walked in. "I don't know what's wrong but I don't think I did it."

Booth took one look at me and raised his eyebrows. "Who'd you bloody your knuckles on?"

"Billy Novak." I spit out his name like it was actual shit. Glaring down at my bruised knuckles, I wished I'd hit him more.

"Billy? Okay, shit." Fisher leaned against the cabinets and nodded. "I'm sure he was asking for it."

"He had his hands all over her." I braced myself against the island and couldn't stop thinking about how I was going to have to watch Ella continue to give herself to my best friends while I got nothing from her. I didn't think I could do it. I would lose my mind.

"What? What are you talking about? He had his hands on Ella? *Our* Ella?" Fisher moved closer, his own anger flaring to life.

I laughed. "She's not *our* Ella."

Booth's voice was quiet when he spoke again. "What do you mean, he had his hands all over her?"

I heard the worry in his voice and realized they thought I was saying something other than what I was saying. They thought I was implying it was mutual, the touching. I had every chance to correct them. I should've told them that she wanted nothing to do with Billy, the same way she wanted nothing to do with me. I couldn't make my mouth form those words, though.

"Vaughn?" Fisher grabbed my shoulder and searched my face. "What happened?"

"She was with him." I looked away, ashamed of myself and unable to face them. "I beat the shit out of him and she was pissed. She said this was a mistake."

Fisher stepped back like I'd punched him. Booth shook his head and stared at me with disgust clear on his face. "She was with him. Where?"

"The Swamp. In front of a fuck ton of people. He was all over her." I wanted to throw up. I could see that I was hurting my best friends but I couldn't handle her shunning me and still being with them. I couldn't be the one on the outside, wishing that she'd let me in. "I'm sorry."

"She said this was a mistake?" Fisher rubbed his chest and deflated. "She said mistake?"

I closed my eyes and nodded. "Yes."

"I need a drink." Booth moved past me to open the fridge. He leaned down and came up with three beers. "I thought we were getting somewhere."

"Me too." I downed half the beer in one drink. "I don't want to be sober for this."

Fisher shook his head and used his teeth to open his bottle. "I don't want to be alone in this house tonight. Not when I thought... Never mind. It doesn't matter what I thought."

I finished the rest of my beer and threw the bottle in the sink, enjoying the way it shattered. "Then let's not be alone."

It didn't take long for word to spread that we were throwing a party. The team showed up with a shitload of liquor and we took the challenge of drinking as much as we could before the party really even started. Booth and Fisher were drinking to deal with their feelings being hurt. I was drinking for that and for the suffocating amount of guilt I felt. I'd never done anything so selfish to my friends. Any time I thought I should tell them the truth, an image of them with Ella flashed through my head and I couldn't do it, though.

By the time the party was in full swing, I was drunk enough that I couldn't remember why I needed to be so drunk.

46

Ella

In true chicken fashion, I stayed away from the house all day. I left campus and walked around for a while before Paul called me. He wanted to take me to lunch so I let him. I did my very best to act normal while picking at a club sandwich and listening to him talk about a new woman he was seeing. I even rode with him when he had to meet one of his lawyers to sign some paperwork. I was doing anything to avoid going home and facing the mess I'd made.

I spent the whole day wishing Vaughn would show up to see his dad. I wanted him to appear so I could apologize. I'd panicked and acted without really thinking. If I'd taken some time to calm down I never would've been so cruel to him. I wouldn't have called him a mistake. I didn't feel that way. I was just scared. Having Paul show up and talk about me like I really was still his kid had freaked me out. I needed to find Vaughn and explain that to him but I was worried he wouldn't care what I had to say. I was worried I'd messed everything up.

Paul noticed I was being weird when he tried to drive me home and I nearly chained myself to his passenger seat. Instead of forcing me to talk about what was going on right away, he drove to his hotel and we sat in the lobby. He waited for me to say something for so long that I finally cracked.

Only, once again, I didn't say what I really felt. Or what was even on my mind.

"It's weird that you still call me your daughter."

He sat back in the understuffed lobby chair and raised his eyebrows. "Oh?"

I shifted in my seat, more than a little uncomfortable. "We barely talk. I left Penn and you didn't know. I mean, you were only married to my mom for a few years. You don't really think of me as your daughter. If you did, you'd be in my life more. Do you do it just to try to make me feel better about not having a dad?"

Paul cleared his throat and shook his head. "Okay. I can't say I saw this conversation coming."

I shrugged. "Sorry. Just forget I said anything. I'm just in a weird mood."

"No." He sat forward and rested his elbows on his knees. "Ella, your mom was parent enough to make up for your dad being a piece of shit. That woman didn't give you a chance to suffer with daddy issues. Me calling you my daughter isn't some pity move I make out of guilt for leaving your mom. I guess I deserve your skepticism, though. I don't call enough. I barely call at all. Maybe it's not fair of me to show up and act like I've been father of the year to you. I do still feel like your father, Ella. I know you might not understand that, but I looked after you for three years. I thought of you as my daughter back then, same as I do now.

"Hell, I met you when you were just a little kid, Ella. I tucked you into bed with your mom and tried to read you bedtime stories. You were already too old for that but it didn't stop me from trying." He smiled. "I'm sorry that I don't call more often. I know it's going to sound stupid but I feel a little silly still hanging on to you after all these years. Like I'm a foolish old man. I guess I worried that you were going to stop answering my calls one day. Or that you were going to think I was a weirdo for calling after all these years."

"I never would've thought you were a weirdo. I loved when you called and we talked, Paul. I just... I think I'm just having a bad day. I shouldn't have said anything." I forced out a deep sigh and shook my head. "You're not silly. You were the best man Mom ever brought around. You still called and checked on me after you two imploded. That was important to me. It kept me from feeling abandoned. So maybe thank yourself for me not having daddy issues, too."

He laughed. "I will thank myself for that, I guess. Do you want to talk about what's really bothering you?"

I looked out the window next to us and watched as a palm tree swayed in the wind. The sky was getting dark with rain clouds and I could tell it was going to pour any minute. "It's nothing. I just... I argued with Vaughn. I feel bad."

"So, nothing has changed then?" Paul leaned forward and patted my hand. "If there's one thing that was true of your relationship with Vaughn, it's that you two could really push each other's buttons. I was shocked when I saw you here last night. You could always get under his skin so easily. And vise-versa."

I shook my head. "I was never the problem. Vaughn was a bully back then. But this fight might've been my fault."

"Vaughn was the same as every other stupid boy who's been led to believe that pulling a girl's hair is cute. He used to follow you around all over the place just waiting for a chance to annoy you. As soon as you paid him any attention his whole face would light up. As much as he loved to fight with you, though, he was your fiercest protector. I don't know how many times I had to pull him off one of the neighbor boys for teasing you."

I frowned. "I don't remember that."

He sat back again and shrugged. "It's true. I swear the families in that neighborhood celebrated when your mom and I divorced and I moved away with Vaughn."

I flinched as a loud clap of thunder echoed through the lobby. Feeling even worse than ever, I glanced at my phone, hoping for a missed text or call from him. "He doesn't feel like a brother to me."

Paul's eyebrows climbed higher on his forehead. After a few seconds, he cleared his throat. "Well. Whatever he feels like to you, Ella, I hope you two sort out your differences."

"As soon as the rain stops, I'll head back. I should apologize before I lose my nerve." I rolled my eyes. "I'm sure you remember how hard it was for Mom to apologize. Turns out, I take after her."

He laughed and nodded. "Oh, your mother was a pain in the ass but she was a lot of fun. You'd do well to take after her. She rarely apologized but when she did, she made it count."

I faked a gag. "Gross."

He snorted out a laugh. "Not what I meant, Ella."

"Sorry. You just never know with Mom." Another clap of thunder had me sighing. "This doesn't look like another five minute Florida storm."

"Nope. You might be here for a little while. Should we get room service dessert and watch TV until it ends? I saw a molten chocolate cake on the menu last night."

I nodded. "Yes, please. With ice cream. Lots of ice cream."

47

Ella

I took an Uber back to the house when the storm finally passed. It was already dark out and I was anxious to get home and find Vaughn. My head was full of thoughts about young Vaughn beating up neighborhood kids for me and present day Vaughn beating up Billy for me. I was desperate to tell him that I was sorry and that I didn't think he was a mistake.

When the driver slowed down before he got to the house, I looked up and saw that the street was packed with cars. People, too. "I don't think I'm going to be able to get closer than this. It looks like someone is having a party."

I frowned. "Um, this is fine. Thank you."

As soon as I opened the car door, the sound of a party filtered in. I was confused as I made my way down the sidewalk and had to step around drunk people coming from our house. A sinking feeling settled in my stomach when I saw the state of the front yard and driveway. The house was wide open and music pumped out from inside. Red solo cups were all over the ground and on top of our vehicles. There was a couple making out against the side of the house and another rolling around in the ground. I'd never seen a party like it outside of frat row. There had never been a party at our house while I lived there so I had a bad feeling about why there was a party happening that night.

Getting into the house was miserable. I had to push past people and the smell was disgusting. Sweat, beer, and something eerily similar to vomit reeked but I was the only one who seemed to notice. I couldn't spot another sober person anywhere. Searching for the guys room by room led me out the back door and onto the patio at the rear of the house. No one ever used it but the party had made use of the space. An impromptu dance floor had been born out of the large square of concrete and in the middle, towering over everyone, I spotted the guys.

Beers in hand, arms waving overhead as they danced to the music, it was clear from the glassy eyes to the goofy smiles that they were all hammered. I'd never seen any of them so drunk and it freaked me out. It freaked me out enough that I pushed my way through the crush of bodies to get to them. I didn't notice the women dancing on them at first. When I did, I ignored the pang of hurt I felt because I was convinced that something was wrong.

"Hey! Fisher! Booth!" I finally got close enough that I could just reach past a blockade of women to grab Fisher's shirt. When he swung his head in my direction, I watched the goofy smile turn down and his nose crinkle as he pulled away from me. I still didn't get it, though. "What's going on? Can we go somewhere and talk?"

"He doesn't want to talk to you!"

I shot a glare at the brunette yelling at me and turned back to Fisher. I expected him to see that it was me and smile at me like he always did. Instead, he scowled at me.

"Go away, Ella!" He looked over at Booth and rolled his eyes. "Tell her, Booth. Tell her to go away."

Booth locked eyes with me as he slung his arm around the woman dancing on him. "Go away."

I was forced to fight my way closer, taking more than one elbow to the boob because of it. "What the hell are you talking about?"

"We don't want you here. In case you didn't get the message, I'm breaking up with you, Ella! You've got a wandering eye and I heard all about it." Fisher slurred his words and jabbed his finger in my direction. "Wandering eye!"

I stared at him in shock, so confused about what was happening. I felt like I'd stumbled into an alternate universe, one where nothing made sense. I expected Vaughn to be angry at me but Fisher and Booth had never been anything but kind to me.

A woman dancing with her arm around Fisher's neck laughed cruelly, the sound so clear over the music. "Yeah, a wandering eye for her stepbrother!"

The music might as well have screeched to a halt. My head spun as people laughed and turned to me, staring and jeering at me like a bad teen movie. I shook my head, so horrified by everything happening that I was sure I was having a nightmare.

"What kind of girl cheats on her boyfriend with her stepbrother? God, what a disgusting slut."

More taunts went up as I looked around, so ready to wake up from my bad dream. My eyes found Vaughn in the crowd and I saw him laughing as a woman rubbed herself all over him. I wanted to scream at him to make it all stop but it just got worse.

"Vaughn, was she at least good?"

Vaughn smirked and shrugged, the look on his face all but confirming that he'd fucked me. More laughter went up around me and I was jolted forward by someone behind me. I stumbled into a guy I didn't recognize and was met with his arm banding around my back when I tried to move away.

"I'm not your brother, baby, but I can pretend!"

I shoved him away and looked at the guys one more time, hoping they'd snap out of it and stop the hell that was erupting around me. Instead, they were all laughing with their friends and dancing like they hadn't just crushed me. Turning around, I fought my way back to the house to a chorus of name-calling and a barrage of pushing and more than one hand grabbing my ass.

I didn't cry until I was in another Uber on my way back to Paul's hotel. I doubled over and tried hard to hide the sounds of my pathetic whimpering. Feeling like a fool and like my world was ending made it nearly impossible, though. I pinched my leg over and over again, praying I'd wake up and that I hadn't just been called a stepbrother fucker in a public setting.

The driver handed me a mini pack of tissues when he parked in front of the hotel and wished me good luck as I stumbled out of his car. I took the stairs up to Paul's floor and when he opened the door to my desperate knocking, I rushed into his arms and sobbed into his chest.

"What's wrong? What happened, Ella?" Paul's voice was desperate and full of fear as he walked me over to his couch. "Talk to me, sweetheart. Are you okay?"

I looked up into his kind eyes and it all came blubbering out.

48

Ella

Morning came after another terrible night of sleep. I'd tossed and turned on Paul's couch until finally I gave up and just sat outside on his balcony in the dark. I'd cried all the tears I could cry the night before on Paul's shoulder and I felt like an old sponge that'd been left out in the sun. I was dried out. Even if I wasn't, I'd reached a point of hurt and anger that didn't call for tears. I'd been sobbing in my bathroom over Billy just a few months earlier but what I felt that night was so far beyond heartbreak. There was plenty of that, too, but it was more. It was worse.

Paul joined me on the balcony later that morning and sat down next to me with a heavy sigh. "How are you doing, kid?"

I forced a smile and shrugged. "I don't know."

He rubbed his jaw and stared out at the morning sun coming up over the city. "I thought about what you said about not wanting to go back there. I have a friend with rental properties here and I called her before coming out here. She's got something available right now. It's tiny but she said it's nice."

"If I can afford it, I'll take it." I'd already made up my mind. I wasn't going back to that house.

"She's going to do me a favor and let you rent it for less than what she'd usually charge. Whatever you can't make, I'll cover, Ellie. Don't worry about it."

I turned to face him. "You don't have to do that, Paul. I know that I put you in an awkward position by coming to you, crying about your son. You don't have to do anything more than what you already have."

"Just let me help. You did the right thing, coming here. It makes me feel a little less like a failure to be able to help you." He saw me start to argue with him and held up his hands. "I don't need you to comfort me and try to make it better, Ellie. I should've made more of an effort for you."

"Thank you. For everything. I don't know what I would've done last night without you." I stood up and stretched, ready to force myself to do anything besides sitting and stewing. "When can we see the apartment?"

"Right now, if you want. She gave me the lockbox code."

I nodded. "If it's okay with you, I'd like to get out of that house as soon as possible."

"Of course, it's okay with me. Let me get changed and we can go." He looked at my rumpled dress and frowned. "Do I need to swing by the house and get you something to wear?"

"Unless you'd rather not be seen with a mess, I'm okay going like this. I want to get my life sorted as soon as possible."

"You're not a mess, Ellie." He reached out and squeezed my hand. "Alright. Let's face this day."

The apartment was just off campus and it was in a historic building that had serious haunted vibes. It wasn't so much an apartment as it was a large closet but I loved it for all the things it wasn't. Like how it wasn't next door to the guys and how it wasn't on campus where everyone had seemed so eager to trash me the night before. Paul set everything up with his friend and I had a new place to live before lunch.

"I'm going to pack up your stuff." Paul stood in the open doorway and blew out a quick breath. "It'll be a little while before I'm back. Are you going to be okay here?"

I nodded as I turned in a circle, looking at my entire apartment in that one move. "Yeah, I think so. Thank you so much, Paul."

"Even if I didn't love you, kid, I made the demon spawn who hurt you. It's the least I can do. Call me if you need anything while I'm out." He wrapped me in a tight hug and ruffled my hair. "I'll be sure to have Connie right shotgun on the way back."

I squeezed him hard and swallowed a lump of emotion. "Thank you."

After he left I called Mom. She answered and before she could say anything, I just blurted out the entire story. I realized I could still cry, and did. When I finished, she'd already booked a flight to come be with me for a few days.

"You can show me around campus and we can throw bricks through those jerks' windows. You know, the normal mom's visiting campus activities." She sniffed. "I love you so much, Ella Rae. You are so special and you deserve the world. I never wanted you to learn how much men suck but it seems that lesson doesn't skip anyone."

I cringed at the name and dug my fingers into the naked mattress that came with the apartment. "I love you too, Mom. Besides making a monster of a son, Paul isn't so bad."

She grunted. "Yeah, yeah. Paul's great. We all love Paul. I'm glad he was there for you, baby, but I'm coming now. This is a mom project."

"I'm glad you're coming."

"I'll always come when you need me. No matter how old you are, I'll always be your mom, Ella." She sighed and I could hear her going through her drawers as she spoke. "My mom wasn't always there for me when I went through hard things. She had this idea that to be an adult, I needed to face everything on my own, no matter what it was. I know I raised you right,

Ella. You're more of an adult than I'll ever be. But you'll never have to face life alone as long as I'm still kicking. I will always come when you need me. Even when you don't need me, sometimes. You know that, right?"

My eyes burned with unshed emotion. "I know, Mom. I love you. Thank you for coming. I think I really just need your hug."

She groaned and I could hear that she was crying. "Maybe I won't murder those boys after all, not since I got to hear that because of them."

There was a knock on my door. "Someone's here, Mom. I'll call you back."

"I'll see you soon!"

I opened the door, expecting Paul. Instead it was Natalie. I'd texted her to let her know that I was moving to a new apartment but I hadn't stopped to explain anything. She was already there, standing in front of me with a tub of ice cream bigger than her head and two plastic spoons.

"Can I come in?"

"Yeah! Sorry. I'm just surprised to see you. What are you doing here? With ice cream?"

She looked around and nodded. "This will be nice. I like it."

"Nat?"

She finally met my gaze and sighed. "I heard a few rumors around campus. I don't care what's true or what's not true. I just want to be here for my best friend."

I sank onto the mattress and wrapped my arms around myself. "I guess this is what I get for involving myself with guys that this campus is obsessed with."

"Fuck all of that. Let's just eat this ice cream and talk about whatever you want to talk about. You can help me pick out a new football team to cheer for. God knows I'm done with this fucking team. The Crocs? Really? What? Are we a school of rubber shoes? Lame."

49

VAUGHN

I woke up with a splitting headache and was so disoriented that I didn't know where I was. Dad was standing over me, shouting, and I had a weird moment of feeling like I was still a kid living at home with him. I sat up and rubbed my eyes, trying to understand what he was shouting about.

"Look at this place! Son, I don't know what got into you, but this isn't right. I'm ashamed of the way you acted and I've never had to say that before."

I looked around and felt a wave of horror and nausea as I saw the state of the living room. There were people passed out all over the place and the house was wrecked. I was on one end of the couch and there was a girl I didn't recognize on the other end, curled up without a shirt on. Dad's words started to sink in just when I saw Fisher stumble to his feet and run towards the kitchen.

"Honest to god, Vaughn, I want to shake you. Get the hell up and get these people out of there. Right now. I'm just getting started ripping you a new one and I can't imagine you want your fan club to hear what I have to say. Although, I don't know why I'm affording you any privacy and dignity when god knows you didn't give any to Ellie last night."

Ella. I grabbed my throbbing head and groaned. "Where is she?"

Dad stood with his hands on his hips. "Not here, Vaughn. And she's not going to be here ever again. I'm going to pack her stuff up. These people need to be gone when I get back down here."

He stomped away and I forced myself to get up. The room spun around me for a few seconds before I could take my first steps. I didn't make it five feet before Fisher came back, pale and shaky.

"I've never felt this close to death before." He leaned against the doorway and dry heaved twice before he managed to swallow down the urge. "Was that your dad shouting?"

I nodded, still processing everything I'd heard.

"What was he yelling about? Why's he so mad?"

Booth came charging down the stairs, eyes red and face just as pale as Fisher's. He flung open the front door and Fisher and I watched as he leaned his head off the porch and threw up.

"All three of you! Get the hell up here! Right now!" Dad's voice was angrier than I'd ever heard it. He was furious and a wave of doom hit me. His earlier words started to sink in.

"He's packing Ella's stuff up." I didn't wait on Fisher or Booth to follow me. I figured whatever Dad wanted to yell about, it was only fair that I take the brunt of it. He was *my* dad, after all. I stopped short outside of Ella's bedroom, though, and that feeling of doom grew larger.

"What the fuck?" Booth stumbled past me and ran his hand over the bright red paint smeared across Ella's door. In giant, bold letters, the word *slut* was written proudly.

I saw Dad sitting on the edge of Ella's bed, clutching something in his fist. I actually took a step back when he looked up at me, the anger and disappointment I saw on his face so jarring.

"Come in here." His voice was hard as he stood up and motioned at the room around him. "Come see what you did."

Walking into the room, my body sagged as I saw why Dad was so angry. Ella's room was trashed. Her stuff was thrown all around the room and it smelled like beer and god only knew what else had been spilled everywhere. More slurs adorned the walls and I finally saw what Dad had in his hands. Ella's stuffed animal.

"I was angry when I came over here. I had to watch Ellie cry her eyes out last night for hours. I didn't want to believe that the son I raised to be a good man could treat anyone the way she was treated." He held the stuffed animal out to me. "What am I supposed to tell her about this? When she's already so hurt over how you treated her? How do I tell her that all of her stuff is basically ruined, but worst of all, the stuffed animal she's had since before we ever knew her was ripped to pieces by *your* friends."

I swallowed, the real weight of everything sinking in. "I didn't know-"

"Shut up." Dad pointed at me with Connie, pieces of the stuffing dangling from his hand. "I could've forgiven you for sleeping with her. I don't love it but I could've gotten over it. I could've forgiven a messy breakup or some bad blood between the two of you. But this? Vaughn, I don't know what I'm supposed to do with this. You three humiliated her. You used her and then you threw her to your wolves. I can't even look at you right now."

I had flashes of memory from the night before. Ella trying to get our attention. Ella being pushed around as people called her names. Her face before she left. I bent forward and covered my face with my hands. Her face. I knew I could live a thousand years and her face would still haunt me.

"You want to know the worst part? She was with me before she came back here last night. She was coming to apologize to you. Whatever happened between the two of you, she was beating herself up about it." He pushed Connie into my chest and stared me down with a look of disgust I'd never seen from him. "I have to go tell her that she has nothing left here.

The silver lining is that she can leave this place without too much trouble now."

"Where is she?" Fisher sounded like he was talking through a ball of cotton, like he was struggling to force the words out.

"She and her wandering eye are safe and away from you three dipshits." He walked out of the room and then turned back to us. "Leave her alone."

"Dad, I... I didn't mean... I was just angry and-" I looked desperately to Fisher and Booth. "She told me that I was a mistake and I-"

"Seems like she was right, son."

I watched him leave and tightened my grip on Connie. Looking down at the shreds of him that remained, I felt my world closing in around me.

"You told us that she said *this* was a mistake." Booth inched closer to me. "You said *this*, not you."

I wanted him to hit me. I wanted to feel physical pain that might take away from the emotional pain I was feeling. "She said I was a mistake. She was going to come back here and be with the two of you while I had to sit back and watch. I... I couldn't-"

It was Fisher who hit me. His fist connected with my nose and right cheek hard enough to knock me backwards. "Did you lie about Billy, too?"

I let my nose drip blood down my shirt as I nodded. "She didn't want him touching her."

Booth stopped in front of me and patted my arm. "Thanks, Vaughn. Thanks for being so goddamned selfish that you didn't care who you took out in the process of making yourself feel better. Great friend."

Fisher rubbed his knuckles as he glared at me. "Fuck you, Vaughn."

They left me alone in her trashed room, trapped with the memory of her distraught face and the words she'd been called. I sat on the edge of her bed and then sank to the floor in front of it. The edge of one of her books stuck out from under it and I pulled it out with a heavy sigh. She had nothing. No clothes, no books, no Connie. It was all my fault.

50

Booth

"You boys should be ashamed of yourselves. This place is disgusting. I refuse. When I took this job, I told you I wasn't going to clean up after parties. Have you even tried to clean up? Have you seen the bathrooms? I quit." Mallory scowled down at Fisher and then turned around and stomped out of the house, slamming the door behind her.

He looked over at me and winced. "Well, that sucks."

We both sat there, staring at the TV even though it wasn't turned on. When Vaughn came in through the front door a few minutes later, he looked confused. "I think I just saw Mallory burning rubber getting out of here."

I crossed my arms and nodded. "She quit."

Fisher decided to turn the TV on finally but quickly realized it was broken. He checked the remote while I watched and I saw that the batteries were missing. He sighed. "Who comes to a party and steals the batteries from a guy's remote? I wanted to turn the volume up so I wasn't forced to talk to our roommate."

Vaughn made a frustrated noise. "I said I was sorry. I'm trying to make it right. With Ella and Dad both hating me right now, I don't need you two hating me, too."

"I don't hate you." I stood up and walked past him on my way to the kitchen. "I just don't want to see or talk to you right now. Maybe ever again."

I gagged at the smell coming from the sink and swore. Four days had passed since the party and we hadn't bothered touching anything. Every time I thought about cleaning I just didn't see the point.

Vaughn followed me into the kitchen and stood in front of the sink. He started pulling dishes out while holding his shirt over his nose. "It's not like I haven't tried to fix things. This isn't what I want."

Fisher laughed angrily from the doorway behind me. "It's exactly what you wanted. If you couldn't have her, we couldn't either. None of us have her. Congratulations."

"Are you beating yourself up as much as you're beating the shit out of me? You were cruel to her, too. You made everyone think she cheated on you, the darling quarterback." Vaughn tossed a plate onto the counter a little too hard and it shattered. "And you, Booth. You think you didn't do any damage? None of us are innocent. Yeah, I fucked up first and started this shit, but you were both eager to trash Ella as soon as you got your feelings hurt. So fuck this. Fuck you. Fuck me. Fuck everyone."

I watched as he stormed past us and out the front door. "Where are you going?"

He stopped and spun around. "I don't fucking know. I don't want to be on campus. I don't want to be here. I'm a grown ass man thinking about running away. Okay?"

Fisher rolled his eyes and shook his head. "Jesus, Vaughn. Just come back inside. You can't run away. We have practice in two hours. We need to clean this place because apparently the only person who hates us more than Ella is our housekeeper. If you're going to be a baby about us being pissed at you... I guess we can be okay again."

Vaughn looked at me and I could see how he was barely hanging on. Sighing, I shrugged. "Whatever. It doesn't mean I'm over it. I just don't have the energy to replace you as a roommate if you drive your truck into the ocean."

Hanging his head, Vaughn slowly came back inside and shut the door. "I know I deserve a lot worse than what you're giving me. I'm sorry. I can't put into words how sorry I am."

"Did you try to see her?" I asked with a great amount of hesitation and worry. So far, none of us had been able to get to her. If she was getting our texts and calls, she wasn't acknowledging them.

"I tried. I spent an hour on the phone with Dad this morning, begging him to give me her address. He's not budging." He leaned against the stair railing and rubbed his tired face. "I walked around campus the rest of the morning, hoping to spot her. Nothing. I did get a message back from her friend, though. Natalie."

Fisher stood up straighter. "What'd she say? She's ignored everything I've sent her."

"Thanks to me, people around campus are being assholes to Ella. Calling her names and being cruel to her. Natalie let me know that I deserve to rot in hell and that she hopes a football gets shoved up my ass and we never win another game." He pinched the bridge of his nose. "I don't know what to do. In all the time I've known Ella, she never retreated. She was alway up for a fight when I pissed her off."

"People are treating her like shit because of me. You were right about me making people think she cheated on me. You started the shit ball rolling down the shit hill but I made it worse." Struggling with his own guilt, Fisher sat on the stairs and held his head in his hands. "I should've known better. I don't know why I believed you. She didn't care about Billy anymore. She cared about us. She trusted us."

I swallowed down the urge to vomit. It was all I felt like doing since waking up and realizing just how severely I'd hurt Ella. I had an ever present memory in my head of some chick dancing on me while Ella watched, her eyes pooling with tears. I'd felt so vindicated at that moment. I was proud of how I hadn't crumbled, despite how weak I felt over the idea of Ella not being in my life. I couldn't stop imagining the look on my face that she'd watched. Proud, cocky, mean.

"I'm going to go out and look for her again. If I hear anyone talking shit about her, someone will have to bail me out of jail." I yanked open the door and looked back to see that they were both coming with me. "Think your dad will bail us out, even though he hates us?"

Vaughn shook his head. "Not a chance."

Fisher shrugged. "My parents would be too ashamed to have a kid in jail. They'd get us out."

"I need you to know something, Vaughn." I waited for him to look at me. "If I hit someone today, at least one of the punches will be me imagining it's you I'm hitting."

He nodded. "That's fair."

51

Ella

I kept my head lowered as I walked away from my last class of the day. What I'd learned about the college campus since things went to hell with the guys was that everyone on it really, really supported the football team. I felt like I was in middle school again with a bunch of kids whose biggest goal in life was to make me cry. Thankfully, spending three years of my adolescents with Vaughn had toughened me up. I cried a lot but it wasn't going to be over a bunch of people I didn't know hating me. Much, anyway.

I still had Natalie on my side. And Chris. Even though Natalie was still refusing to acknowledge that she liked him, he refused to go away. I was thankful. A few times I'd been heckled, Chris was there to call it off. Other times, it was Natalie going rabid on whoever happened to make a nasty comment at me. When I was alone, I did exactly what I was then. I walked with my head down and moved fast. It was harder to catch a moving target.

My apartment was calling to me and all I wanted to do was curl up in my bed and count the days until I could transfer back to Penn. I had to work that night, though. I'd taken on more shifts at the coffee shop to cover the costs of everything I still needed to replace. Paul covered a lot of things, like my books and a new laptop. Mom covered clothes and toiletries. It was the stuff I didn't even realize I needed until I went to grab it that I was left to replace. Then there was the search for a new Connie. I didn't want anyone to know how devastated I was over a stuffed animal so I'd tried to play Connie's loss off as just another frustrating thing that'd happened. In secret, I'd found an exact match to Connie online but the seller was asking a ridiculous price since Connie had been some special edition toy.

I didn't even know why I was trying so hard to replace Connie when the new Connie wouldn't be the same. It wouldn't have the same smells, the same thin spot in the middle where I squeezed it. Not having anything left me feeling so at odds, though. I'd found myself waking up in the middle of the night, trying to find Connie.

Mom had gone back home that morning and Paul had left shortly after Mom arrived so I was officially without parents again. It seemed silly but being so hurt had made me feel like a kid again, like I wasn't sure I was okay on my own.

Lost in thought, I didn't notice two guys walk past me and then turn around to follow me. At least, not at first. Until they decided to make their presence known. Unfortunately, by that time, we were away from the quad and I'd let my guard down since there were fewer people around. My shoulders were just finally starting to sink down from where they'd been up around my ears when the two of them fell into step on either side of me.

"Well, hello there, Ella Daughton."

I hadn't seen them coming so I flinched and tried to step away from him, just to bump into the other one. I glanced nervously from one to the other and started to walk faster. I didn't know either of them and I could tell by their jeering smirks that they weren't there to be kind to me.

"What? Feeling shy?" The one to my left casually put his arm over my shoulders. When I shrugged it off, he laughed. "Aw, come on, Ella. Don't be that way. We're just here to be your friends. You need a friend right now, don't you?"

I shook my head and walked even faster. My heart was hammering away, fear tingling all along my spine. "Just leave me alone."

The one on my right caught my wrist and pulled me to a stop. "Look, we know the kind of kinky shit you're into. We're not family, but we can role play, babe. I'll be your stepbrother and Eric can be your step daddy."

I yanked my hand away and glared up at him. "Fuck you."

"Yeah, that's the plan, honey." Eric grabbed my waist and brushed against my ass. "We know you're a freak. We just want to see it in action. Let me and Brian have a viewing party, huh?"

"Don't touch me!" I screamed at them and backed away. "What the hell is wrong with you? Leave me alone!"

"Don't be a bitch, Ella. We just want some of what you were giving your stepbrother. Just a sample, even." Brian leered at me and grabbed himself through his pants. "I'd be happy with that dirty mouth."

One second they were in front of me, the next they weren't. I blinked and screamed as something large flew across my vision. Stumbling backwards, I watched in with the slow realization that the fast moving blur had been Booth. He was on top of both Eric and Brian, pummeling them with his huge fists.

When one of them got a punch in, Booth growled like an animal and went at them even harder. Fisher ran up to the mess and jumped right in, landing an elbow in someone's side like he thought he was a professional wrestler. I would've laughed if the circumstances weren't what they were.

I turned to look for help to break up the fight and ran straight into Vaughn. He caught me in his arms and looked me over before glancing behind me at the fight still going strong on the ground. I heard someone shout that campus security was coming and Vaughn winced. I could tell he wanted to get his friends away from trouble and I used it to my advantage.

He held up a finger to me. "Wait right here. Don't move, Ella Rae."

As soon as he slipped around me to grab Fisher and Booth I ran. I didn't stop running until I was at my car and I only felt like I could breathe again when I'd been at work for nearly an hour. I'd gone through that whole first hour like a zombie as I replayed the whole thing in my head. I felt violated and dirty. I was glad those two assholes had taken a beating. I just felt wrong that Booth, Fisher, and Vaughn had come to my rescue. They caused the problems. They couldn't be the problem and the solution. They just couldn't.

The next day I saw Eric on campus. With two black eyes and tape across his nose, he looked like someone Booth had taken out with a flying tackle. He glanced up, spotted me, and nearly tripped over himself as he raced to go the other way. I noticed more of the same the rest of the day. I didn't hear any mean comments and I was left alone, even if I was still stared at like a science experiment.

When I had lunch with Natalie off campus, I found out why everyone had backed off. She was eager to share the gossip with me even though we'd instituted a no talking about the guys rule.

"After they beat the shit out of those guys, they did this whole *Braveheart* thing and announced to the quad that anyone caught harassing you would meet the same fate. It was epic, apparently. I know they're assholes and we still hate them, but that softens the hate a bit. Right?"

My face burned red with embarrassment as I thought of the spectacle they'd probably created. I didn't care that what they'd done had seemingly helped. It wouldn't always. Then people would have even more evidence to use against me somehow. And sure, the guys were taking up for me in that moment. But what about the next? What happened when they decided they hated me again?

"I don't hate them. I just don't want anything to do with them." I could see she had more to say but I just shook my head. "I don't want to hear anything else about them, Nat. Please."

She sighed but she nodded. "Sure, Ella."

52

Fisher

Running around campus in our full gear was the coach's idea of punishment for us getting caught fighting. The fact that he made the whole team do it was almost more of a punishment. No one wanted to run the campus and no one was happy that we were the reason they were suffering. Coach wasn't in a forgiving mood, though, with the team heading towards a division championship. One fuck up and the whole season could be over. I knew that but I still couldn't care as much as I should've. Football was what I wanted to do. I loved it. If I wanted to get drafted to a good team after graduation, I needed to keep showing off my best work.

Booth and Vaughn were about as motivated as I was. We all knew what was riding on our performance but it was hard to give a shit when we'd hurt Ella so thoroughly.

As captain of the team, I was at the front of the pack as we ran. Despite the cooler weather, it was hot in our full gear. I was tired and I honestly felt a little like throwing myself to the ground and seeing if a full blown tantrum would get Coach to pity me.

Of course, Coach had us running in the middle of the day when the campus was busiest, too. He wanted us to be embarrassed but I wouldn't feel anything other than satisfied about beating the shit out of the two pricks messing with Ella. They deserved the ass-whooping they got. They deserved another one if I could catch them somewhere private.

Pushing through a side stitch, I let my gaze track from side to side. Unlike the first half hour, I finally spotted the one person I'd been searching for. Ella. I didn't think twice about veering off the path I'd been on to run towards her. It didn't occur to me that everyone would follow me until they did.

Ella looked up and saw me running straight towards her with the entire football team behind me and her eyes went wider than I'd ever seen them. I could see the thoughts racing through her mind as she decided what to do.

"Ella! Just-" The rest of my words trailed off as I watched her turn around and sprint away from me. From *us*. The entire football team was behind me, watching.

I didn't think. I just ran. It didn't occur to me in the moment that chasing after her with the entire football team might not be something she wanted because I just wanted to talk to her so desperately. Ella was surprisingly fast but I was faster.

I caught up with her and, running beside her, I tried to apologize. "Ella, I'm sorry. I just need-"

"What are you doing? Stop chasing me!" She looked over her shoulder and before I had a chance to catch her, she tripped over her own feet and went down hard. A pile up of players was imminent as everyone in front stopped to avoid running her over.

I watched in horror as Ella ended up under a few guys. Flat on her stomach, her ponytail was sticking up like a flag of surrender, waving in the breeze. The guys on top of her tried to move quickly, realizing they were going to flatten her. I helped shove them off and knelt down beside her.

"Ella? Are you okay? Jesus, that wasn't supposed to happen."

She turned her head to face me and blew a few strands of hair out of her mouth. "Ruining my reputation and happiness wasn't enough? You want to leave me physically broken, too?"

I yanked my helmet off and grabbed her under her arms to tug her to her feet. "Where are you hurt?"

Vaughn and Booth, both unhappy runners who'd been at the back of the pack, caught up and got the tail end of the commotion. Booth pushed past everyone and stood in front of Ella. "What happened? You're bleeding."

My stomach twisted as I saw that her elbows were both bleeding, as was her chin. "Oh, god. I'm sorry, Ella. I don't know what I was thinking. I'm-"

Vaughn moved closer and gripped her head to move it so he could examine her chin. "Fuck. We need to get this cleaned out, Ella Rae. Does anything else hurt?"

A few whispers could be heard from the team behind us and Ella recoiled. She pulled away from us and swiped her hand over her chin, wincing as she tried to wipe away the blood. She lowered her head, moved around us, and, without saying another word, hurried away.

Vaughn tried to go after her but Coach appeared, a dark scowl on his face. He stretched his arm out across Vaughn's chest and shook his head. "Take a goddamn hint. I'm assuming she's the one you dumbasses were fighting over? Well, great job! You almost killed her. That's an extra half hour. Get back to it! And stay on the fucking path this time, Hayes!"

When we finally got home that night, I felt like I'd been run over by a semi truck. My body hurt all over from the full practice we'd endured after running for an hour and a half. I had blisters on my feet and I hadn't been paying attention during practice and I'd taken a sack that made me bite through my bottom lip.

I fell into the couch and groaned as my body protested. Booth and Vaughn were in the same shape and they each folded onto the couch on either side of me. I wasn't so sure Coach hadn't tried to kill us.

"Booth. Call your mom and have her come take care of us." Vaughn grunted out the words like it was exhausting to even speak.

"This place is disgusting. She'd murder all three of us for living like this."

I sighed. "Booth. Call your mom and have her come murder us."

He let his head rest on the back of the couch and stared up at the ceiling. "Do you think she's okay?"

"Who? Your mom?" I shrugged. "Why wouldn't she be?"

"I meant Ella." He shook his head. "I can't believe you chased her down."

Vaughn snorted. "No one could."

"What was I supposed to do? Not take the chance to talk to her? It's nearly impossible to catch her. She changed her normal schedule and no matter how many times I call or text, she doesn't answer. I regret the pile up, but I couldn't let her get away without trying." I winced. "Hindsight is twenty-twenty, though. I probably should've stopped when I realized the entire team was following me."

"She hates us. And she has every reason to." Booth pushed himself off the couch and groaned. "I'm going to bed."

Vaughn turned his head to face me after Booth was gone. "She has every reason to hate *me*. I'll talk to her and tell her that you two were just victims of my selfishness."

I picked at a callous on my hand. "I wish that I thought it would help."

"There has to be something we can do." He sounded like he was starting to panic. "Right? She can't just write us off. She cared about us."

"And we turned the whole campus against her. I think she *can* just write us off, Vaughn. I think she has."

OFF-LIMITS ROOMATES 247

He stared off into space as I forced myself off the coach and towards the stairs. I could see a look of determination play across his features but I just ignored it. Ella was done with us.

53

Ella

"And then the entire football team was on top of me. At least that's what it felt like. I bled, Mom. My chin has a big bandaid across it because of him. I had to go back to the nurse this morning and get a bandage change." I could tell she wanted to laugh so I sighed. "Go ahead. If it wasn't *me* it was happening to, I'd laugh, too."

She tried to hide her laugh with a cough. "No, no. It's not funny. Are you okay?"

"I'm fine." I groaned. "I mean, I'm not fine. I'm mortified. He chased me with the entire football team. I'm trying to blend in. I just want to finish this semester already and become invisible until I get back to Penn."

"With a Daughton woman's curves? We don't do invisible, honey. We were built to stand out." She did laugh then. "I'm sorry. It's really not funny. I'm just picturing it and I can't imagine what the hell he was thinking. And why didn't the guys behind him realize what he was doing and stop?"

"I don't know! They're lucky we didn't all land in a pile of shit after how much they scared me. I just looked up and the entire football team, in their helmets and everything, was chasing me down. Now I know how the other teams feel and I'm not surprised they lose."

She laughed even harder. "A bunch of idiots."

I reached behind me on the bed for Connie and then sighed when I remembered he wasn't there. Laying flat on my bed, I stared up at the ceiling and ignored the sneaky tears that slid out of the corner of my eyes and into my hair. "I just want to come home, Mom."

"You will. Thanksgiving is in a couple of weeks. You'll be home before you know it and itching to leave again. It'll get better, Ella. It won't always feel so raw."

I wasn't so sure. "I don't know if it's because there are three of them but it hurts worse than it did when Billy cheated. The public shaming aspect aside, it just feels like someone shot me through the chest. You know that movie with the woman who walks around with that big hole in her chest the entire time? That's me. I don't think her hole hurt, though. Mine does. A lot. And just when I get distracted by something and start to smile, there it is again."

"I have no idea what movie you're talking about. Are you sure it wasn't a porn? All this talk about holes hurting makes me think you're thinking of a porn."

I started to say her name in exasperation, the same way I always did, but then I stopped and took in a breath of air that hurt a tiny bit less. "Thanks for always being you, Mom."

"It was a porn, right? Was I right?"

"I don't think so." Someone knocked on my door and I forced myself out of bed. "Natalie's here with pizza, Mom. I'll call you later. Love you."

"Love you, too, Ella Rae. Keep your head up."

I opened the door for Natalie and was about to close it when I spotted movement in the hallway. I nearly screamed when I realized it was a person and that they were coming towards me. I had the door halfway shut when I recognized them. I slammed it the rest of the way shut and locked it.

"Did you show Vaughn where I live, Natalie?"

She frowned. "No. Why the hell would I do that?"

"He's out there right now." I was whispering at her, hand still on the door, too scared to face Vaughn to tell him to get lost.

Natalie wasn't. She pushed me away from the door and yanked it open. On the other side, fist raised to knock, was Vaughn. "Did you follow me?"

"No." He cleared his throat when Natalie gave him nothing but silence. "Yes. But for a good reason. I need to see Ella."

"That's not a good enough reason to act like a creep!" Natalie lowered her voice. "And I watched you and your buddies at practice yesterday. You all look like shit. If you fuck up this season and don't bring home a championship, I'm going to find a way to shit in your mailbox every day for the rest of my life."

I was behind the door, hidden, and I made a face at her. What the hell was she talking about? Why was *that* her threat of choice?

"Yeah, sure. Great. I deserve it. I just need to see Ella. Please." Vaughn's deep voice was as serious as I'd ever heard it. "I know she doesn't want to see me, but this is important."

Natalie rolled her eyes. "Sure it is, step bro. It's always important with you guys."

"Fuck this. I didn't follow you across campus on a wild goose chase as you walked around in circles and stopped to pick up leaves for a fucking hour just to stand here, talking to *you*." He stopped and I could hear him take a deep breath. "Sorry. I'm sure if I hadn't been so ready to talk to Ella that the walk would've been great. I'm going to move past you now. Excuse me."

I grabbed the door and pulled it open, desperate to stop him from coming into my new home. Nothing in my new space smelled like him or reminded me of him. Nothing except for my own body. I couldn't get rid of that, though. "Stop. I'll talk to you, just not in here."

"Are you sure?" Natalie looked like she was ready to murder Vaughn. "Say the word and I'll get rid of him."

I held up my hand and squeezed past Vaughn to step into the hallway. I was very careful not to touch him. "I'll be right in, Nat."

Vaughn shook his head as she shot him more death stares before shutting the door and leaving us alone in the hallway. He lifted his eyes to mine and looked unsure of himself. He didn't say anything but just stared at me.

I crossed my arms over my chest and looked over his shoulder. "What do you want, Vaughn?"

He took a step closer to me and I saw that he had a bag behind his back. "I need to tell you something. Give me five minutes?"

I let out a humorless laugh. "That's the same thing Billy asked for. I feel like I'm in a cycle of men just needing five minutes of my time."

He winced. "I deserve that. I was an asshole. Worse than an asshole. I'm sorry, Ella. I fucked up. I don't expect you to forgive me anytime soon. I wish you would and after today, I can't guarantee that I won't keep trying to earn it, but I don't expect it."

I gripped my upper arms tight. "Vaughn."

"Just give me a second to get my thoughts together. I, um, I didn't know if Natalie would actually lead me here and I was so caught off guard by the path she took that I didn't have time to plan out exactly what I want to say." He rubbed his jaw and sat the bag down by his feet. "Okay. I don't think I deserve your forgiveness, but Booth and Fish do."

Shaking my head, I looked at my door and considered calling the conversation done.

"It was my fault that they did what they did. They were upset because of me." He stepped closer and put his hands over mine on my arms. "I was upset when you said that we were a mistake. I was jealous of Booth and Fish still getting to be with you and I didn't think I could watch it and be okay. I told them I saw you with Billy and that you said that *we* were a mistake. We, as in all three of us. I couldn't stand the idea of being the only one hurting without you so I took them down with me."

I stared at him like he'd grown two extra arms and a head. I hadn't known what to make of Booth and Fisher turning on me but I thought they were like the Three Musketeers, or something. One for all, and all of that. To find out he'd purposefully turned them against me hurt. It didn't change the rest of the pain I felt, though.

"I'm sorry, Ella. I was scared. I didn't want to lose you and I didn't know how to make you see that I wasn't a mistake. So, I went and proved you right. Booth and Fisher just got sucked into my shithole."

I tilted my head as I stared at him. "Do you want to know what just occurred to me, Vaughn? They expected me to trust them with my body and my secrets but they didn't trust me enough to have a conversation with me that night before writing me off completely. So, no, they aren't just innocent bystanders who got caught in your crossfire. What you did was the catalyst, but they are big boys who made up theirs minds to insinuate that I'm a stepbrother fucking whore to everyone on campus. All of you did."

"No one will mess with you anymore, Ella. I... I'm so sorry. I-"

"I don't know what you expect from me. Do you want me to thank you for stopping the number of guys who come on to me thinking I'll be an easy lay? Or maybe I should thank you for cutting down on the amount of people loudly calling me names? It's much nicer now that everyone is whispering or just thinking all the bad things about me." I forced out a laugh. "I was coming back to tell you that I was wrong. I was coming back to tell you that you weren't a mistake and that I was just terrified of people finding out about my feelings for you and thinking that I was... Well, that I was a stepbrother fucking whore.

"I cared about you. I cared about all of you. And now I just want to leave this place and never look back."

His grip on my hands tightened. "I care about you, Ella. I don't want to lose you."

I stepped out of his reach so his hands fell away from me. "You did this."

"I know. And I take full responsibility for it, Ella. I was a stupid asshole. I hurt you and I let other people hurt you. From the moment I walked into that coffee shop and spotted you I wanted to keep you safe. I wanted to keep you, period. Every stupid fucking thing I said or did to keep you away from my friends was just me wanting you without seeing a way to have you. I've been an asshole to you the entire time you've ever known me and you still gave me a chance."

I shook my head. "I can't do this. I can't, Vaughn."

He dropped his head. "I can't tell you that I'm not going to keep trying."

Tears filled my eyes but I blinked them away. "Can you please leave?"

He looked away and cleared his throat. "I wanted you to have this."

I saw him grab the gift bag and shook my head. "I don't want anything from you."

"It's yours, Ella Rae. I'm just returning it." He saw that I wasn't going to take the bag and put it at my feet. "I tried my best to fix him."

54

Ella

I brought the gift bag home with me for Thanksgiving. I was too afraid of what I thought was inside of it and what it would make me feel to open it but I couldn't be away from it. Mom didn't mention it, thankfully, and it stayed on my side table, just out of reach.

Mom had done a lot of things to make sure I was okay. She only talked about the guys if I brought them up first. She saw that I'd lost a few pounds since she'd last seen me and she made all my favorite foods to guarantee I found those pounds and some. She sat with me on my first day back home and watched hours of court TV, despite hating it. The one thing she refused to give up was football, though. As much as she loved me, football had been her first love. Well. Men who played football had been her first love. The game was a quick second and it stuck long after the men did.

Her daughter's college football team was in a division championship the day before Thanksgiving and she wasn't going to miss it, no matter how many dirty looks I shot her way. Natalie had texted me first thing, just before the game started, to tell me that she definitely wasn't going to watch the game. Not a chance of her doing anything like that, she'd assured me. I couldn't help rolling my eyes at her antics as I told her to watch the game.

I could've stayed in my room for the length of the game but that felt like a punishment in itself. Sitting there with a gift bag that I wouldn't open, straining to hear the names that I desperately did, and didn't, want to hear from the next room, it sounded miserable. Instead of hiding, I paced behind the couch and drove Mom crazy during the first half of the game.

Every mention of the guys made my heart thump a little harder. The amount of air time they gave Vaughn and Fisher from the sidelines was wild and I found myself critiquing the cameraman. Chris would never. The continuous shots of them, helmets off, faces and hair wet with swamp, was almost enough to send me running to my room. Mom kept shooting me looks, though, like she was waiting for me to run and I dug my feet in.

It was a shot of Booth that hit me hardest. He was sitting on the bench with his head hung low, no trace of happiness on his face. His dimples were gone as he shot a look at the camera and glanced away just as quickly. His team was winning, most of his teammates were buzzing with energy. Booth looked like his pet had just been put down.

Mom even sucked in a sharp breath at the sight of him. "Oh."

I crossed my arms and glared at her. "Don't say a word."

"I wasn't going to." She cleared her throat and continued to stare at the TV. "It's just that he looks heartbroken."

"Mom." Coming around to sit next to her on the couch, I curled my legs under me and shook my head. "Don't."

"I'm not!" She managed to stay quiet through the halftime show and then cleared her throat again right after the third quarter started. "So."

The Crocs were playing defense so the guys weren't on the field. I looked over at her and raised my eyebrows in a silent question.

"How are you doing?"

I leaned away from her on the armrest of the couch and scowled. It wasn't at her, just at the world in general. "It's Thanksgiving and I'm supposed to focus on the things I'm grateful for, right? Well, I'm grateful for you and for being away from that campus."

The opposing team scored on the TV and Mom shouted. "What the fuck, ref? How did you miss that holding call? Do your job!"

I rolled my lips into my mouth and then felt a pang of sadness as the camera panned to Fisher completing a few practice throws on the sideline. He looked up and it was like he was staring straight at me before he glanced away. My next breath was a little harder.

"Oof. That kid can do broody, can't he?" Mom saw my look and held up her hands. "Sorry! It was just an observation."

I'd never seen Fisher attempt anything close to brooding before the night of their party. He was usually so quick with a charming smirk. The few times I hadn't been able to hide from them on campus, he'd been nothing like the guy I'd first met. Just thinking about it made me feel guilty, like I'd helped take away something fun from the world. That thought always sent me down a spiral of anger and frustration, though, because I hadn't caused the whole mess. They had.

We watched the rest of the third quarter in silence. I was lost in my feelings while Mom was on the edge of her seat. The other team had gotten fired up during halftime and they were giving the guys a fight. They went into the final quarter tied.

"I swear to god if they lose this game, Ella, I'm going down there and I'm going to kick all their asses." Mom stood up and took over my pacing. "I want to see a national championship with a team I have ties to. Even if those ties are a little loose currently."

"Loose? Mom, they're not loose. They're non-existent." I turned my glare on the TV as they showed Fisher throwing a perfect touchdown pass to Vaughn. "Yay. Touchdown."

Mom winced at my sarcastic tone. "Ella, I'm not sure you-"

"There's nothing to talk about, Mom." I was being an ass but seeing the guys was cutting deep. I'd celebrated almost every win with them. I knew how much they loved the cookies I baked for them. They came home after each game, happy to see me and my baked goods.

"The second this game is over, you and I are going to have a hard talk, young lady." She could barely look away from the screen as the Crocs defense fought the other team's offense from moving down the field. "Interception! Interception! Holy shit! Yes!"

I nearly had a heart attack from her sudden screaming. Holding my hand over my chest, I watched as the camera panned to Vaughn and Fisher walking onto the field and I saw what a massive contrast there was between them and the rest of the team. The rest of the team was losing their minds in excitement. Vaughn and Fisher looked like they were marching in a funeral procession.

I sat there with that image in my head for the rest of the game. Mom lost her mind as our team won and then she sat down calmly next to me like none of it had happened.

"Okay. Time for that hard talk." She reached to mute the TV but we both froze when the shot switched from an overview of the field, where students had run onto the green to celebrate, to a close up interview with Fisher just to the side of the chaos. Confetti rained down behind him, some of it catching in his sweaty hair. He was red-faced and his uniform was stained with grass and dirt. He was the picture of the champion athlete, if you didn't look at his eyes too closely.

The journalist interviewing him was a pretty blonde in our school colors. "We just watched you break the passing record for your division, Fisher. How are you feeling right now, after this win?"

Fisher stared into the camera and I saw him catch his breath before speaking. "Honestly?"

55

Ella

Mom looked my way but I couldn't tear my eyes away from Fisher.

The journalist smiled at the camera and looked back at Fisher. "Of course! I'm sure you're elated. This is a big win for you guys. I know you felt cheated last year and you've surely redeemed yourself now."

"Yeah, sure." Planting his hands on his hips, he ducked his head. "Redeemed."

"Fisher, I couldn't help but notice that your usual flair was missing during the game today. The announcers pointed it out a few times. We're used to seeing your signature grin after every score. Was today just a matter of being serious and staying focused for you?"

Mom swallowed so loudly that I heard it over the TV. "This kid's making me nervous. He looks like he's ready to cry."

Fisher lifted his eyes to the camera. "You know, it's hard some days to not let personal life get to you on the field. I fought for my team but I struggled today."

I sat up, my heart lodged securely in my throat. What was he doing?

"Oh?" The journalist seemed as lost as I felt.

"Yeah. There's this girl... She should've been here today. Usually after the games, she bakes me and my roommates cookies with our names on them. I never knew that someone could make a cookie taste so goddamn good." Fisher was so in his head that he didn't notice the panic on the woman's face at his swearing. "She's not here, though, and none of this is very much fun without her. It's crazy how someone can come into your life and make things that seemed amazing before look so dull without them. You know? What's the point of all of this if she's not here?"

I couldn't breathe. I wasn't sure Mom was breathing, either. The journalist looked thrown as Fisher just turned and walked away, leaving the interview as if he'd forgotten he was even doing it.

"Well, folks." The woman was a trooper. She shook her head and smiled at the camera. "It seems that even the best quarterback in the division can't escape love's fickle ways. Let's all hope that Fisher Hayes gets his happy ending because everyone here in Starn Stadium is cheering for him today. Everyone except for the Hanover Hooks, that is. This is..."

Her voice trailed off as Mom lowered the volume. She turned to me with wide eyes. "Okay. Wow."

I wasn't sure I remembered how to breathe.

"I mean... Wow." She shook her head. "That changes things. I mean, this entire day changes things. I was imagining them playing today and being out there like a bunch of little shits, having a blast even though they hurt my baby, but they didn't look like they were having fun, Ella Rae. They looked like they wanted to run away."

I finally sucked in a shaky breath. "Stop."

"No. I said we're going to have a hard talk and we're going to have a hard talk. Don't interrupt me, either." Mom turned so she was facing me head on. "I taught you that Daughton women never take men back. We are strong women who don't need men and we don't forgive easily. We suck at apologizing and we don't do second chances. I accidentally taught you that men are not all that great most of the time. I brought home a lot of duds over the years. You never saw me have a reason to forgive a man, Ella. After your father left... I guess I just started going for men who I couldn't love. Paul was almost the exception but even that was doomed before it started.

"I like my life. I like changing men like I change my panties. It's fun and it keeps me on my toes. You've never been like me in that way, though, honey. You're steady and strong. You crave something real and rock solid, probably from years of seeing man after man pass through here without any semblance of normalcy. I still don't believe that most men deserve second chances. But..."

I saw the way she glanced at the TV and closed my eyes. Her words battered around in my head but I couldn't make sense of them yet.

"Don't get me wrong, Ella. I think that what they did was idiotic and hurtful. I think they deserved to spend the last month suffering because god knows you have. I'm seeing these kids on TV, though, and it's probably one of the most exciting days of their lives so far, and they look beyond miserable." With a heavy sigh, Mom reached over and took my head. "It's been a long time since I knew Vaughn well, Ella, but I did know him very well for a while. He was a little shit but he was a good kid. He did stupid things sometimes, of course, but deep down, I never worried about him murdering us in our sleep."

I snorted out a laugh at her unexpected ending. "Is that the bar we're using?"

She smiled. "No. I just wanted to make you laugh. And it worked."

I hugged my knees to my chest and rested my chin on them. "So, I'm just supposed to unlearn the lessons you taught me and forgive them?"

"If you think that they're truly sorry and regret hurting you, yeah. You know them, Ella. You've seen them during the last month. Do you think they'd repeat the same mistake?" Mom stood up and stretched. She went to the kitchen and poured herself a glass of water and I was still just staring at the spot she'd vacated when she got back.

"I think it would've been easier to forgive them if the entire school hadn't gotten involved. Being harassed by everyone else made their betrayal so much harder to deal with." I shook my head. "But the school did get involved. Because they lashed out at me in public."

"Yeah, it turns out that men's egos are pathetically weak and they go to extreme lengths to make them feel a little better." Mom rolled her eyes. "Not an excuse. Just a fact."

"They tried to fix it. Afterwards, they tried to make people leave me alone. I know they didn't mean to cause what they did. The very next morning I had missed texts and calls from them." I hugged myself tighter. "I just want out, Mom. That school turned on me so quickly. People think I'm some incest perv and they don't even know I was with all three guys. That's what this is. Me and three guys. That's never not going to cause a ruckus."

"Oh, now you're just reaching for straws." She stood up again and held up her finger. "Wait one second. I'll be right back."

I felt tears pepper my eyes when she came back a few seconds later with my gift bag in hand. "Mom..."

"I know it's from one of them, with the way you carried it in here like it was made of glass. Open it."

The thick paper of the bag crinkled in my hand as I clutched it. "I can't."

"Why not?"

"Because. If it's what I think it is, I'm not going to be okay." Tears pricked the back of my eyes anyway. "Vaught brought it to me. He said he tried his best to fix him."

Her eyes went wide. "Open the fucking bag, Ella."

"What if it's him? What if it's Connie?"

"Then you're going to have to forgive him and the other two. Because if he saved Connie, he's worth keeping, Ella." She nodded at the bag. "Open the damn thing. I'm on the edge of my seat."

With tears streaming down my cheeks, I opened the bag and reached inside. My hand was met with the familiar flattened fur that I knew so well but also something rougher, something that hadn't been there before. I pulled it out and Mom gasped in horror. To be fair, Connie had seen better days. I knew he'd been ripped to shreds but Vaughn had sewn him back together. Not well, but it was Connie in my hands, in one piece.

"Oh, my god." Mom covered her mouth with her hand. "I mean, it's a beautiful gesture, but... God."

I laughed through my tears and traced my finger down line after line of rough stitching. Lifting him to my nose, I inhaled deeply and smelled Connie, the same as always, with a bit of Vaughn. He was still mostly flattened in the middle when I squeezed him to my chest.

"Don't squeeze him too hard, Ella. He doesn't look built to withstand a lot." She winced and tilted her head to stare at it from a different angle. "I mean... Bless him for trying."

I clutched Connie even tighter. "Whatever happens to him, it can be fixed."

"Yeah, but... Should we order a new one and put this one in a locked box so it won't kill us when it comes to life?"

"Mom!" I laughed and stuck my leg out to gently kick her. "Connie's perfect just the way he is."

"Yeah, yeah. Vaughn did an amazing thing and I'm proud of him for doing it, but would it have killed him to watch a video about sewing?" She grinned and patted my leg. "Does that make your decision a little bit easier?"

My stomach twisted with nerves. "I don't know."

"Yes, you do. Don't try to play it cool, Ella Rae Daughton. I can tell you're already halfway back together with them in your head." She stood up and clapped her hands. "Thank god. Thanksgiving won't have to be so dark and moody now."

56

Vaughn

I met Dad at the front door of our house after the game. I'd been watching for him, impatiently waiting for him to show up so I could play my hand. I knew he was still pissed at me but he'd shown up to the game, which was a good sign that he hadn't written me off completely.

When I opened the door before he could knock, Dad raised his eyebrows at me. "I expected you three to be out celebrating."

I glanced over my shoulder and saw that Booth and Fisher had joined us. They each had a duffel bag in their hands and mine was sitting on the stairs next to them. "Um, yeah. About that."

"What?" Dad looked at our bags and started shaking his head already. "No. Whatever it is you're going to ask me, don't. I'm still pissed at all of you."

"We need you to take us to Ella's." I watched his face drop in surprise. "We'd drive ourselves if we thought there was a chance in hell we could get the address. And we're hoping that having you there will make it harder for Ella to turn us away."

Dad laughed. "You're joking, right?"

"No. We've been trying to talk to Ella for a month and we're not getting anywhere individually. So, we're going to try to talk to her all together. We want to be with her, Dad. We care about her and there's something real between us. We're supposed to be together. Even if you don't like it. Even if other people won't get it. We don't give a shit."

Booth stepped forward. "We're desperate here, Mr. Adler. We need to make it right."

"And you think showing up the night before Thanksgiving is the way to make it right?" Dad looked skeptical but he wasn't outright refusing us.

"We're going to think of a plan once we're on the road. A grand gesture, you know?" Fisher winced. "We're trying here. We're here, trying to go to her, after the biggest win of our lives because it didn't feel like much of a win without her. Take us. Please."

Dad looked around us at the house. "Well, at least you cleaned up after yourselves. The place looks better than normal."

"Mallory quit after the party, sir. Fairly." Fisher managed a wry grin. "We lived in filth for a while but if we're going to bring Ella back here, we wanted to make sure it was good for her."

"Dammit. I'm a romantic at heart, boys. Get in the truck. Pee now because I'm not stopping unless it's for gas once we're on the road. I'm supposed to be meeting a friend at a cabin in the mountains on Friday and this is going to be a tight turnaround." Dad squeezed my shoulder. "I'm proud of you for trying."

"I'm not sure I deserve that."

"You do." He pulled me into a hug and sighed. "We all fuck up. It's how we come back that makes us men. You could've gotten your feelings hurt by how much she's turned you down and given up. You didn't, though."

I shook my head. "She's worth it."

"Yeah, well, you better know that I love you because you're forcing me to drive to my ex's the night before Thanksgiving."

"I love you, too, Dad. Thanks." I grabbed my bag and we headed out. It was only once we were on the road that the three of us looked at each other and realized we had nothing in the way of a grand gesture, not even an idea.

Two hours in and Dad had started offering his ideas. Once he suggested we buy her a puppy, we cut him off, though. We were trying to be realistic and I was pretty sure Ella, the busy pre-law student, didn't have time to raise a puppy. When I started rethinking the idea, I cut myself off.

Somewhere in North Georgia, Dad turned on the radio and we drove another hour like that. When he got out to get gas in Tennessee, Fisher leaned forward from the backseat and pointed at the radio. "What if we did the cheesy boombox outside her window thing? We watched that one movie together with the guy and the lawn mower. Remember? They rode away on the lawn mower together?"

Booth nodded. "She liked that movie a lot."

"When the hell were you watching movies?" I glared at them for a few seconds and then sighed. "Whatever. Just tell me about the movie."

Dad was silent as he listened to us agree to singing outside of Ella's window. He was silent as he listened to us pick a song. He was silent as he listened to us practice the song for an hour straight. He didn't break that silence until we were right outside of Ella's hometown. "Well. This is either going to work because she really cares about you guys or it's going to put the nail in your coffin. There is no in between."

"What the hell? Dad! It's a good idea. Right? It's a good idea, because if it wasn't, you would've said so hours ago!" I looked back at Booth and Fisher with a growing sense of panic. "This will work, right? She liked the movie. It has to work."

Fisher swallowed and I saw his whole throat bob with it. "It'll work."

Booth rubbed his hands over his thighs. "My hands are sweating. A lot. Why are my hands sweating so much?"

"Yeah, now that you mention it, I'm feeling a little warm back here. Is the heat on too high?" Fisher grabbed his shirt and pulled it out to fan himself with it. "Wow, I'm burning up."

"I think I need to reapply deodorant before we do this." Booth sniffed his armpit and groaned. "I think I'm going to throw up. Whose idea was this again?"

"It's too late to change your plan now, boys. We're here." Dad sounded way too happy about sending us into a full blown panic. "You'd better hurry. If word spreads that Vaughn Adler is back in town, Ella won't be able to hear you over the screaming."

I glared at him. "You're not helping."

"Never said I would." He singsonged with a giant smile on his face. "Go get her, boys."

Fisher made a sound that was suspiciously similar to a gag and opened his door. "God, I hate us."

"Which window is hers?" Booth looked up at the small cottage house and looked at my dad. "Do you know?"

"I texted and asked for the address, kid, not a blueprint of the house."

I glared at Dad. "You're enjoying this too much."

Fisher was in control of the music. He had the song ready on his phone. Booth and I stood on either side of him and we positioned ourselves in front of the left window, taking a guess on it being the right room. We'd just won a championship game that morning and there we were, all about to vomit while singing a Taylor Swift song.

Fisher didn't give us longer to panic. He hit play and we went for it.

57

Ella

I'd just put on my pajamas and washed my face when I heard what sounded like cats fighting from somewhere outside the house. I knew out neighbors didn't have cats so I slowly moved closer to the sound and ended up in Mom's doorway. "What *is* that?"

She was kneeling on her window seat, peeking out of the blinds. When she looked back at me, her face was bright red and she was laughing so hard she had her legs crossed and her hand pressed over her middle.

"What?" I walked over and pulled one of the blinds down, just to let it snap back into place. My entire body lit up with a mixture of excitement and horror. "No."

Mom pushed me away. "Go out there and make them stop. They're going to wake the dead."

"What are they doing?!" I looked out again and saw a neighbor's lights turn on behind them. "Oh, my god. How are they here? What is happening?"

"Go! Here comes Mr. Daniels! He's never going to shut up about this."

I rushed to the front door, full of nerves, and quietly stepped outside. Booth, Vaughn, and Fisher were standing in front of Mom's window, their attention focused there so they didn't notice me standing there, watching them. Fisher had his phone over his head and they were screaming "*Lover*".

I covered my mouth to stop a laugh as more of our neighbors started coming outside to shout at the guys to shut up. Mr. Daniels was in the middle of the street, shaking his cane at them.

"People are trying to sleep! What do you even call yourselves doing out here? Is this some sort of gang thing?"

The quiet neighborhood had been disrupted in a big way. Dogs barked, people shouted, and then there was just the sound of them continuing to sing. I realized quickly that they were blessed with a lot of things but harmony wasn't one of them. And then there was the sound of laughter coming from the end of our driveway. Paul was standing next to his truck, doubled over as he cackled.

Vaughn stopped singing to turn on his dad. "Jesus Christ, Dad! Stop laughing! We're trying!"

"Shut the hell up!" That shout came from Mrs. Conner, two doors down.

When someone shouted that they were calling the police, I found my voice again. "Did you guys come here just to get arrested for disturbing the peace?"

Three heads snapped in my direction and the singing stopped just like that. I watched as they each sent a hopeful smile my way before slowly moving closer to me.

"We want you back, Ella Rae. We care about you and we'd do anything for you. Including going to jail for disturbing the peace." Fisher turned his phone off and winced. "I'd really like to stop singing now, though."

"Please, do." I saw that Mom had opened her window and was hanging out of it. "You're lovely boys but you're never going to make it as singers. At least not together."

Vaughn ducked his head and lifted his hand in a surprisingly shy wave. "Hi, Ms. Daughton."

Mom rolled her eyes. "Focus on my daughter. I'm just here for the show."

"Same. Got any popcorn?" Paul called out as he came closer.

"I didn't know you were coming, too. What a surprise." Mom was smiling despite how sarcastic she sounded. "Let yourself in. There's a bag of chips on the counter."

"Mom!"

"Dad!"

Paul hurried up the driveway and gave me a tight hug and a kiss on the head. "Give 'em hell, Ellie."

I watched as he went inside and the four of us remaining outside waited to see if he was going to appear in the window next to my mom and we weren't disappointed. Paul stuck his head out and gave the guys a thumbs up.

Vaughn groaned and turned to me. Before he could say anything, the sound of a siren in the distance clued us all in on the fact that someone really had called the cops.

I reacted like I was hiding drugs on my body. I sprinted to the front door, yanked it open, and motioned for them all to get inside. They ran inside and I slammed and locked the door behind them before turning out the lights on my way to my room. "If the cops come, you have to deal with them, Mom! Not it!"

The guys followed me into my room without prompting and I shut the door behind them, locking that one, too. I switched my bedroom light off, leaving just my bedside lamp on. The four of us were in my small room, in what could pass as mood lighting, and we were all breathing faster from the excitement. I looked at each of them and tried to cover my mouth to hide a snort but there was no helping it.

We all erupted in laughter and it was fun until I started crying. It was so random and embarrassing that I tried to play it off but Booth pulled me into his chest and held me tight. I held him just as tight as I cried into his chest.

"It's okay, Ella. We're here." He took a deep breath and I sniffed and shot him a curious glance when I realized he was smelling me. "Sorry. I just missed the way you smell."

"It's okay." I shrugged and breathed his scent in like I wanted to. We stood there, sniffing each other, for probably longer than was acceptable, before Fisher got impatient and pulled me away from Booth.

He hugged me but it didn't seem like enough for him so he picked me up and held the back of my thighs as I wrapped my limbs around him. "I've missed everything about you. I just want you back, Ella. I would do anything to erase the last month. Everything is gray without you."

I clung to him as I just let myself enjoy being held by them again before talking. I waited for Vaughn to demand his turn but when he didn't, I glanced over and saw that he was standing next to the head of my bed, running his hand over Connie. Fisher let me down and I inched closer to Vaughn. "You fixed him."

Vaughn shrugged. "It was my fault he was hurt in the first place. I'm sorry I didn't do it better. There-"

"He's perfect." I closed the gap between us and gently wrapped my arms around his waist. Pressing my cheek to his chest, I could feel his heart racing. "I opened the bag this morning finally. I wasn't ready before."

He stood with his arms at his sides still, not holding me back yet. "And you are now? Ready?"

I just had to nod and he grabbed me in a fierce embrace. He bent to me, burying his face in the crook of my neck and letting out a groan filled with pain.

"I'm so sorry, Ella. I swear that I'll never knowingly or willingly hurt you again." He ran his nose up my throat and pressed a kiss to my jaw. "I just want to take care of you and listen to you laugh. I never want to be the reason you cry again."

I tipped my mouth towards his, desperate to feel his lips on mine but before we connected, a loud knock on my door made me flinch away. "Yes?"

Mom swung the door open and smiled sweetly. "This is going to be an open door house tonight. While I appreciate a good round of makeup sex, I can't know that it's happening to my daughter, just a room away from me. You boys will be sleeping in the living room tonight and Paul will be sleeping in the hallway, in case you get any ideas."

"And what if Paul gets any ideas?" It wasn't that I wanted to do anything sexual when my mom was in the next room but I wanted to be held and it was too weird to do even that where my mom could see.

Paul stuck his head in next to Mom. "If Paul gets any ideas, your mother's door will be locked. I've been informed that the only Daughton woman that takes a man back is in this room tonight."

I shrugged. "I'm not making any promises yet but these three won a championship game today. What have you done lately?"

Vaughn wrapped his arm around my waist and then immediately let it fall away when Mom shot him a look. "Yep. Too weird. Sorry."

"I'm not going to remind you that the last time you were in my house, you were my step-son, young man." Mom wagged her finger at him. "And I'm not sure I've forgiven you three just yet. You made my baby cry. And, Vaughn, if whatever you did to Connie makes him come to life and start cutting people, I'm going to be pissed."

Fisher laughed a deep belly laugh. "I told him he needed to watch a video."

Paul eased past Mom and looked at Connie. His eyes were damp when he looked at his son. "You did good, son."

58

Ella

"You said you weren't making any promises yet." Booth looked up at me from where he sat on my bedroom floor, the only place they could be without my mom fluttering by every five seconds. "You don't have to do anything you're not ready for. I just want to know if you're willing to give us another chance. I need to hear you say it."

I hugged Connie tighter, fighting every urge to be in Booth's lap. "I'm giving us another chance, Booth. Mom gave me a lecture about forgiveness today that kind of made sense. And I think… I think it was just time. I was running out of steam. What you did sucked. What happened because of it sucked. I don't think you would make the same mistake again, though."

Vaughn reached up and rested his hand on my knee. "Never."

I swallowed my pride and laced my fingers through his. "I'm sorry for what I said to you. You were never a mistake, Vaughn. I never should've said that. When that stuff happened with Billy in The Swamp, I was just panicking and I could see people looking at us and it felt like the end of the world for people to find out about us and judge me."

"Then I went and made your fears come true." He rested his forehead on my bed and sighed. "You don't have to apologize. This whole thing was my fault. You wouldn't have been panicked about people finding out if I hadn't gone psycho when Billy touched you. I caused all of this. I'm sorry to each of you."

I had to touch him. Running my fingers through his hair, I gently scratched his scalp and watched Booth and Fisher. "Did he tell you that he tried to throw himself on the sword for you guys? He tried to shoulder the blame for everything and send me back to you two."

Fisher leaned over and punched Vaughn in the thigh. "Fuck that. We're a package deal. We all fucked up. We all made choices that hurt Ella."

Mom strolled by. "Language, boys."

"Shit. I mean, sorry. Sorry, Ms. Daughton." Fisher flinched when Mom reappeared in the doorway. It seemed like he was a little afraid of Mom.

"I'm fucking kidding!"

I waited until she left to slip to the floor between them. "I like that, what you said. You guys *are* a package deal. I don't know how I would pick just one of you."

Fisher inched closer. "You don't have to. This is okay with us."

"Just us, though. To be clear." Booth looked at me with a sternness that I wasn't used to from him and it sent a shiver down my spine. "We accept each other getting to share you. No one else."

I gave up fighting the urge and crawled into his lap. I sat sideways, though, in hopes that Mom would leave us be. "Have I ever given you the impression that I would ever want anyone else? I have what feels like half of the football team here. I'm not *that* greedy."

He pressed his forehead to mine. "Just making sure."

Fisher rubbed my back but I could see that his mind was still on Vaughn. "You would've sacrificed yourself like that for us?"

Vaughn nodded. "It was my fault."

Booth kissed the tip of my nose and sighed before lifting me and settling me back down in Vaughn's lap. "If you were willing to do that for us, the least we can do is let you two take a moment to make sure you're okay.

Fisher and I will try to distract the parents for a few minutes. Think they'd fall for me and Fish insisting on doing live replays of the game?"

Fisher scoffed. "Who wouldn't? We're division champions, man!"

Vaughn brought my hand up to his lips and kissed my fingertips as they left. I glanced over and saw that they'd pulled the door shut before shifting so I was straddling him. He groaned but kept his touches PG.

"Are we okay?" He searched my face. "I feel like I'm up against a mountain because of the ex step siblings thing. I heard what people called you. And I know that no one said a thing about me the whole time, when I'd done the same thing as you. Me being a part of this makes shit harder for you. I don't want to hurt you in any way, Ella, but what if me just being me hurts you?"

I nodded because he was right. To an extent. "It does make things a little harder. It just doesn't change the fact that I want to be with you, Vaughn. I won't pretend like it wasn't brutal to be called the things I was called, but I made it through it. Partly because of you three threatening to maim or murder people. At least that's what I assumed you threatened because they all just stopped doing it to my face immediately.

"Maybe some people will always hear that you were my stepbrother for three years and think less of me. Those same people would probably think less of me for something, no matter what. At least if it's this, I'll be able to face them knowing you have my back. And that this thing between us is worth it. At least *I* think it is."

He shook his head as a slow smile stretched his lips. "How do you do that? I should be begging you for a second chance and you've already gotten past that and are onto facing the future. For someone who isn't supposed to be good at forgiving, you're damn good at it."

"For you." I shrugged one shoulder at him. "And for them."

"Thank you. I'll earn that forgiveness."

I ran my hands through his hair and gripped it tight so I could lift his face to mine. Lowering my mouth until our lips were a breath apart, I tried to be as clear as possible. "You don't need to earn anything. It's already been given. Now it's time for you to forgive yourself. You're not less than Booth or Fisher to me. I love each of you-"

Vaughn cut me off with a kiss that was possessive and made me feel worshiped. He held my face in his hands and stroked his tongue over mine, tasting me like he'd never get full. He hardened under me and I rolled my hips over him, forgetting where we were entirely. It was Vaughn who kept his composure.

He eased the kiss to an end and gripped my hips to keep me still. "You have no idea how much I need to bury myself inside of you, Ella Rae, but our parents are in the next room and I'm pretty sure your mom's crazy enough to hurt me."

I pressed my forehead to his shoulder and whimpered. My body didn't understand where the orgasms had gone for a month and why it couldn't pick them back up already. "I just want-"

"You said you love us." He felt me stiffen and laughed, a sound of pure happiness. "You said it, Ella Rae. You said you love us!"

I covered his mouth with my hand and glared at him. "Be quiet! I didn't mean to say it. It just slipped out. I'm not ready to scream it to everyone. I mean, we're just getting back together. It's too soon. I need to get to know you guys even better. We need to date. We haven't even been on a date. I can't say it yet. That's crazy, Vaughn. So you just have to stay quiet about it. Okay? *Okay*?"

He licked my hand and when I yanked it away, he grinned at me with pure chaos in his eyes. I barely realized we were moving until he'd dumped me on my bed and ran to my door. I jumped up and chased him and quickly found myself in a pile of bodies just outside of my door.

I heard Mom groan in pain. "Someone's knee is on my boob."

"Someone's boob is on my knee." Paul grunted back at her.

I gave up and just let myself lay there, on top of them. "This is my second human body pile-up and I have to say, I much prefer being on top."

"That's what she said?" Fisher let out his own groan of pain. "Sorry. If I don't joke, I'll cry. I think my dick is broken. I mean penis. My penis is broken."

"Shut up, man." Booth crawled out from the pile and easily scooped me up. "I prefer you on top, too."

"Hello?! Her mother is right here, big boy!"

"God, no, I just meant... I didn't mean it like that." Booth's face was a nice, deep red.

"Don't call him big boy like that, Mom. It's weird."

"Oh? Is it weird? Well, I'm pretty sure it's weirder that I have my head nearly up one of your boyfriend's asses while somehow straddling another of your boyfriend's dad." Mom held up a hand. "Get me out of this human centipede in the making, big boy."

Booth grabbed her and pulled her up. "Yes, ma'am. Sorry about that."

Vaughn was across Fisher's back and he rolled over his shoulders and head to get up. Fisher grunted and punched him. It was a calamity of massive proportions. When everyone was back on their feet, I looked around and narrowed my eyes.

"Why was everyone just outside of my bedroom door?"

Mom crossed her arms. "Why was your door closed?"

"I asked you first."

Fisher surprised me by wrapping his arms around me and picking me up. "You said you love us."

I groaned. "You guys were spying? What the hell? I expect it from my mother, but et tu, Paul? Fisher? Booth?"

"And I heard that line about you being inside my daughter, Vaughn. Not cool." Mom slapped his chest and then looked at Paul. "He gets that from you. You always had a filthy mouth, too."

"Mom!" I pushed away from Fisher and tried to push Mom into her room. "Go to your room, young lady."

She reversed the move and pushed me into my room. "Nice try. It's late and we've got a big meal to cook tomorrow. I can't trust you four to not push the rules. Everyone, go to sleep."

I groaned. "Wait. I need-"

"You don't need anything. Say goodnight." Mom pushed me out of the way and shut the door, cutting me off before I could say anything else to the guys.

I sighed and crossed my arms. I'd forgiven the guys and I was ready to spend time with them to make up for the month we'd been apart. Mom wasn't having any of it, though. I knew her tones well from years of pushing her and I knew she meant business. I also knew that I'd just accidentally told Vaughn that I loved them and I felt an urgent need to make sure it wasn't too much, too soon.

"I can still hear you breathing next to the door. Get in your bed and go to sleep or I'm not making the green bean casserole tomorrow." Mom knew my weakness.

"Fine, fine. I'm going."

59

Ella

I slept like the dead for the first time in a month. When I did wake up, it was close to noon and the house was alive with the sounds of Mom bossing the guys around. I took care of my bathroom needs and brushed my teeth before venturing out to join everyone.

Mom had the guys bent over the kitchen island, picking through a giant mound of pecans. She swung her way over to me and wrapped me in a tight hug when she spotted me. "Good morning, baby. Or should I say good afternoon? How you do feel?"

I stretched and blushed when I saw Vaughn's eyes drop to my exposed midriff. "I feel good. What are you guys doing?"

"They're picking out the best pecans." Mom grinned at me. "For the pecan pie."

Booth straightened and rubbed his back. "Your mom is tougher than Coach. She woke us up bright and early to start this."

I laughed out loud and shook my head. "Stop! She's just messing with you. She buys our pecan pie from a bakery in town. Even if she did make it from scratch, you wouldn't need to go through all these pecans. Where did you even get so many pecans?"

Vaughn slowly stood up and blew out a slow breath. "Are you shitting me?"

Mom circled the island, patting their butts with a cookie sheet and shooing them away. "Think about this next time you consider making a choice that could make my daughter cry. This is nothing. The punishments I can come up with would make the CIA wet."

I groaned. "Mom. Jeez."

Paul strolled in from outside with a grocery bag in hand. He kissed the top of my head and then strolled over to Mom and did the same to her. "Hey. I missed you while I was out."

Mom giggled and wrapped her arms around his waist. "You were barely gone, sweet cheeks. I missed you, too, though."

Vaughn's gaze crashed into mine and we both turned to our parents, horrified looks firmly in place. "Dad. What the hell?"

"You can't do this! Vaughn and I were together first this time so you have to cut this out. I can't actually sleep with my stepbrother. Dear god, no." I shook my head hard enough for it to knock my ponytail loose. "You two need to stop it. Put some distance between you and remember why you got divorced in the first place."

Mom and Paul stared at me for a few seconds and then they both laughed like I'd said the funniest thing ever. Paul took a few steps away from Mom, thank goodness, and both of them wiped their eyes as tears of laughter leaked out.

Vaughn looked at me and frowned. "We'll just disown them."

"I'm not ready for this yet. I'm going to go shower and get ready for the day and when I come back, this won't be weird anymore." I started to leave and then stopped. I moved to each of the guys and kissed them on the cheek before going back to my bedroom.

The next time I entered the kitchen I was better prepared for my mom's antics. Dressed in my favorite sweater and leggings, I felt cozy and the appreciative looks on the guys' faces made me feel cute, too.

They were sitting on the couch, half of their attention on the TV, where a football game was on, and the other half on me. I felt a wave of awareness and need coursing through my body. I wanted to be alone with them desperately.

"Do the potatoes, baby." Mom handed me the potato ricer and nodded to the stove. "Cooking wasn't half as bad with Paul's help. I forgot how good he is in the kitchen."

I expected an innuendo so I waited but when she didn't make a joke, I couldn't help staring at her. "Are the two of you really-"

"God, no." She grinned. "It was fun to mess with you kids, though. The boys have been shitting themselves all morning. Vaughn's eyes nearly popped out of his head every time Paul touched me."

I shivered. "Not a funny joke."

"You know I don't take men back. Paul's great, but he seems happy with his new girlfriend." Mom shot a look over her shoulder at me. "Plus... I've been out on a few dates with Charlie Mallard. He's nice."

I barely caught the ricer after I dropped it in shock. "Nice? You just called a man nice? Holy crap. You like a guy."

"Yeah. He's coming over later tonight to have a late Thanksgiving dinner with me." Her smile was softer than I'd seen it in years.

"I get to meet him already? Wow. It took you over a year to introduce Paul to me."

Paul slipped into the kitchen and ruffled my hair. "That's because your mom was afraid I was too good to be true. These looks? A good job? Funny and charming, too? How could she not be afraid I wasn't real?"

Mom snorted. "And I was right. Turns out you farted and didn't clean just like the rest of them."

"Ignoring your mother's nasty comments regarding my hygiene... You actually won't be meeting your mom's new boyfriend tonight."

"He's not my boyfriend."

"Why not? Are you guys going to lock me in my room again? I'll agree if you let the guys come in with me."

Paul grinned. "I was supposed to be spending my holiday with my girlfriend in a remote cabin at the top of a mountain. Since those plans were hijacked by young love, I'm just going to meet her at her place. Since you kids need some time to talk without your parents listening in, I thought it would be nice for you to take the cabin."

I forgot all about the potatoes. "You're letting us go to a cabin? Today?"

"Yep. Your mom and I have ulterior motives, of course, but just consider us the best parents ever. We're supportive of your untraditional relationship and we're progressive enough to not even have nightmares about what might happen at the cabin." He made a face and cleared his throat. "You'll have to drop me off at the airport first, but then you'll be free from us."

"Do the guys know?"

Paul nodded. "They seem pretty excited."

"Of course, they are. My baby is a catch and they know they're lucky that she forgave them." Mom sniffed and wiped her eyes. "You're going away for your first sex trip and I'm just so proud of you."

"Jesus Christ." Paul shook his head and took over the potatoes. "Go be with the guys, Ellie. I'll help your mom finish up here."

I hugged them both tight. "I love you guys. I'm going to drag them away from the TV. We'll be outside."

"We'll come get you when it's done. Try not to scandalize the neighbors' kids, honey." Mom pushed me away and sniffed again. "Too many onions. I'm not crying."

I hurried into the living room and crooked my finger at the guys. "Come with me."

60

Ella

It was shockingly easy to steal them away from the TV. They all followed me with matching expressions of eagerness. I led them around the side of the house and to the picnic table in the backyard. It was a lot colder than it'd been on campus and it only took one teeth chatter for Booth to take his hoodie off and pull it over my head.

"You're going to be cold now." I lifted the neck of the hoodie to my nose and inhaled his warm scent. "But I'm never giving this back."

He wrapped his arms around me from behind and leaned against the side of the table. "Good."

"So..." I looked back and forth between Fisher and Vaughn. "We're going to a mountain cabin?"

Vaughn smirked. "Excited?"

I nodded. "I don't know what I'm more excited about. You guys or the cabin itself."

Fisher stepped closer to me and gently cupped my face. "Be more excited about us."

I shrugged. "Maybe."

He closed the distance between our mouths and kissed me then, putting all of his effort into making sure it was him that I was most excited about.

He only pulled back when the sound of a kid screaming broke the silence around us. "I hate that kid."

Laughing, I looked over and saw one of our neighbors watching us with her mouth hanging open. I covered my face and laughed. "Oh, god. We're causing a scene."

Vaughn tugged me into his arms and dipped me. Smiling down at me, he looked happier than I could ever remember seeing him. "Let's really give her something to talk about."

I weaved my fingers into his hair and nodded. I'd already faced a month of ridicule on campus. One shocked neighbor wasn't going to scare me away. I drank in his kiss and smiled into it, the feeling of everything being okay so nice that I didn't think I'd ever stop smiling.

"You're happy?" He pulled me up and kissed me once more. "Really happy?"

"Really, really happy." I moved back into Booth's arms and stood between his thighs while stretching up to kiss him. His big hand cupped the back of my head and I moaned when his other hand cupped my ass.

"When we get to the cabin tonight, we're going to talk about what you said last night." Booth trailed kisses down my jaw and growled. "About how you love us."

I clutched his shirt in my hands and tilted my head to offer him more of my neck. "We don't have to do that. We can just cuddle in front of a fire. Yeah? Yeah. I'm glad we agree."

His hand moved lower on my ass until he was cupping the bottom curve and his fingers dipped between my thighs. "We'll cuddle. After we talk. And probably after we figure out just how this is going to work."

I hadn't been touched in far too long. I squeezed my eyes shut and nodded. "Sure. Whatever you say."

"Are you ready for all three of us, Ella Rae?" Booth tightened his grip and then let me go completely at the sudden sound of my mom's voice coming from the front of the house. When I shot him a frustrated look, he smiled sheepishly. "Your mom is scary."

"Ella Rae!" Mom came around the side of the house just as I separated from Booth. She put her hands on her hips and shook her head. "Did you eat the bag of marshmallows? Those were for the sweet potatoes."

I groaned. "I'm sorry! I was sad!"

Vaughn stepped forward. "So it's my fault. I'll run to the store and buy some."

Mom suddenly smiled and walked over to pinch his cheeks. "You were always such a good boy. Even when you weren't. I already sent your dad. I had to get him out of my hair. He wouldn't stop talking about his new girlfriend. I'm starting to think he made her up."

"Does your neighbor always scowl like that?" Fisher nodded to the neighbor who'd been staring the whole time we were outside and lifted his hand in a wave. "Oh, shit. Here she comes."

The woman was a new neighbor that I didn't recognize and from the look on her face, she wasn't very happy about us. "There are children in this neighborhood and what's happening here is shameful."

My mom was a lot of things. She was wildly inappropriate, way too into talking about sex, my most loyal supporter, and she was one hundred percent momma bear. She was wearing a frilly pink apron and had her hair curled to perfection, all while wearing a pair of heels that I would've died in. She looked like the picture of a lady that I was sure our neighbor expected. Until she opened her mouth.

"Look here, lady. If you think you're going to come into my yard and judge my daughter and her boyfriends, you're sadly mistaken." Mom yanked off her apron and marched closer to the woman. "I suggest you take your shitty ass attitude and your bad perm back home before you piss me off. Shameful. Ha! What's shameful is your lack of ability to see something you don't like and shut the fuck up."

"I see all the men coming and going at all hours of the night. It's no wonder she turned out like she did. *Slut*. You need Jesus." The woman's face had gone bright red. "And watch your language!"

I hurried after Mom and wrapped my arm around her waist. "Okay, let's not go to jail on Thanksgiving for beating up an old lady, Mom."

"Ma'am, I think maybe you should go back in your house before my girlfriend's mom opens up a can of whoop-ass on you. I think your open ignorance and pride in that ignorance is pushing her buttons." Booth had silently moved across the yard and put himself between Mom and the neighbor. "Also, Jesus doesn't like ugly."

"And in case my buddy's kind suggestion doesn't cut it for you, here it is with a little more directness." Vaughn crossed his arms and stood next to Booth. "Beat it. Your opinion isn't wanted and if you call my girlfriend or her mom a slut again I'm going to let her take a few swings at you."

Fisher was all grins as he picked both me and Mom up to carry us towards the house. "I feel like I never left Florida at all."

Mom flipped off her neighbor as we were carried away like rowdy toddlers. "If she calls my daughter a slut one more time I'm going to go Florida Man all over that lady!"

I couldn't help laughing. It was the most ridiculous fight ever but seeing my support system in action was heart-warming. "To be fair, I think she was calling *you* a slut."

"You're not too old to spank, Ella Rae Daughton. It was definitely *you* she was calling a slut." Mom patted Fisher's arm when he put us down inside the house. "Wow. You're strong."

I sniffed the air and frowned. "Mom? Is something burning?"

"Fuck!" Mom took off towards the kitchen, grumbling all the way. "Stupid woman. Made me burn my Thanksgiving dinner. I should get a dog and let it shit in her yard every day. My damn green bean casserole is ruined and she's worried about my language and who I screw. There are more important things in the world, asshole!"

Fisher's grin stretched from ear to ear. "This is the best Thanksgiving ever."

61

Ella

The casserole wasn't salvageable. I stared at the place it would've sat on the table and sighed. It was my favorite part and our rude neighbor had ruined it.

"I swear to god, Ella, if you don't stop sighing over that green bean casserole, I'm going to kick our neighbor's door in and lose my shit on her." Mom shoved the sweet potatoes at me. "I'll make you one for Christmas. A personal one, just for her."

"Do you think *she* has green bean casserole?"

Paul cleared his throat. "Ellie, you're going to get your mother locked up for murder if you don't give it a rest. How about we go around and talk about what we're grateful for? It's cheesy but I'd suggest smoking crack right now if I thought it would lower your mother's blood pressure."

"My blood pressure is fine. Everything is fine. I'm just thinking of ways to get back at that woman." Mom saw Paul shake his head and shoved a piece of turkey into her mouth. "I'm super grateful that I didn't burn the turkey."

"There you go." Paul looked to me. "Ellie?"

I sat up straighter and smiled at Mom. "I'm grateful that I have a mom who'd literally fist fight someone for insulting me. And even if the green bean casserole got burned, I'm grateful for the leftover bag of dried onions."

"Okay. Vaughn. Your turn." Paul pointed to his son with his glass of wine clutched firmly in his hand.

"Sorry if mine isn't as sour as the first two." Vaughn laughed as both me and Mom shot him a dirty look. "I'm grateful to be here. I wasn't sure I would be."

The green bean casserole was forgotten. I reached under the table and took his hand. "That's really sweet. I'm grateful you're here, too."

"I'm grateful that you didn't give up on us. And for you, Ms. Daughton, for being so accepting of us. Sure, you made us pick through pecans for hours, but we deserved that." Booth cleared his throat. "I've had to spend every Thanksgiving away from my mom because of football and normally I spend the day feeling like shit. Like crap, I mean. Today hasn't been like that at all."

I could feel Mom melt at the same time as me. Booth was a massive guy who looked like he could take on the world but he was such a teddy bear inside. A teddy bear who missed his mom. Before I could get up to hug him, Mom did. She ended up squeezing his head against her chest and gently rocking it back and forth. I heard Vaughn try to stifle a laugh as we watched Booth try to figure out what to do with my mom's boobs in his face.

"Mom. Boobs." I saw Booth's cheeks turn bright red and snorted the water I'd just taken a sip of up my nose. Choking and sputtering up water at the Thanksgiving table wasn't exactly how I planned the day to go, but it fit in with everything else happening.

Mom let go of Booth and rolled her eyes. "They're not boobs when a mom is hugging a kid."

"They are when the kid isn't your kid." Paul grinned. "This is coming from a guy who had a lot of friends with hot moms."

"I'm grateful for how bizarre today has been!" Fisher's raised voice silenced the rest of the room, minus my random coughs. "Maybe it hasn't been a traditional Thanksgiving, but it's been real. My family dinners have always been so stiff and proper. No one would've ever dared to talk about boobs. And no one would've ever gotten into a fight with the neighbor and threatened to kick an old woman's ass. I want to spend all my holidays here."

Mom moved over to him and hugged his head the same way she had Booth's. "You boys are just so sweet. I'm so glad you came to your senses and came crawling back to my daughter."

Fisher's voice was muffled as he spoke. "This also definitely wouldn't happen at my family's dinner. We don't even hug, much less boob hug."

I looked over at Vaughn. "Don't say anything sweet or you'll be next with the boobs."

"Does it work on you?" He wagged his brows and then winced when Paul smacked the back of his head. "What? What'd I say?"

"I'm grateful that in just a few hours, I'm going to be with my girlfriend and away from this circus. Not that I don't love you guys. I do. I just love my sanity, too." Paul barely dodged a roll Mom tossed at his head.

"We get it. You have a girlfriend. We totally believe you." Mom sat back down and picked up her fork, pointing with it as she spoke. "I'm pretty excited about my Charlie coming over tonight. He's actually real."

While Mom and Paul dissolved into an argument about who was more likely to create a fake partner, I reached over and took Mom's wine glass. I took a long sip and looked around. Paul was right about it being a circus. It was *my* circus, though, and I'd never been happier.

"Think we could just sneak out and get on the road?" Vaughn scooted his chair closer to mine and leaned in to whisper in my ear. "I'm also very, very grateful that I'm going to be buried inside you in just a few hours. Probably the most grateful out of anyone here. I'm just riddled with gratitude over it."

I blushed and pushed him away. "You can't say things like that at the same table as our parents. I think that's probably illegal. At the least, it's morally questionable."

"You can sue me when you're a big time lawyer." He sat back in his chair when he noticed our parents coming to the end of their argument. "What time do we need to drop you off at the airport, Dad?"

A knock came from the front door and all of our heads turned to stare in the direction of it. I sank down in my chair as I assumed it was the cops coming to arrest us for threatening our neighbor. When no one else moved, Paul stood up.

He drained his wine and shook his head. "Nobody hurt yourself racing to get the door."

Mom met my gaze. "If it's the cops, we were never outside. We're innocent and we've never even seen that lady next door."

"I heard from a different neighbor that she's not well." Fisher nodded gravely. "It's sad, really. She used to be such a presence in the neighborhood. Now she spends her days in imaginary fights with her neighbors."

I had to pick my jaw up off the floor. "That's terrifying. You're bad. I mean, you're amazing, but you're bad."

Vaughn grunted. "He'll never lie to you but lying *for* you? He's the best. He's gotten us out of so much shit."

"Um... April?" We all turned to look at the man standing next to Paul with a bouquet of flowers in his hand. "Did I get the time wrong?"

Mom stood up so fast that her chair fell over backwards. "Oh, Charlie! We were supposed to meet later today... You're here, though. Which is great. Let me introduce you to everyone."

I watched in awe as Mom blushed when Charlie hugged her and gave her the flowers. I couldn't remember a time when a man made her blush.

"This is my daughter, Ella. These are her boyfriends. Booth, Fisher, and Vaughn." Mom cleared her throat. "And this is my ex-husband, Paul. He's only here because he's Vaughn's dad."

Paul snorted. "And here I was thinking I was here for my charming personality."

Charlie looked a little shell shocked but he recovered fairly quickly. "Nice to meet everyone. I'm really sorry for intruding. I can go and come back later. I don't want to take time away from your daughter."

I smiled at him, liking him already. "We're leaving soon, anyway. I'd feel a lot better knowing I wasn't leaving Mom here alone. Especially after she tried to fight the neighbor earlier."

"Ella!" Mom groaned. "I didn't try to fight her. She called Ella a terrible name, though."

"She called *you* a terrible name." I laughed, thoroughly enjoying getting to embarrass Mom for a change. "Stay for dinner, Charlie. I hope you don't like green bean casserole. Mom burned it."

62

Vaughn

I glanced in the rearview mirror at Ella and saw that she'd nodded off. We'd dropped Dad off at the airport and gotten on the road to the cabin but we'd spent more time with Ella's mom and Charlie than we'd meant to, so it was late. The mountain road leading up to the cabin was only lit by the truck's headlights and the full moon overhead. It curved and wound around the mountain as it slowly took us higher and higher. Just when I was starting to worry that the GPS was broken, I saw the sign for the cabin.

Booth breathed out a sigh of relief from next to me. "I was convinced that we were lost."

"Dad couldn't have picked a more remote cabin. There hasn't been another house for miles." I turned down a narrow driveway with trees on either side, encroaching into the dirt road. "Well, if this is where we die, at least it'll be under a pretty cool night sky."

Ella woke up when the road got rough and the truck jolted her. "Where are we?"

Fisher leaned forward from the back seat and grunted. "Pretty sure Vaughn's dad is a serial killer and this is where he was going to kill his girlfriend."

"Nice, Fish." I fought to keep the truck from sliding off some of the deeper ruts and scraping along the line of trees. By the time the road opened up and revealed a cabin, my shoulders were tense and I was silently cursing Dad for renting a murder cabin.

"Whoa." Ella unbuckled and scooted forward. "It's cute!"

I shot Booth a look after I parked in front of the small cabin. I wasn't sure it was cute. With no lights on, the place looked creepy. I didn't get a chance to look more than a quick glance, though, before Ella threw open her door and rushed towards the porch. "Ella!"

Stopping in the truck's headlights, she looked back at us and grinned. "Come on! I want to see the inside! Do you think there's electricity or will we have to light candles? That'd be so pretty!"

Booth swore under his breath as he rushed after her. I waited to cut the truck off until I saw him grab a key from the lockbox next to the door and unlock it. Once I saw a light come on inside, I cut the headlights and grabbed our bags.

Fisher hung back with me and looked around at the pitch black forest surrounding us. "This is going to be embarrassing but tell me why I'm feeling more anxious about what's going to happen inside the cabin than I am about what's in these woods out here."

I stopped with one foot on the first step of the porch. "What do you mean?"

"Have you ever shared a woman with two of your buddies? Because I haven't. There's a lot of logistical shit that I'm worried about." He sounded stressed. "It's got to be good. If it's bad and she decides this isn't a good idea, I-"

Ella poked her head out of the cabin. "Come on, slow pokes! It's so cute! There's electricity and running water, so don't worry about that."

I smiled as she disappeared into the cabin again. "She loves us."

He took a deep breath and slowly blew it out. "You're right."

"We'll figure the rest out." I rolled my shoulders. "I'm nervous, too. There's a lot of dicks in my near future and I can promise you that I never thought I'd say anything like that."

"The time with me, Booth, and Ella was easy. It's not like we're going to be swinging our dicks all over the place. If our dicks touch, we're doing something wrong." He shuddered. "Just to be clear, that's not what I'm signing up for."

I punched him in the arm. "No shit, asshole. What in our four years of friendship would make you think that I might be signing up for touching dicks with you?"

Ella stuck her head out again. "Okay, I'm hearing parts of your conversation and I feel like I'm hearing a lot of talk about touching each other's dicks."

"What the fuck is going on out there?" Booth's voice boomed from inside the cabin. "That's not what I signed up for."

"None of us signed up for that! Jesus." I stomped up the porch steps and stopped in front of Ella. "You're a pain."

Her lips turned up in a wide smile. "I know."

Fisher followed me inside. "For the record, we were talking about *not* touching each other's dicks."

Booth shot us a glare from across the room. "That isn't something we need to clarify. I don't need to state that I'm not going to touch fire but you know I'm not going to touch fire."

"We were talking logistics, asshole." I dropped the bags on the big leather couch separating the living room from the small dining room. "This place doesn't look so murdery inside."

Ignoring our dick talk, Ella spun around in a circle as she looked at everything. "It's not murdery at all. It's adorable. Look at the fireplace. And there's a hot tub on the back deck! The shower in the bathroom is big enough for all of us, too. It's huge!"

I smiled at how genuinely excited she was. "The hot tub sounds pretty good."

She stepped into my space and rubbed her hands up my shoulders. Her mouth turned down as she dug her fingers into my tense muscles. "You're all tight. Let's get in the hot tub and loosen you up."

I settled my hands on her hips. "You really want to get in the hot tub, huh?"

She kissed my chin. "Yep."

I looked over at her bag. "Do you have a swimsuit in there?"

She shook her head. "Nope."

Fisher pumped the air behind her. "Let's hot tub."

63

Ella

I watched the guys strip down to their boxer briefs and climb into the hot tub while I shivered from the cold. The hot tub seemed like a good idea when I wasn't standing on the back porch with an icy breeze chilling me to the bone. The only thing that motivated me to pull my clothes off was the vision of the guys and their bare chests.

Stripping down to just my panties, I quickly climbed into the tub and sank down to my neck. The water melted me and I groaned out loud. "Oh, my god. That's heaven."

Fisher was closest to me and he took advantage of it by pulling me into his lap. He wrapped his arms around my stomach and nuzzled his mouth against my neck. "That's a sight I'll play over and over again in my head for the rest of my life. Your body is beautiful, Ella Rae."

I shivered and tried to sink lower into the water. "My body is freezing cold. Am I an idiot?"

He grunted. "Well. You're here with us, so...maybe?"

I laughed and then locked eyes with Vaughn. "For that, Fisher, I'm leaving you."

Vaughn let me pull him away from the corner seat he was on and laughed when I took his spot but pulled him back so he was almost sitting in my lap. "This is weird."

I dug my fingers into his shoulders, doing what I could to loosen him up. He immediately sank farther into me and groaned. Rubbing him until my hands were too cold to keep out of the water, I listened to the sound of his moaning and felt my body responding. "Thanks for driving us."

He leaned into my chest and gripped the outside of my thighs. "I'm glad you came with us. And that you forgave us."

"I'm glad you guys showed up for me. The last month has been hard. I missed you so much." I pressed my cheek to Vaughn's shoulder. "I don't know how you three did it, but you made me care about you. So, please never do anything stupid again."

Booth reached out and ran his thumb over my bottom lip. "Did you mean what you said?"

I knew exactly what he meant. He wanted to know if I loved them. I swallowed my nerves and nodded. "I do love you. Each of you. I didn't mean to fall for you guys but you're each so funny and sweet in your own way. You make me feel more like myself than I've ever felt before."

Vaughn stood up and climbed out of the tub. I thought I'd said something wrong but he reached over the side and scooped me up. "Time to figure out the logistics, Ella Rae."

I shivered as he carried me inside and to the giant shower. While the water warmed up, he put me down on the bathroom counter and the three of them stood in front of me, looking not unlike a pack of hungry wolves.

"I love you. I don't have the pretty words to explain to you how much right now but I will someday." Vaughn smiled. "Until then I'll just have to show you."

"I love you, too, Ella." Fisher cupped my face and searched my eyes. "I'm crazy about you. The amount of shit I would do for you to prove it is scary."

I bit my lip and looked up at him through my lashes. "You don't need to prove anything. I believe you. The three of you are willing to all be with me selflessly. It would be so easy for you guys to demand that I choose one of you. It would be the expected thing but you guys never made me feel like I had to choose one of you."

Booth tested the water and edged the other guys out of the way so he could pick me up. He carried me under the stream of hot water and kept me plastered to his chest. "I will never let anything bad happen to you again. I love you and I only ever want to make you happy."

"I feel so lucky to have you guys."

Fisher gently took my hair out of its ponytail and tipped my head back so he could wet it. "We have a lot of making up to do."

I held onto Booth's neck as Fisher massaged shampoo into my hair, rubbing my scalp as he did. "As much as it pains me to say this when you're washing my hair for me, you don't have to make up anything. I forgive you. That's the end of it."

Vaughn watched us from the back of the shower. "You should let us make it up to you, Ella Rae. Tonight."

The way his tone dropped and got all warm made me tingle. I was nodding before I could even think 'yes'. "Okay. That sounds okay."

Booth held me the whole time Fisher washed my hair and then Fisher stepped back and let Booth take over washing me. He slowly peeled my panties from my body and took his time stroking every inch of me with his sudsy hands. By the time they were drying me off, I was wetter than ever.

I bit my lip to stop the groan of displeasure from escaping when Booth put me on the counter again instead of carrying me to the bed. I had to grip the counter as they each fussed over me. They brushed my hair and even rolled on my deodorant for me before they each took their time rubbing lotion into my skin.

"Are you trying to kill me?" I was breathless from the nonstop stimulation. "Seriously. I tell you that I love you and then you torture me?"

Vaughn stepped back and smiled at me. There was something hesitant playing in his eyes. "I'm getting up the nerve to pull out my dick in front of my best friends."

My heart swelled at the vulnerability he was showing. I slipped off the counter and hugged him. "We don't have to do anything. We can take our time."

He scoffed. "Fuck that."

I gasped as he picked me up and carried me to the bedroom. "Okay, then. Pull it out."

Fisher laughed as Vaughn dropped me on the bed. I went up on my elbows and watched as, one by one, the three of them pushed their wet briefs off. I swallowed audibly as I looked at each of them.

"Okay. I'm realizing just how much penis I'm supposed to take and I'm a little worried." I sat up and licked my lips. "So, I'm excited about the prospects here. Let me start there. I'm just having some concerns about where you're going to put all of that."

Vaughn tugged me over to him and kissed me hard. "One step at a time."

I opened my mouth to ask him what he meant but he was faster in showing me. I was flat on my back and his face was between my thighs fast enough to make my head spin. My mouth fell open as he stroked his tongue over my clit.

64

Booth

"Vaughn!" Ella called out his name as Vaughn ate her out. Her hands clutched the blanket beneath her and her thighs wrapped around his head. "Oh, god!"

I blew out a shaky breath as I watched, fully taking in the experience of seeing our best friend with the woman we loved. It was intoxicating. I moved onto the bed and leaned over her so I could kiss her. I tasted her pleasure as she moaned into my mouth. I stroked my tongue past her lips and groaned as she sucked at it.

"You taste so good, Ella Rae."

I sat back and watched as Vaughn pushed two fingers into Ella's drenched sex. She moaned and rocked her hips back and forth, her neediness so plain to see. Fisher settled on the bed on her other side and cupped her breasts, stroking her nipples with his thumbs until her hips moved faster. I reached down and circled her clit, hungry for her pleasure.

"Yeah, I'm seeing the benefits of this." Vaughn gripped her thigh in his free hand and pumped his fingers faster. "Look at how much attention you're getting, Ella Rae. And you still want more. You're such a greedy little thing."

"More. I've missed you guys too much for teasing." Her voice was breathy as she made it clear that she wanted more from us.

Vaughn looked up at us and nodded. Both Fisher and I motioned for him to take her first. Fish and I knew we could share. Our ability to make the complicated relationship work depended on Vaughn's willingness to share Ella.

He stood up and flipped her over so she was on her hands and knees. Instead of going straight to fucking her, he bent over and ate her out from behind. Ella cried out his name and hung her head forward, letting her hair fall in her face. I nodded to Fish and he moved to kneel in front of her, stroking her hair out of her face and waiting for her to be ready for his dick.

Vaughn straightened and lined their bodies up while Ella lifted her head to look at Fish. He dipped his head to kiss her as Vaughn sank deep in one stroke. She screamed into Fisher's mouth and Vaughn's face pinched as he swore loudly, right along with her.

"So fucking tight." Vaughn ran his hands up her back and back down to grasp her waist. "Fuck, Ella. You're soaked for us."

I pulled her hair back in my fist and watched as Fish kissed her one more time before he sat up and gripped his dick. He pressed it against her lips and she opened to take him in as deep as she could. The sight was enough to make my balls ache. She gave herself to us so willingly.

Vaughn was just as affected as I was. He groaned and couldn't tear his eyes off of her mouth stretched around Fisher's dick. He thrust faster, his hands tightening as he did. "Fuck."

Fisher swore at the ceiling as Ella sucked him deep. I reached under her body to play with her clit once he gripped her head to take control of her movements. I stroked her in tight circles and then pinched it between my fingers. I kissed her shoulders and back, starving for the warm taste of her in my mouth.

Ella moaned around Fisher's dick, her eyes squeezed shut as she took everything we gave her. Vaughn slid his hands lower and cupped her ass, pulling her cheeks apart and pressing them together again. I watched as he stroked his finger over her asshole and her entire body shuddered.

"Can you take me here, Ella Rae?" Vaughn pressed his finger past the tight ring of muscle and into her ass. "Can you take all of us?"

Fisher pulled out of her mouth long enough for her to say she wanted to try. I rubbed her clit faster as Vaughn eased a second finger into her ass, stretching her so she could take his cock. Ella panted around Fisher's cock and a red flush worked its way down her back and over her entire body just before she screamed and came hard. Her body went limp after the strong orgasm and Vaughn took advantage of her relaxed state. He pulled out of her sex and pressed the tip of his dick against her ass, using her own juices to ease the way.

Fisher and I both watched as inch by inch, Vaughn slid his cock into her ass. Ella clutched the blanket under her and came again from the intrusion. He gave her time to adjust to his size and then he started moving, pulling out of her ass and then thrusting deep again. Slowly, at first, he fucked her ass with his hands tightly gripping her hips.

Fisher groaned and pulled out of her mouth. "I need to stop or I'm going to come. Jesus."

I switched places with him and smiled down at Ella as her eyes widened at the sight of my cock, the same way it always did. I pressed just the tip past her lips and let her lick me like that until she wanted to take more. I gripped her hair and held it tight as I watched her face. She opened her eyes and looked up at me as Vaughn fucked her faster. His deep thrusts pushed her mouth farther down my cock until my tip was brushing the back of her throat. She gagged and I started to pull out but she lifted her hand to grip the inches she couldn't take into her mouth and squeezed me.

Vaughn growled and drove himself harder into her before pulling out completely and stumbling back a few steps. "Fuck. I can't come that fast. Jesus."

Fisher wasted no time in positioning himself behind Ella. He slid into her core and grabbed her shoulders, holding her tight as he fucked her harder. He groaned and shook his head. "She feels too good."

I stroked my fingers down the side of Ella's face and cupped her cheek. "Are you going to try to take all of us, Ella Rae?"

"Her pussy just clamped down on me harder than ever. I'd say she likes the sound of taking all of us." He curved his body over hers and kissed her back. "I'm going to finish in your perfect mouth, Ella Rae."

Vaughn looked at me and then down at Ella. "No way you're going in her ass, man. You'd kill her."

I pulled out of Ella's mouth and let out a short laugh. "Thanks, I think."

Ella sat up on her knees and reached out to stroke my cock. "I'd try. For you."

I shook my head. "We're not breaking you tonight, baby."

She bit her lip and smiled. "I like when you call me baby."

I laid back on the bed and pulled her down on top of me so I could kiss her. "Take me, baby."

She sat up and gripped me so she could lower herself on my cock. We both groaned as she sank lower and lower. Her nails bit into my chest and she gasped once I was fully inside.

"Now open that beautiful mouth for Fish." I cupped her breasts and teased her nipples as she leaned forward and twisted to the side so Fish could push his dick to the back of her throat.

She pulsed around my dick and the sensations just grew stronger as Vaughn settled behind her and slowly eased himself into her ass. It made her pussy even tighter around me and the sounds she made were wild. We all held perfectly still as he took her ass. Her eyes watered and I was worried she was in pain so I reached down and rubbed her clit, desperate to make her feel better. She surprised all of us as she came harder than ever, screaming and shaking between us.

The feeling of her walls fluttering up and down my length was too good. Vaughn grunted and started fucking her. Fisher gripped her hair tight and fucked her mouth. I thrust into her from below, finding a rhythm with Vaughn so we were fucking into her at the same time. Ella's orgasm never stopped. She was trapped between us, taking everything we were giving her, and coming from it the entire time.

Vaughn was the first to tense and come. He thrust himself deep into her ass and froze as he filled her ass with his come. I couldn't last much longer and when her walls squeezed me tighter than ever, I lost my control. I shot my seed into her, coming more than I ever had. I growled and stretched up to rake my teeth over her shoulder as I came, needing to mark her even more than my come in her pussy did.

Fisher came just seconds later, growling her name as he did. He pulled out once he was done and sank onto the bed beside me. Vaughn settled on my other side as Ella slumped onto my chest with my dick still buried inside her.

Her body continued to shake with aftershocks of her orgasm for minutes after it was all over. Her breath was warm against my chest as she slowly caught her breath. I wrapped my arms around her and held her tight.

"Yeah, it works." Vaughn reached over and lightly slapped her ass. "You're stuck with all of us for sure now, Ella Rae."

She let out a weak laugh. "Thank god because I'm pretty sure I'm ruined for any other man now."

"Don't even talk about other men." Fisher groaned. "I'm too tired to prove a point by fucking you again right now. Give me five minutes."

I grinned. "What he means to say is that we love you."

Her walls fluttered around my shaft. "I love you guys, too. I never want to leave this cabin."

"Move back in with us, Ella Rae." Vaughn pushed her hair out of her face. "Please."

"Okay, but I'm not doing your laundry or cleaning up after you. Cinderella is dead and gone." She couldn't help smiling despite the toughness she tried to portray. "Right?"

"Cinderella got you into our bed, baby." I laughed as she scowled at me. "You don't have to clean up after us, of course. You just have to keep baking for us."

Fisher nodded. "The only thing better than your baking is your pus-"

"Oh, my god." Ella sat up and winced. "We're going to need a bigger bed."

"We just proved that we can squeeze into tight spaces." Vaughn grunted when she slapped his stomach. "Fine. We'll buy a giant bed."

"And whatever else you want." Fisher grinned. "And maybe those diamond encrusted brass knuckles."

Ella sighed. "I'd settle for more of this."

"Done."

65

Epilogue

Ella

Six Years Later

Traffic was terrible as I tried my best to make it across town in time to watch the kickoff. Fish was starting his third season as a starter for a professional team and each game was just as exciting as the last. Normally, I would've already been at the arena, sitting with a few of the other girlfriends or wives as I waited for the game to start but I'd had an interview that morning. Tucker, Foltz, and Williams was a large firm that did a lot of corporate law but they had a small sector that did pro bono work to relieve the public defender's office. I interviewed for that sector and it'd gone well. I was hoping I'd hear something within the week.

"We're almost there, Ms. Daughton." Larry, the driver that Fisher insisted I use, glanced at me through the rearview mirror. "We'll be there before the kickoff."

I smiled at him. "Thanks, Larry. I didn't think the interview would go on so long."

"That's a good sign, isn't it?"

"I hope so." I ran my hands over my dress and looked up at him. "Do you think this is too much? I've had so much free time since passing the bar exam and Fisher's coach said I was making him fat with all my baking so I switched to sewing. This is a lot, though, right?"

He laughed. "No, ma'am. It's nice. Have they seen it?"

"No. I wanted it to be a surprise. I'm not a seamstress, though. I'm petrified that I'm going to sit down and bust the seams during the game." I'd taken some material with the team colors and used it and one of Fish's old jerseys to make a sundress. I was worried that I looked like a Pinterest fail. "Maybe I should change back into my interview uniform."

"Don't do that, Ms. Daughton. I think they'll like the dress. My wife is a seamstress and you could tell me she made that dress and I'd believe it."

"You're sweet, Larry, but I think you might be a liar." I laughed and looked at my phone. I was going to be cutting it close. I always gave Fish a good luck kiss before each game. I'd never missed one. "Are Vaughn and Booth already there?"

"Yes, ma'am. Vaughn went with Fisher earlier to do some last minute work on his shoulder and Booth went with them."

Vaughn had left the game to work on the sidelines. He worked as a physical therapist for the team and stuck close by Fish to make sure he didn't hurt himself. Booth had gone in a different direction. He taught science at a local high school but the students were begging him to coach their losing football team. All three of them had found their way into careers that they loved and it was finally my turn after years of undergrad and law school.

Of course, I was fighting an uphill battle. No matter how much a firm liked me, I knew they were seeing my stomach and debating whether or not I was worth taking a chance on. I was six months pregnant with twins and my baby bump had turned into a baby mountain. We hadn't planned to get pregnant for another few years but apparently my birth control was only so strong when I was testing it so often. I was excited about our babies, of course, but I planned on going to work as soon as I could. I hadn't worked so hard to become a lawyer just to give up at the first sign of hardship.

"Almost there, Ms. Daughton."

I slipped my feet into my matching flats and fluffed my curls. I wanted to look good when I saw my men. It'd been hard to still feel sexy while growing two little beings inside me. The guys were good about showing me how much they liked my body, though. They never stopped touching me. I smiled as I thought of them and how they'd refused to let me out of bed that morning without a handful of orgasms first.

"Alright. Here we are." Larry parked and tried to get out to open my door.

"Stay inside, Larry. I can get the door myself. Thanks for the ride!" I only struggled a little bit to get out of the car with my belly but I made it.

He'd pulled right up to the back entrance to the locker room. Inside security lines, the entrance was private and it was how I typically got in. Before I could swipe the key card that being Fish's girlfriend had gotten me, the door swung open.

Booth let out a relieved breath when he saw me. "There you are. How'd it go, baby?"

I swooned as he took me in his arms and kissed me deep. He'd grown his beard out and it was soft against my face thanks to the beard oil he used. I pressed my body into his and groaned when he pulled away. I was in the stage of pregnancy that made me want to hump my guys nonstop. "It went well, I think. They were really nice."

He took my hand and pulled me towards the locker room. "If they're smart, they'll call you back with an offer. They'd be lucky to have you. I like that dress, by the way. It's highlighting some of my favorite parts of you."

I struggled to keep up with his long stride and when he noticed, he picked me up. I laughed and wrapped my arms around his neck. "I can walk, Booth."

"We're on a time crunch, baby."

I expected him to stop outside of the locker room but knocked and someone opened the door for us and then he carried me inside. I slapped my hands over my eyes, not wanting to see any of the other guys' nakedness. "Booth!"

He laughed and put me down. "Good choice, baby. Keep those eyes covered."

I gasped when he stepped away from me. "Booth? What are you doing?"

"There's a lady in here, assholes! Put your dicks away!" I recognized Coach McDonald's voice and winced. He was a scary man when things weren't going his way. "Well, don't you look pretty, Ella."

I still had my eyes covered. "Booth brought me in here, Coach. Blame him if you're upset about the intrusion."

"I like how fast you threw him under the bus." He'd never gotten over Booth turning him down. He wanted Booth on his team but Booth wanted to help kids more than he wanted to play ball.

"Hey, Ella. Looking good, ma."

"Are you in here to see a real man, Ella?"

"Get rid of that loser's jersey, momma. I'll let you wear mine instead!"

I grinned at Fish's teammates called out things to me to get under my guys' skin. The other players loved watching Fish get cranky over me and they knew it'd only gotten worse since I'd gotten pregnant. "Hello, boys. I hope you're bringing home another win today. It's wrong to disappoint a pregnant lady."

"Don't even talk to these assholes, Ella Rae." Fish's voice came from somewhere in front of me. "Come here, sweetheart."

I smiled as he pulled me into his arms and hugged me. "Let me give you your kiss and get out of here."

"There's something I have to do before you can go." He let me go. "Count to five and open your eyes, Ella."

I did what he said and when I opened my eyes I screamed. Booth, Vaughn, and Fisher were kneeling on one knee in front of me, a beautiful diamond sparkling up at me from the ring box in Fish's hand. I covered my mouth and let out a hysterical sounding laugh. "What are you doing?"

The entire team was watching and tears filled my eyes when I saw one of them holding a tablet with my mom's face filling the screen. As I watched, Booth's mom edged my mom out of the frame and wiped her eyes.

"We love you, Ella Rae. We've known you were the woman we wanted to marry for a very long time. Nearly every wish we've ever had has come true because of you. We wanted to wait for you to finish law school before we did this and the dates just added up for today to be the day." Fish grinned up at me with tears in his eyes.

"Six years ago today, you called me and asked me for a place to stay." Vaughn's eyes were suspiciously moist, too. "You started all of this that day, Ella Rae. You came into our lives and changed everything. You've made every day special since that day."

"I knew I loved you the first time you baked us cookies with our names on them." Booth's smile was bigger than I'd ever seen it, except maybe the day I told them I was pregnant. "You make life fun, Ella. You make it special. You're going to be the best mom to all the kids we have and you're going to be the best wife. Make us the happiest men ever and marry us, baby."

I laughed through my tears as the team around us broke out in cheers. I moved to kneel in front of them and Fish jumped to his feet and stopped me.

"It's still a locker room floor, Ella Rae. We can kneel on it. You can't." Fish wrapped his arms around me and kissed me. "Marry us, baby."

I nodded and peppered kisses all over his face. "Yes! It took you long enough to ask!"

Booth and Vaughn took their turns holding and kissing me until Coach McDonald cleared his throat and tapped his watch. "We can be a little late but if we don't get out there soon, they're going to think we're too scared to face them."

Fish slipped the beautiful ring on my finger and pointed at the tablet where my mom's face had taken center stage again. "You've got guests waiting in our box for you, Ella Rae."

I gasped. "They're here?!"

Booth took my hand and nodded. "Our moms are very excited to see you, baby."

"Dad, too." Vaughn winced. "Plus his new girlfriend. Of course, that means your mom had to bring a date, too."

"Not even our parents' obnoxious dating habits can ruin this. We're getting married!" I kissed Fish again and brushed my nose over his. "Go out there and bring home another win, fiance."

He cupped my belly and grinned. "For you."

Booth picked me up again and carried me out of the locker room to a chorus of cheers and calls from the rest of Fish's team. He and Vaughn stopped just outside so we could watch the team run down the ramp to the field. It was one of my favorite parts. The crowd always went crazy when they saw Fish and his team. Their excitement was almost as wild as mine.

"This is the best day ever." I sighed wistfully and rested my head on Booth's shoulder.

Vaughn slid his hand up my thigh and winked. "It'll be even better later. Celebration sex with you is my favorite. Along with makeup sex. And angry sex. And sleepy morning sex. Pretty much any sex."

"Our parents are all staying the night at the house tonight." Booth laughed at the crestfallen look on Vaughn's face. "Which is why I got us a room for the night."

"God, I love you guys."

66

FREE PREVIEW OF GRUMPY MAKES THREE

I can catch more flies with honey. I could also catch a bear with honey. I gripped the counter that separated me from the rest of the diner and did my best to keep my smile in place. My mom's constant reminder that I'd get as far as I wanted in life as long as I kept sweet played in my head but it was facing an uphill battle against the shitstorm of a day I was having.

On a scale from one to attacked by an ape at the zoo and publicly ridiculed for the ape having to be put down, I was climbing into that ape exhibit. I'd started my day counting pennies from my childhood piggy bank to have enough money to pay the water bill and then I'd quickly gone into finding my boyfriend cheating on me. It was so cliche that I wanted to scream. I didn't scream, though, because I was a freaking ball of sunshine! Also, I probably didn't scream because the relationship had run its course. I just didn't know how to end it. Thankfully, Camden did. He'd ended it with a busty blonde who lived in the upstairs apartment. The only thing about it being her that really pissed me off was that she'd kept me awake so many nights by having loud sex right over my bed. It was just insulting that she'd ruined my sleep *and* slept with my boyfriend. *Ex*-boyfriend.

I'd grabbed a bag, shoved a few things inside, told Camden's bare ass that I'd come back later to get the rest of my stuff, and I'd blown out of there. The water bill money was going straight back into my piggy bank. I had to find a new apartment. Or maybe just a room in someone else's apartment. If I really had time to think about everything, I was lucky that Camden cheated on me. The water bill wasn't the only thing that was about to get cut off at his apartment. Worse than that, the red notice taped to the front door had been there for a few days already and the apartment manager was only going to give so many eviction warnings before he actually made a move. Camden was probably going to be as homeless as I was soon. We'd both be searching for single rooms in someone else's apartment.

That all had really set the pace for the rest of my morning, though. Even if I was okay with the relationship ending, being cheated on still stung. The sex that I'd walked into that morning had been a lot more vigorous than the sex I'd had with Camden. It left a nasty feeling nagging at the back of my brain that maybe I was the problem.

I was late to work and Henry, my boss, was on a warpath because the cook had called in sick and somehow, that was my fault. I'd been chewed out while I stood perfectly still, clutching my piggy bank to my chest because my car doors didn't lock and I didn't want to risk losing the little bit of money I had in the world. Henry was no fly, nor was he a bear. He was a tiny man with tiny man syndrome and no amount of honey from me changed that. He hated me. I secretly believed it was because I towered over him at my above-average height.

So, broke, cheated on, yelled out, and clutching a porcelain pig I'd named Pig-Pig, I considered myself to be having a really, really bad day. Life thought that was funny, though, and I was pretty sure it said 'hold my beer' before sending in the Carrington brothers.

Henry's niece, Megan, normally waited on them. They were particular about how their breakfast was served, how long it took them to get it, the way the bill was left on their table, and even how long the waitress taking their order could stare at them without them getting cranky about it. Not that they ever really looked up from their phones to notice any of those things. It was like they just knew when something wasn't exactly right. They had a Karen sixth sense and Megan had perfected the art of keeping them as happy as they seemed to be capable of getting.

The few times I'd waited on them, I'd had Henry barking orders in my ear like a Pomeranian, making sure I didn't mess anything up. That morning, Henry was in the kitchen covering for the cook. I was on my own. I made it through taking their order, dropping their order off at their table, and I'd been on my way to setting their bill down when I noticed a dark scowl on the face of the oldest brother. Looking down at his plate, I saw that there was a hair clinging to the side of it. My stomach sank faster than an anchor.

I thumped the bill down harder than I meant to and practically ran back to the kitchen. I was struggling to stay positive when I looked at Henry, cooking without a hairnet, and waved my arms at him. "A hair!"

He frowned at me. "What?"

"There was a hair on one of their plates! A hair, Henry!" I tugged at my own hair, making it stand out more than it already was, and then pointed at it. "A hair. A human hair. On a Carrington brother's plate."

Henry's face went white and I watched as he reached up to feel his head. No hairnet. He registered what I'd already seen, glanced over at my hair, and his jaw hardened. "It was obviously one of yours."

I gasped. "Do you know how much product I have in my hair to keep it from growing to the size of a basketball, Henry? More than you can imagine. My hair doesn't fall out until I brush it out at the end of the day."

"It must've been yours." He cleared his throat and wiped his hands. "Did you say anything to them?"

"No! I left the bill and came in here to tell you." I pawed at my neck and grimaced, an expression not approved by the official Little Miss Sunshine committee, but I was breaking out in hives. I didn't know what else could go wrong. Even the more positive spin I'd tried for earlier were souring. Camden's cheating suddenly felt a lot worse.

"I'll go speak to them. We can't lose their business."

I watched Henry leave and chewed at the corner of my thumb nail. The lore around the Carrington brothers was never-ending. I'd heard so much about them over the years. The main thing I'd heard was that messing up with them wasn't an option. Waitresses better than me had vanished after spilling a few drops of their coffee on the table in front of them. If Henry blamed me for Hair-Gate, I was a goner.

Peeking out of the kitchen, I saw Henry speaking animatedly with his hands. He mostly blocked my view of the Carrington brothers with his movements but I could tell the oldest brother was staring at Henry, his face hard.

I waited for the gavel to fall and when it did, I was still surprised.

Henry slammed open the kitchen door and didn't blink when it nearly took my head off. He glared up at me and bared his little teeth. "You're fired."

My mouth fell open. "What? But I didn't do that, Henry. That wasn't my hair and you know it."

"I don't give a shit. You should've noticed it. You're fired and I never want to see you in this building again. If you cost us their business, I'll find you and sue your ass." He waved his hands like he could blow me out of his presence with the light breeze he created. "Out. Now."

Just like that, something snapped in my brain. I could only keep smiling through so much. I patted Henry's head, flicked the tip of his nose, and shouldered my way past him. I grabbed Pig-Pig, my purse, and a single dry pancake before stomping out to my car. The Carringtons were already gone, but I could see the back end of their fancy SUV and it filled me with rage. They'd cost another waitress her job and were just going to ride off into the morning sun without another thought? I didn't think so.

Continue Reading Grumpy Makes Three for $2.99 or FREE with Kindle Unlimited!

Printed in Great Britain
by Amazon